Key Witness

Key Witness

by Willo Davis Roberts

G. P. Putnam's Sons
New York

Key Witness

[1]

THE HOUSE seemed impossibly huge and empty as I moved between my room and the car, hauling out my belongings. I was unaware of the richness of the furnishings; the paintings in their gilt frames were strangers rather than old friends I'd lived with for fourteen years.

It was raining, which was rather fitting, although I no longer thought of rain as being God's tears, and I noted that I'd tracked mud across the front hall carpet. It was beautiful carpet, rich and deep, welcoming one into the broad hallway with its graceful sweep of stairs and its brocaded wallpaper. Except that it wasn't welcoming me—it was bidding me good-bye, forever.

I hesitated over the mud, then hardened my heart. It was someone else's carpet now, let them deal with the mud.

"One more load and I'll have it," I said. "Except for the books. I'll let you know where to send them as soon as I know."

Maudie regarded me with pale, sad eyes. "I wish you'd think about it a little longer, Brenna, before you go rushing off this way."

I shook my head. "I've thought. I'm going."

"You grew up here." She shook her head over my involuntary glance around me. "Not in this house so much as in this town. Ever since you were twelve years old Hampton has been your home. Your friends are here. . . ."

"I have no friends. Haven't you noticed, Maudie? They all crawled into the woodwork, except for the few who came nosing around in curiosity."

"That's not true and you know it."

1

I did know it wasn't *quite* true, but I hadn't finished feeling sorry for myself. "I can't live here anymore," I told her, and *that* was certainly true enough. "I can't face anybody anymore."

Maudie had been Aunt Stell's housekeeper and confidante for more than thirty years, and when I joined the household, she added me to the list of people she loved. She was as much my mother as Aunt Stell had been.

"Honey, people stand what they have to stand. You can, too."

"Do they?" I didn't try to hide my bitterness. "Aunt Stell couldn't. Well, I'm not going to kill myself, Maudie, but I won't stay here either. I have to go." I was wild to be on my way, to cut the tenuous cords that held me to Hampton, to this house, even to Maudie.

She was well past sixty, a round, soft, sweet-natured woman. I'd never seen her with trembling lips until the past few days. They were trembling now.

"Brenna. Listen, love, don't do anything hasty . . . think a bit before you do anything . . . irrevocable."

I laughed and was surprised at what a hateful sound it was. "There's not much time for thinking, is there? Unless we go to a hotel to do it." I flung out a hand, taking in the opulence around us. "This isn't ours anymore. We have to get out."

"Not right away. Probably not for weeks actually."

"Do you want to sit here until they come and toss our suitcases out on the sidewalk? After checking them to make sure we haven't taken any of the silver, of course, or anything else that doesn't belong to us."

The sorrow in her face was for me, not for herself, although an era had ended for her, too. "Brenna, don't. Nobody suspects *you* of anything wrong. Look, you know I'm going to my sister's, and I'm sure she'd be happy to have you come there, too, for a bit until you've had a chance to get your breath and figure out the best thing to do. . . ."

"Your sister lives on a pension, the same as you'll be doing, and she doesn't have room for me, even for a short time. Oh, Maudie, it isn't fair that you should have nothing! All these years, and I know Aunt Stell intended. . . ."

I couldn't keep back the angry, frustrated tears, the tears I hadn't shed for myself but could, for Maudie.

"I'll be fine. I know what Mrs. McCaffey intended, and she'd have done it, had there been any way. I know what they wanted for you, too, and you're the one that matters. I'm an old woman, ready to settle for a rocking chair with my feet up, but you've got your whole life ahead of you. . . ."

The tears were already gone. "Well, I won't spend it here. I've got one more box, Maudie, that will fit into the trunk."

"You'll let me know where you go, and keep in touch."

"Yes, of course I will."

"You have my sister's number."

"I have it. I'll be all right, Maudie, I'll be fine."

She managed a rather watery smile. "Yes, of course you will. God bless you, dear."

I thought rather grimly as I stowed the last of my belongings in the trunk of my small Toyota that He hadn't exactly been showering me with blessings of late, but who knew? Things just might get better once I'd shed the dust of Hampton.

We kissed good-bye, quickly, awkwardly, both of us knowing that it might be the last time we'd meet. And then I was driving away, purposely not watching her small figure in the rear-view mirror.

Ever since I'd decided not to stay and stick it out, a voice had been whispering to me, *Coward, coward.*

Yet it wasn't a mistake to run. I knew that because of the way my spirits began to rise immediately. I hadn't even reached the outskirts of Hampton when I realized that I was humming under my breath.

I was right to go. My hands firm on the wheel, I accelerated to the speed limit and headed east, to the sea and Bascom's Point.

I don't know why I hadn't told Maudie where I was going. I knew at once, when I decided to leave, where I would have to go. Maudie wouldn't have told anyone.

Yet I kept it a secret, almost even from myself, as if I had had plenty of time to make up my mind, and I hadn't yet decided.

The one thing I had salvaged from the wreckage of those lovely years with Aunt Stell and the Senator was the inn.

The lawyers had confirmed that—my half-interest in the property that had belonged to my father's family for over a hundred years. It hadn't been lost with everything else; it was still mine, as Aunt Stell had intended it to be. It was to be my refuge, my sanctuary.

In spite of the rain, I had the window open, because it was warm, and I caught a glimpse of myself in the mirror, sun-streaked brown hair flying, dark eyes bright for the first time in weeks. I imagined that already there was a touch of color in cheeks that had grown wan.

I drove steadily, keeping to the limit posted on all the signs. There was no

3

hope of getting to the coast in less than two days' traveling time, but that didn't bother me. I was in no hurry to begin living again. I needed a little time to cut completely the ties with the past, and then I would cope with the future.

I'm not sure when I first noticed the car behind me. There were other cars, of course, although traffic wasn't heavy on this early September morning. But this one in particular, a white sedan, appeared several times in my rear-view mirror, sometimes nearly catching up to me, then dropping back until I didn't notice it anymore, then showing up again.

I didn't think much of it because I was on the main highway. Lots of people who were going all the way to the coast would use the same road.

The rain had slowed to a drizzle when I stopped for lunch at one of those roadside places. The white car happened to be fairly close behind me when I turned off; it hurtled on past and I saw without particular interest that the driver was a man.

I ate methodically and was surprised to find, when I'd finished, that I'd left nothing on the plate. It was the first time in days that my appetite had approached normality.

I went back out to the car and proceeded on my way, and a short time later a routine check of the road revealed the white car once more behind me, several cars back.

I found myself wondering idly where he'd been, to have fallen behind after passing me. So far as I could remember, the roadhouse where I'd eaten had been the only eating place, and there hadn't even been a gas station where a traveler might have stopped, except the two flanking the restaurant. I knew he hadn't stopped at either of those.

Still, it didn't yet occur to me that there was anything significant about my traveling companion. It wasn't until I pulled off the road once again for gas, only to see the white car swing into the station on the opposite side of the highway, that uneasiness stirred.

I stood beside my own vehicle, staring across the road while the attendant washed my windows. The other driver had gotten out, too, and was checking his tires. I didn't get a very good look at him, but enough to see that he was a man in his forties, rather stocky and dressed in a blue suit.

"You going far?" My attention returned to the uniformed youth filling my gas tank.

"To the coast," I admitted.

He nodded. "Thought you'd been on the road quite a while. Bugs really build up on a long trip. You all alone?"

4

I'm not normally a skittish person, but that bothered me a bit, that the young man was aware of my aloneness. Yet it was obvious that the car contained no other person, and this precluded a denial; no doubt it was simply a casual question.

"Don't bother you, being alone?" he asked, accepting my proffered bill.

"No," I said, and up to now it hadn't.

He counted out my change from the device he wore on his belt, then eyed me speculatively. "Wouldn't want company, would you?" Before I could voice a protest, he qualified this so that I felt rather foolish. "You like dogs? We got this dog, somebody dumped him off here two days ago, and we're trying to find somebody to give him to. Just a pup, really, and a nice dog, but I already got a collie and my wife won't take another one. We got him tied out back."

A dog. I nearly laughed. "No, thanks, I don't think I want a dog."

"He's an Airedale, real good-looking. Wouldn't be surprised if he was a purebred, from the look of him. Be a great watchdog, a good protector for a girl alone."

Without thinking, I glanced across the road to where the white car and its driver were still delaying, although I could see he'd concluded his business transaction.

It was absurd to think the man had any interest in me. Yet a girl alone on the road *was* vulnerable. A dog would frighten off a casual male, any but the most determined. And I was lonely as well as alone. I hadn't had a dog since my cocker spaniel died when I was nine; the Senator hadn't cared for dogs.

The attendant saw my indecision. "Come around and look at him. Won't hurt to look."

I followed him around to the rear of the building and gaped in dismay at the animal we'd come to examine. "I thought you said he was a puppy!"

"Bet he's less than a year old," I was assured. "See, he likes you!"

I stared at the oddly square-jawed brown and black dog, which was leaping with delight and trying to lick my hand. "I suspect he likes everybody. That wouldn't make him much of a watchdog."

"Oh, no, once he knows he belongs to you he'll run off everybody, no kidding. I bet he wouldn't let any stranger get within a mile of your car, like if you stopped to sleep alongside the road or anything."

"I have no intention of sleeping in my car, thank you," I said. The dog had made contact with my hand with a warm, rough tongue. "He's as big as a horse."

"A pony, maybe." The man grinned. "That's not a bad thing, in a

5

watchdog. Gives him a little authority, you know. Young as he is, he's got a bark on him enough to stop anybody in their tracks.''

I stared down at the dog, already feeling that tug I remembered from all those years ago. "What's your name, boy?''

"Got a collar says *Rudy.* No license, though, must have lost it, if he ever had one. What do you say? We got him some dog food, couldn't let him go hungry. I'll throw that in, and the hubcap we're using for a dish for him. What do you say? He needs a good home.''

So did I. But I didn't voice the bleak thought. We talked a few more minutes, and the next thing I knew I had an Airedale, sixty pounds of him, in the back seat of the Toyota, along with most of my worldly possessions.

It wasn't until I was actually driving out of the station that I remembered the man in the white sedan and glanced across the street. Darned if he wasn't still there, seemingly studying a map.

The uneasiness returned, intensified, and I purposely speeded up past the posted limit to see what he'd do. The white car dropped back a little but stayed in sight, which wasn't especially reassuring.

Rudy lolled against the window, making smudges on the glass. Would he be of any use if I got into trouble? I wondered. But what trouble would there be, so long as I kept moving? By tomorrow night I'd be in Bascom's Point, with the old aunts. Just thinking of them brought a smile to my lips, and for a time I forgot about any possible pursuer.

Some of my relatives had been Bascoms, many years ago. The aunts who occupied and operated the inn were St. Johns, the same as I was. Aunt Stell had been a St. John, my father's younger sister. Callie, Egg, and Zell were her aunts, my great-aunts. I didn't know them well, having seen them only a few times as a child. Sometimes they'd come to Aunt Stell and the Senator's for Christmases. Even as a child I'd sensed their uneasiness in the luxurious household; they weren't used to maid service and all the other things that a great deal of money made possible. My memories of them were vague except that they'd seemed incredibly old.

Well, everybody looks old to a child. They had been kind to me and brought me hand-knit slippers and scarves and mittens, and Aunt Egg had made fabulous cookies, even better than Maudie's.

Was that what I was looking for? A return to childhood, to the protection offered by adults who would see that I was shielded from the hurts of life?

I sighed, hoping I was more realistic than that.

Rudy suddenly plunged toward me, nuzzling my neck so that I nearly slewed off the road.

6

"Sit!" I commanded angrily, feeling shaken, and was relieved when he obeyed the command. "Stay," I told him, and he subsided against the cushions, unabashed, grinning at me in a very human way.

A few miles farther on the white car passed me. I wasn't expecting it and therefore didn't glance at the driver until he was pulling ahead, so again I didn't get a clear look at him. Middle-aged, blue suit . . . that was all I saw.

Still, I felt better with him ahead of me and I relaxed. With the dog in the car I began to talk, about anything or nothing, and I thought he liked it. It was less lonely for both of us that way.

I picked a quiet motel on the outskirts of some small city whose name I don't remember; there was a coffee shop in connection with it where I could have dinner. The man in the white car had vanished somewhere along the road.

I splurged on a small steak, saving the bone and scraps for Rudy. He chewed greedily, swallowing most of it whole.

"I hope you have a cast-iron gut," I told him, "or you're going to be sick."

He wagged his tail enthusiastically, looking for more. I dumped dry dog food into the hubcap . . . from a Cadillac, I noticed . . . and followed that by water from the tiny bathroom. The room was an ordinary one, impersonal but comfortable. I felt better not being alone in it.

A shower, a TV movie watched in a slow unwinding of tension, and I was ready for sleep. Rudy curled beside the bed as I turned out the light.

And then it started again.

As it had every night since the funerals.

At first I fought it, fought the sick compulsion to relive the entire horrible episode, fought the tears I knew would be the conclusion, and then, as before, I gave in.

Was it a little easier now? Did remembering hurt a little less? Was I toughening up?

Of course I was. I'd left Hampton, hadn't I? I'd left behind all the memories, all the people who'd looked at me and whispered behind their hands. I'd made a positive step in the right direction, away from the past, toward . . . what? Toward something, at any rate, that had to be better.

I lay awake in the darkness and let the memory roll like a film, just the way the events had happened.

7

[2]

I REMEMBER thinking, while watching the news about the scandals in Washington involving all those high government officials, *how terrible this must be for their families.* For the men who had somehow deluded themselves that they were justified in breaking laws and betraying the trust of their countrymen, I felt little sympathy. For all their rationalizing, their attitude of "the end justifies the means," I thought they knew full well what they were doing, and how wrong it was, and they'd simply thought they wouldn't be caught.

But though their families were innocent, *they* were perhaps suffering most of all. I read a magazine article about one of those women, a loyal, trusting, church-going wife; the list of charges brought against her husband was twenty pages long, and some of the items were so personally damaging that the man persuaded his prosecutors to eliminate the more embarrassing ones because they would be so crushing to his wife.

I watched another one of the women on television, a slim, fair-haired, sweet-faced woman in her early forties (I don't recall, anymore, who she was, but I'll never forget the pain in her eyes) who had caught my attention to the point that I forgot to listen to the commentator or the questions and answers.

She looked so tired. She hadn't slept the night before, I thought. She lay awake and wondered how it could be possible that the man to whom she'd entrusted her entire life and the lives of her children could have done the terrible things they said he'd done. Maybe she'd prayed that he would be found innocent; only now it was becoming clear to her that such a prayer

8

couldn't be answered. Did she feel anger and resentment as well as horror for what they must all go through before it would be finished?

Oh, yes, I'd thought about the families. I never dreamed that I would one day be among them, those humiliated and helpless women.

We heard about it on the six o'clock news. It wasn't that either of us was addicted to the news . . . God knew it was usually too depressing for either of us . . . but when the Senator was home he never missed a newscast, and the habit was set.

I wasn't watching the screen, being engrossed in my own activities, which at that moment meant some last-minute stitching on the lingerie for my trousseau. I heard the newsman's voice without letting the words register until Aunt Stell made a queer strangled sound that brought me around in my chair.

She was sitting in her yellow recliner, leaning forward with her fingers digging into the padded arms, her bulging eyes fixed on the screen.

At first I thought she'd had a seizure of some sort.

"Aunt Stell? Are you. . .?" And then I heard his name.

"Senator Harold McCaffey had nothing to say to newsmen regarding the indictment, but it was clear that he was under great physical and emotional strain as he headed for his plane. We will bring you reports on further developments as soon as our staff relays them to us. And now, on the home scene. . . ."

I was looking at the woman who had reared me after my parents died. She was a small, gently rounded woman, not exactly pretty but always neat and attractive. For several years now she'd been using a faint blue rinse on her white hair, which made her eyes bluer. She was wearing blue today, too, and normally it was very becoming.

At the moment her skin had a grayish tinge that brought me out of my chair and to her side, reaching for her hands. They were icy.

"Aunt Stell . . . what. . . ?"

Her mouth worked soundlessly for several seconds before she could say it. "Harold. They've indicted Harold. . . ."

"The Senator? For what?" I sank back on my heels, still holding one of her hands, which was infecting my own with its chill.

"They said . . . conspiracy and fraud . . . oh, God, Brenna, it can't be true. . . ."

"Of course it can't," I agreed quickly, but I knew it was. Already that appalling chill was creeping through me as it must have invaded all the others, those women whose men had taken the law into their own hands.

9

She stared at me, in no way comforted by my foolish assurances. "Oh, Brenna, not Harold . . . not Harold. . . !"

I murmured something meaningless, feeling the sickness spread through me.

"He's been a Senator for twenty-four years." Even though I was only a few feet from her, I could scarcely hear the words. "This will kill him, Brenna. He's always been such a proud man. This will kill him."

Not, at first, a thought for herself. Her world had revolved around Harold McCaffey for forty-three years, and the habit was strong; the Senator came first.

"Miss Stell, I can put the roast back a little if you think. . . ." Maudie had come to the doorway and was staring at us, knowing at once, of course, that something was wrong. "What . . . what is it, is she ill?"

For Aunt Stell didn't turn her head, didn't respond, and the tears were beginning to trace erratic channels down her cheeks.

My knees were trembling so that it was hard to get up. "It was on television . . . they've indicted the Senator for . . . for conspiracy and fraud. I wasn't listening, I didn't get it all . . . Maudie, I think we'd better call Dr. Andover."

She swallowed and nodded. "Yes. Do you want to call him? I'll get her upstairs. Miss Stell . . . come with me, love, I think you need to lie down. . . ."

I don't know how Maudie got her to her room. I do have a vague memory of speaking with the doctor once I'd managed to track him down. And I recall being glad that Larry was out of town until Monday, so I wouldn't have to talk to anyone, face anyone.

I really thought someone would come, or call, from the church. Aunt Stell was very active, and very generous, in her church. They must have known how terrible it would be for her, as I had known with the unknown blond wife of one of those others, but no one came, no one called.

Maudie was still upstairs with Aunt Stell when the doorbell rang, so I went to answer it.

The Senator muttered something about being unable to find his key. He stepped into the front hallway, quickly closing the door behind him.

Uncle Harold was nearly always referred to as "the Senator," even by those closest to him. He was a senior member of Congress, and he liked everyone to be aware of, and to acknowledge, that. Aunt Stell and I often addressed him as "Senator" in fun.

It was impossible to think of him now in any connection with fun. He was

10

a big man, in his mid-sixties, a bit paunchy, but not really fat. It seemed to me that the familiar, congenial face had somehow gathered flesh that had melted and been recast in thick folds. It was probably only that I was used to him smiling and today he wasn't smiling.

He looked sick. No, I amended, not sick . . . scared. Senator McCaffey, scared to death.

He licked his lips, one of the first signs of uncertainty I had ever observed in the man. "Where's Stell?"

"Upstairs. Maudie's with her. Dr. Andover gave her a shot."

Pain glazed his eyes. "She knows."

"Yes." I felt wooden, unresponsive. I had lived in this man's house, partaken of his bounty, for fourteen years. He was away a good deal of the time, but when he was at home he was amiable, generous, fun to be with. He had seldom spoken a cross word to me or punished me in any way. Yet here I stood, in his time of trouble, totally unable to make the smallest gesture of sympathy, to utter the briefest word of comfort.

His voice was husky. "She's taking it real hard."

There was no reply to that but the obvious one, so I didn't make it. I did follow him to the doorway of the study and watch while he poured himself a very stiff brandy. I wouldn't have minded one myself, but I couldn't voice the request. His hand shook so that I wasn't sure the glass would make it to his mouth.

It was another's voice who spoke; I didn't recognize it as mine. "What's going to happen?"

His snowy hair, usually so carefully waved or so artfully wind blown, stood up in odd tufts where he ran his hand through it. "God only knows, Brenna."

"Is it . . . will you go to trial?"

"To trial and probably to jail," he said savagely, pouring another drink, which he tossed off with as little effect as if it were water. "I thought I had some friends, goddamn their eyes, but they've thrown me to the wolves." There was more profanity, which rolled past me without impact.

"But they can't send you to jail unless they prove. . . ." I was stopped by the expression in the gray eyes.

"That's what I'm saying, girl, none of my friends are going to come through and bail me out. Nobody wants to be tarred by the same brush. Why, Senator Carlson wouldn't even speak to me on the phone, the son of a bitch, after all I've done for him! He'd never have been elected if I hadn't given him my support!"

11

I was chilled, cold, shivering a little. "What . . . exactly did you . . . do?"

The gaze he turned on me was like nothing I'd ever encountered from the man. Angry, contemptuous, hard. "For Christ's sake, Brenna, grow up! You've lived in a political atmosphere for over half your life; you can't be such an innocent as to think fortunes are made without getting the hands dirty! I've left a call for Graden; let me know when it comes through. I'm going to take a shower."

"What about Aunt Stell?"

For a moment misery overpowered the anger. "I'll see Stell when I've . . . calmed down a little. If Andover gave her a shot, maybe she's asleep."

I doubt if he believed that. I didn't. It was indicative of something that he didn't dare go to her yet.

"This will kill her," I said, without realizing it was exactly what she had said of him.

"Don't you think I know that, Brenna?" he said very quietly, and then he walked past me and up the stairs, out of my sight.

Why had I said it? Had I deliberately wanted to hurt him, Uncle Harold who must already be experiencing the torments of hell?

He hadn't denied anything. He'd admitted he would probably go to jail. Senator Harold McCaffey serving out his remaining years in prison? And what would Aunt Stell be doing? I wanted to cry and my eyes burned with unshed tears, but there was no release there for me. Maybe there was no release anywhere, for any of us.

That first weekend was agonizing. I don't know what the Senator said to Aunt Stell, whether he was as blunt with her as he'd been with me. She came downstairs on Saturday looking as if she'd shrunk so that the clothes hung gracelessly on her, though I knew that was impossible. It must be the way she held herself, no longer proud and happy but hurt and humiliated.

Maudie fussed about her because she wouldn't eat. I finally told the housekeeper to leave us alone, that it was unlikely we'd starve to death if we missed a few meals, for none of us could swallow past the lumps in our throats. Stell wandered around the house, touching things here and there, rearranging books or vases, staring without seeing. Most of the time the Senator was locked in the study; I thought he was drinking heavily, for I could smell it on him when he emerged, but it wasn't making him drunk. Graden, his lawyer, came and they were in conference for hours. When he left, Aunt Stell and I were in the hallway and I think she almost asked him what he thought would happen, but his face was so grave she hadn't the nerve.

We didn't want to read the papers or watch the television, yet it was impossible not to. We had to know the worst. Nothing was very clear, but the accusations flew thick and fast. There were allegations that Senator McCaffey had taken bribes, that construction contracts had been granted to particular firms for financial considerations, that the construction was shoddy and wouldn't have passed inspection without the Senator's intervention. My uncle wasn't the only one involved and he wouldn't be the only one to be pulled down, but he was the one at the top.

The Senator himself watched the screen with glazed eyes. Once in a while he'd mutter something about the sons of bitches who were throwing him to the wolves. Mostly he didn't say anything.

The Senator and Aunt Stell had always been very affectionate. I remembered how reassuring it was to me, when I came to live with them, that they were a couple who really loved each other. They were always casually touching or patting, and I often saw them exchange kisses.

Now they didn't touch each other; they scarcely looked at each other. Each of them suffered in his own private hell, as I did.

For after the news exploded across the country, Larry came back early from his business trip. I wasn't ready for him; I hadn't yet thought what to say or do. Maudie told me he was waiting for me in the music room because the Senator was in the library and Aunt Stell was in the living room.

I didn't want to go down, but that was too cowardly, and what good would it do to wait? Larry . . . there was nothing I could do to lessen the terrible impact on him, any more than I could think of a way to ease my own burden.

He had been playing a one-fingered melody on the piano when I came in, and he turned quickly as if he'd been caught in some forbidden act. He was tall and slim and dark and good-looking . . . all the things a fiancé is supposed to be, including clever and wealthy. I could imagine how his parents were reacting to this.

"Brenna . . . God, what a mess! How are you?" He touched the dark smudges under my eyes. "Not sleeping, obviously. Nor eating. How's Stell holding up?"

I shook my head. "I can't bear to watch her, Larry. I suppose your mother is regretting she ever introduced us. . . ."

"My mother, thank God, is in Chicago. She called me, just in case I

13

hadn't seen the newscasts, but I'd already made reservations to come home. What's going to happen? He'll fight it, naturally."

"I suppose so." I sounded dull and tired. "But from the look of Graden's face . . . it's going to be worse before it's over, I'm afraid. He told me, himself, that he'll probably go to jail."

I moved into his arms then and felt them fold around me in the old way, but there was no comfort for me there either, and after a moment I moved away. "I intended to send out the invitations the middle of next week. I suppose now I'd better wait."

What did I hope for? That he would say, "No, of course we won't wait, send out the invitations to our wedding"?

Larry said nothing, and I made myself turn to look into his eyes.

"Don't you think so?" I pressed, hating myself, hating him because I knew what he was going to say.

"Yes, I suppose you'd better. Until we know what's going to happen," he agreed.

Until we knew what was going to happen. Even then, I think I knew it was all over between Larry and me. He was a young lawyer with political aspirations; his father headed a large and rather staid legal firm that wouldn't want to be contaminated by a connection with Senator McCaffey.

"Just for a few weeks," Larry said. "By then, well, maybe we'll have a better idea what it's best to do."

In less time than that the entire world would have crumbled around me, but I didn't have to wait for the rest of it. I knew the truth right then, that afternoon with Larry.

Sunday, that last weekend we had together, was a waking nightmare. For the first time in over twenty years, except for a few times when she'd been ill, Aunt Stell didn't go to church. Maudie woke her as usual and asked what she would wear, and Stell only turned her face to the wall.

"I'm not going," she said, "ever again."

Shaken, Maudie appealed to me.

"How can you blame her?" I wanted to know. "She's been a saint, an absolute saint, Maudie, for years and years. Next to the Senator, her church has meant more than anything else in her life. But after what's happened I certainly understand why she can't face them . . . it's as if she's responsible herself for the things he did."

"But *she* didn't do anything. . . ." Maudie's eyes were blurred with tears. "Brenna, she needs her church now more than ever."

14

I shook my head. "I don't think so, Maudie. Maybe her God, but not her church. Nobody even called to see how she was or if she needed anything. She's an embarrassment to them and she knows it. She won't go back."

"Pastor Allen's down with the flu," Maudie said. "His wife called; he'll come when he's able."

My voice was chill. "That isn't why the rest of them are staying away. Leave her alone, Maudie. If she doesn't want to go to church, just leave her alone."

Aunt Stell stayed in her room. Uncle Harold holed up in the study with the door shut. I paced the house, fighting my own emotions. None of my friends called either, with the exception of Nancy Elliot, who was to be my maid of honor when I married Larry. She asked, rather uncertainly, if there was anything she could do.

I told her there was nothing, which was true, and then hung up to realize I was resenting the fact that she hadn't just come over so I'd have someone to talk to. Talking would, I knew, have eased the horror of it a little, but I knew, too, that I didn't really want to talk to anyone.

Around one o'clock Maudie approached me to ask if I'd find out if the Senator would like a bite of lunch. I was no more anxious to speak to him than she was; I'd scarcely begun to sort out my feelings for him. There was resentment, certainly, for the position he'd put us in, Stell and Maudie and me. Yet in the midst of all this animosity I suddenly remembered the first Christmas after my parents died, when he'd done so much to make it a truly happy holiday for me.

I lifted a hand to tap on the closed door and then heard the voices. I couldn't bring myself to interrupt him if he were with the lawyers again, so I wandered back out to the kitchen to tell Maudie.

She stared at me. "Who's with him? I didn't let anybody in, did you?"

"No. He probably answered the door himself."

"Maybe he was only on the phone. I don't know, I guess I'll just wait until he asks for something to eat," she said, and we left him alone.

It was early evening when Maudie poked her head into the living room where I was trying to work up an interest in a TV movie. She looked strained and tired.

"Brenna, Larry's here. He wants to see you."

I got up and turned off the set. "There's no reason why we can't talk here." I was surprised he'd come and not as numbed as I'd thought because my heart began to hammer. Maybe he'd changed his mind and wanted me to go ahead with the wedding plans, after all.

15

Maudie had neglected to mention that Larry's mother was with him. Maybe it was because they were within hearing distance and she was afraid of what I'd say.

I couldn't claim that I really liked Mrs. Engle. She was a beautiful woman with dark hair like Larry's, and she looked much younger than she was. She always made me feel rather gauche because she wore elegant clothes and valuable jewels with such careless ease. Being born to such things did make a difference, I supposed.

She had seemed happy enough when we announced our engagement. After all, the Senator was an important and influential man, and the Engles with their inherited wealth were aware of the value of connections in high places.

Her patrician face was as lovely and controlled as ever, but I didn't make any mistake about it; she no longer thought me suitable as a daughter-in-law.

I made polite sounds and offered them drinks, which were declined; they did sit down. Pamela Engle sat as if she didn't intend to stay long.

"I'm sorry about all this, Brenna," she said. "It must be very distressing for you."

That was an understatement and I didn't have an appropriate reply. I never seemed to think well when talking to Pamela.

"I thought you were in Chicago," I ventured.

Her eyebrows rose fractionally. "Naturally I flew home immediately. In a crisis, one rallies around."

Since we'd heard the news Friday night and this was forty-eight hours later, I couldn't think it was *us* she was rallying around.

Larry cleared his throat. "I told Mother we'd decided not to send out the invitations right away, Brenna."

Pamela was nodding. "A very wise decision. A wedding would undoubtedly be turned into a three-ring circus by the newsmen. Every reporter who mentioned Brenna would comment on her relationship to . . . the Senator."

For the first time I felt a flicker of defense mechanism on my uncle's behalf. "He's feeling very badly about this whole thing, for Stell and me more than for himself, I think."

Pamela's glance was coolly appraising. She didn't say that he ought to have thought of us before he decided to dirty his hands, but I knew she was thinking it. It was true, of course, but that didn't make it any more palatable, coming from one who'd never had any reason to dirty her hands.

"Larry and I have discussed the matter of the wedding," she said, "and

16

we feel the best thing would be an indefinite postponement. Until everything has died down completely.''

I looked at Larry, who was studiously tracing the pattern of the carpet with the toe of one shoe. Larry was no mama's boy; he wouldn't knuckle under to her unless it suited him.

"It would be very bad business to have the Senator and Engle and Lawford mentioned in the same sentence,'' I observed.

"I'm glad you agree. Of course, eventually. . . .'' She let that trail off while Larry lighted her cigarette. There was no ashtray because Aunt Stell objected to the smell of tobacco and tried to confine the smoking guests to areas where she didn't have to endure it herself. Rudely, I ignored the need and sat where I was.

"Eventually,'' I prodded. I don't know why I felt the compulsion to keep poking at it, when I was already sure it was a dead dog, as the Senator would have put it.

She didn't catch up with the end of the proffered idea. She took a different tack, and I saw the muscle jumping uncontrollably in one cheek and knew this was why she had really come.

"There's one thing that bothers me, Brenna.''

I twisted my lips into a parody of a smile. "Only one, Mrs. Engle?''

"I'm wondering about the advisability of a big formal wedding, under the circumstances. I don't mean just the Senator . . . I mean the previous marriage. We've only just learned of it. I really think that was unfair of you, not to tell Larry about it. In many cultures, you know, such a thing would be cause for invalidation of any promises made regarding marriage.''

My jaw dropped before I could stop it. "If you're referring to my marriage to Max Von Rys, it happened nine years ago, when I was barely seventeen, and it was annulled. From a legal standpoint, I have never been married. And Larry certainly didn't just learn of it; I told him myself, a long time ago.''

Her smile held a touch of frost, and I knew that whatever else my regrets might be, they didn't include the loss of Pamela Engle as a mother-in-law. "You told him the marriage had been annulled, certainly. I don't believe you mentioned that you spent nearly a month with the man before your family found you and . . . annulled it.''

I was shaking and I sat on my hands to hide them. "I told Larry everything he needed to know about it, Mrs. Engle.''

"Including the fact that that youthful marriage *was* consummated, Brenna?''

17

I felt the heat suffuse my face and then recede, leaving me cold and still. "I didn't ask Larry for a certificate of virginity when he proposed to me." I shot a look at him, and he still hadn't the guts to look at me. "Which is a good thing because he certainly couldn't have produced one."

I had the satisfaction of seeing the spots of color now in *his* face.

Pamela rose in a graceful, fluid motion, cupping a hand under the cigarette just before it lost half an inch of ash. There was no longer any pretense of humor or goodwill.

"I think this conversation has gone on long enough. We do understand each other, don't we, Brenna?"

I rose, too, wanting nothing more than to be rid of them, both of them. "You'll excuse me if I don't see you out."

"Of course. Good evening, Brenna."

Larry's eyes met mine for a few seconds before he followed his mother out, and I read it all there. He cared for me, but not enough. Not enough to risk his own legal and political career by the taint of a connection, however tenuous, with Senator Harold McCaffey.

The trembling was so uncontrolled that I had to sit down again once they'd left the room. There was, perhaps, some justification for what she said. I *had* been married to Max; I had spent twenty-five days with him before they found us. I never knew if the Senator had to pull strings to have the marriage annulled. I only knew that I was taken tearfully home and I never saw Max again. I *had* told Larry, however, and he knew I'd scarcely thought about it in years; we had decided that since no one knew about that first marriage but my family and the two of us, and since legally I did not have to report it as a marriage in applying for a license, there was no reason to let it spoil the big wedding the Senator had insisted upon.

I was glad I'd found out, I told myself. I was glad the wedding was off, glad I would never be part of the Engle family.

Maudie found me there, huddled on the sofa, my face wet and ugly. She didn't ask any questions; she simply drew me into her arms and held me as if I were a child, while I cried.

[3]

WE SAW it on television, Maudie and I. Oh, the wonders of modern technology, where you can sit in your own home and watch your loved ones murdered hundreds of miles away.

It was a form of flagellation, watching the newscasts, yet we couldn't seem to help it. I never knew what took place between Aunt Stell and the Senator during that last weekend. They did talk privately, but Maudie told me he slept across the hall rather than in the king-sized bed with Stell. When Maudie and I were around, they scarcely exchanged a word, but they must have said something because it was Stell who told Maudie on Sunday night that he'd flown back to Washington for some sort of hearing.

He was news, of course, so there were television cameras there, and we saw it all in color as he went up the broad marble steps, surrounded by men we didn't recognize except for Graden and his associate.

Even when we saw him fall we didn't believe it, not at first. Not until the announcer, jarred out of his complacent recital of the facts of indictment and the list of charges being brought, blurted, "My God, he's been shot! Oh, my God, the Senator has been shot!"

We watched in paralyzed horror as the others gathered around him, all those men in anonymous business suits with their briefcases and their stunned expressions when the cameras swung in for close-ups. There was a close-up of the Senator, too, sprawled on the steps with an awkwardness he had never displayed in life. We knew he was dead. He would never have allowed himself to be photographed in such an unbecoming attitude had he been alive. And, of course, we had seen assassinations before, several of

19

them. Assassination was becoming the American way of death for those in the public eye.

Assassination. That's what they called it. Not murder.

Not that it mattered what they called it. He was dead. The shocked faces showed it. Of course there was an ambulance and he was lifted carefully and taken away, with the promise by a newscaster that as soon as there was news of his condition it would be relayed to us on this channel.

We didn't need to wait for the report. We knew.

Maudie held a hand pressed tightly to her chest, as if to suppress the pain there. We looked at each other, speechless, and the turbulence of my emotions almost stopped my breathing.

I had felt nothing but sorrow. Sorrow for Aunt Stell, who must be told; I prayed she hadn't been watching on the little portable in her bedroom. Sorrow for the man who had, after all, been a second father to me, whatever else he might have been.

There would be no trial now. No prison sentence. No long-drawn-out news coverage, no television close-ups of strained faces, no pretense that we were able to hold up our heads.

"Poor Miss Stell," Maudie said, almost inaudibly. "She said to me last night, as she was getting into bed, 'I don't think I can bear it, Maudie, it's hurting him so badly, he can't even talk to me.' It's him she's thinking about, not herself, and now he's left her to bear it all alone."

So Maudie, too, I thought, had her resentments.

We went up together to tell her. I had already called Dr. Andover; he swore softly and promised to come as soon as he could.

She lay in the big bed looking peaceful and relaxed. She didn't move when Maudie opened the door, and it wasn't until we reached her and Maudie put out a hand to the limp wrist that we knew we wouldn't have to tell her.

The empty bottle of sleeping capsules in the bathroom was mute testimony to the truth of her statement that she couldn't bear it. She must have taken them all, hours ago, after Maudie left her.

"At least neither of them had to know about the other," Maudie said quietly. "Ah, poor Brenna, I know they wouldn't have left you this way if they'd known anything else to do."

Poor Brenna. Left to face the reporters, the photographers, the mortuary, the double funeral, the crowds of the curious. I moved through it like a robot, unseeing, unfeeling, unthinking, with Maudie at my side to push me in the right direction.

Even when the men came to the house to ask questions, questions to which neither of us had any answers, I remained remote from reality, insulated by my own shock. Afterward I couldn't remember their names, all those courteous but incisively probing men who wanted to know how and why and by whom the Senator had been killed. Their faces blurred in my memory, the faces to which I said over and over again, "I don't know. I don't know."

I heard the news reports and absorbed the information that whoever the assassin had been, he had gotten away, leaving very little in the way of clues. It didn't matter. The Senator was dead, Aunt Stell was dead. If the police and the FBI and the Justice Department combed the building from which the fatal shot had been fired, if they scraped up dust or looked for threads or fingerprints or shell casings that might lead them to the killer, it meant nothing to me. I had been loved and protected and cared for by the McCaffeys, and they were gone and a stage in my life had ended; nothing that happened to a murderer would ever bring back what I had lost.

The only sharply clear thought I remember having had during that time was one of anger and resentment that I had to do it alone, that Larry was not beside me as he should have been, to act as a buffer between me and the men who seemed determined to drag out of me any stray bit of information I might have garnered along the way. Larry, who could have made it so much easier simply by his presence and the touch of his hand, who never came at all.

Until at last I emerged from the cocoon of numbness and began to function again. Until I decided the best thing for me was to run . . . or, to put it less dramatically, to pack up and leave town, to find a place where I could start over.

Bascom's Point. I owned half an inn, sharing with the great-aunts. It would be a place to stay until I'd sorted out my thoughts; it might be a place that needed a dishwasher, or a cook, or a desk clerk. Not that I knew anything about being any of those things, but in my simplicity I supposed they were not any of them very difficult, and that even I could easily handle such tasks.

I was on my way, and the few hundred miles separating me from Hampton were beginning to insulate me from the troubles I had known there.

I slept.

Rudy woke me, whining to go out. I wasn't used to attending to the needs of a dog, but he was quite capable of making them known, and it was rather nice to have something that needed to be done and someone to insist that I do it.

I put my new companion through a series of test commands and found that he responded reasonably well to most of them. That was particularly gratifying when it dawned on me that the great-aunts might not be prepared to have their inn invaded by a sixty-pound Airedale. I had a sneaking suspicion that they were cat people.

I was watching Rudy and was not my usual attentive self when I stepped backward off the walk in front of my room and collided with someone.

I heard the grunt of his breath, a muttered apology, and the man was moving quickly away from me. I turned with my own apology, only to stare after him in disturbed bewilderment.

Did he seem vaguely familiar, a rather stocky man in a blue suit? He got into a car in front of one of the units near the office and drove quickly away without looking toward me, turning east on the highway.

It was a white car.

I couldn't have said whether or not it was the same one I'd kept seeing behind me the previous day. I'm no expert on cars; the makes or models are no more recognizable than the engine parts would be.

"Heel," I told Rudy, and he trotted beside me, tongue lolling happily, as I walked up to see which unit the man had occupied. "Number six. I don't think that car was there when we checked in last night." Already I was getting used to talking to the dog as if he were a person. I think lots of people have pets just for that reason, so they won't seem to be talking to themselves.

I don't know what impulse led me into the office to inquire. I didn't, at that point, really believe the man was following me. It was only that it struck me as oddly coincidental that a middle-aged man in a blue suit and driving a white car kept showing up in my vicinity.

"Number six? Mr. Tolman? Charles Tolman?"

"When did he check in?" I asked, not admitting that I didn't know the name.

"Oh . . . about half an hour after you did, last night. Around six thirty, it was. Did you know him?"

"I thought I did, but maybe not. I didn't see his car last night; it looked like a friend's car."

"I believe he was having some work done on it, at a station down the street. He didn't pick it up until this morning." The desk clerk smiled uncertainly. "I'm sorry if you missed him, if he was a friend of yours?"

I hesitated, then asked, "Was he from Hampton? My hometown?"

22

He had to consult a card for that, then shook his head. "No. His home address is Georgetown, D.C."

I shook my head. "Not my friend, then. Well, thank you." I turned in my key and made my way back to the car, Rudy obediently at my heels. Georgetown. In Washington, D.C. I knew plenty of people there, through the Senator, but none of them well. And there was no reason why any of them should have any interest in me. No doubt the stranger was simply having car problems and just happened to be pacing me.

The rest of the trip was uneventful. I saw no more of the man in the blue suit or his white car. The weather had cleared and warmed so that it seemed summer had returned; however briefly.

I hadn't been to Bascom's Point since the fall my parents died, and my memories of that long-ago time were dimmed. I remembered the inn as a large, rambling place fresh with white paint and green shutters, but mostly I recalled the long sandy beaches where I had been allowed to run free with my cousins and my small dog.

I realized that I was looking forward to renewing the association with more pleasure than I would have thought possible. Aunt Stell had seldom come home . . . never, in the time I'd lived with her . . . because the Senator disliked informal beach living and was always too busy for leisurely vacations anyway. But she had loved it from childhood, too, and often spoke of Bascom's Point and the fun she'd had there as a little girl.

Fun. God, I'd almost forgotten there was such a thing! For a moment I dwelled on Larry and all the plans we'd made. But he'd made it clear I wasn't important enough; he wouldn't jeopardize his future in politics because of me. In a very distant way I could see that it would be uncomfortable, down through the years, to find constant references to his wife's squalid connections . . . *Governor Engle, whose wife is the former Brenna St. John, niece of the notorious (or infamous) Senator Harold McCaffey. . .*

Oh, they wouldn't say it or print it quite like that. But everyone would know. I tried to be fair and think how I would feel if it were Larry's father who had resorted to illegal and unethical acts, but I couldn't believe *I* would ever have broken our engagement for such reasons. After all, *Larry* wouldn't have been guilty of anything, and neither was I.

Thinking about Larry was futile and only aroused bitterness and antagonisms that were better forgotten.

It was nearly dusk when I finally saw the sign: BASCOM'S POINT, POPULATION 732.

23

That small? I suppose that up till then, in the back of my mind I'd considered the possibility that if there were no need for my services at the inn I might find another office job, such as the one in the insurance office which I'd given up in the expectation of marrying Larry. There wouldn't be many jobs available in a place the size of this one, though.

It was a pleasant and only vaguely familiar village, with small neat houses, most of them with fenced yards and whatever flowers would grow in the sandy soil. The business district straggled over four full blocks, none of the shops looking large enough or prosperous enough to warrant the hiring of clerks or secretaries.

I remembered that we'd turned off the main road by the little red brick schoolhouse . . . only it no longer seemed to be standing. I'd run through the town and reached the waterfront with its crumbling docks and scattered small boats, and I wasn't sure how to find the inn.

An old man came along the sidewalk, limping with the aid of a cane. He came to attention like a soldier when I let the car roll to a halt beside him.

"Excuse me, can you help me? I'm looking for the St. John place . . . on North Spit, I think it is, the old inn?"

The old man scratched at a sparsely covered scalp. "If you're looking for a room, there's better places. Here in town. Up to Mrs. Edmonds', for one." He gestured along the deserted street.

"No, I want the St. John's. They're my aunts. Callula, Eglantine, and Grazielle St. John." I smiled a little because those absurd names had always amused me and now that I was two days' traveling time from Hampton my sense of humor was returning.

"Oh." His voice had a flat sound, as if he didn't approve but was determined to mind his own business. "Well, it's out on North Spit."

I refrained from pointing out that I'd already admitted to knowing that only seconds earlier. "And how do I get to North Spit?"

He gave me directions, pointing out the road that wound northward along the curve of the bay. "There's a sign, says North Spit, if the damned kids haven't knocked it down again." He rethought the profanity and apologized. "Begging your pardon, miss."

I nodded. "Which place is it?"

"The only one there is. You can't miss it, it's the only building left out there." He was staring at me peculiarly so that I wondered if he was retarded or something. Not that he sounded retarded. And it didn't matter anyway. All I wanted was to reach the inn and make myself known to the

24

aunts and fall into bed. I felt as if I'd been driving for weeks, rather than for two days.

When I glanced in the rear-view mirror he was still standing there, looking after me. Oh, well. Bascom's Point was off the main roads; maybe they didn't see many strangers here. I turned my attention to the waterfront, which wasn't much. It didn't look as if there were any commercial fishing from this bay; the boats were all pleasure craft so far as I could see, small sailboats and motor launches and dinghies.

Once I passed beyond the docks there was nothing but sand and coarse beach grass. Because the road was in poor repair, I had to drive at a low speed; driving slow was just as well, for it enabled me to enjoy the expanse of water and dunes. Solitude—was that what I craved right now? I hadn't decided; I only knew that I had needed a change of scene and of pace, and this place offered both.

The light had nearly gone when I topped the last of the dunes and saw the inn. From a distance it seemed much as I recalled it from all those years ago, except that I thought then there had been other houses and buildings around it. It was a big place, looming against the background of sand and sea, dominating the narrow spit that ended half a mile beyond the structure.

There was a veranda all around the ground floor, where we had played on rainy days. I caught myself smiling, remembering a time with my parents on that twenty-years-past vacation. It had been an inn in those days, too, although I had no recollection of anyone being there except dozens of relatives.

As I drove into the yard, my smiled faded.

The sound of the motor died as I sat staring at the inn . . . *my inn* . . . the only piece of property that hadn't been lost as a result of the Senator's bad judgment. The half-interest had been Aunt Stell's, the lawyer told me, and the reason it hadn't vanished like everything else was that she had signed it over to me some years before, although she continued to pay the taxes on it and hadn't told me about the transaction.

I had envisioned it as a going business place, which made a profit and supported the aunts and could perhaps be made to contribute to my support as well. What I was now looking at was not encouraging.

The house was huge, but there all resemblance to the mansion of my memory ended. Its weathered siding and shingled roof bore no trace of paint. Perhaps that wasn't unusual here on the coast because the wind and the sand would combine to scour paint away.

25

The signs of neglect were obvious in the sagging steps and the broken porch railing. There wasn't even a light that I could see.

I fought to control the surge of alarm. What if it were all locked up, empty? Abandoned? Why hadn't I thought to call before I left home, to speak to the aunts and let them know I was coming? I had sent a telegram, though, notifying them of the funerals, and I knew they'd received it because they sent a wreath for each of the caskets.

I listened to the wash of the surf on the far side of the dunes where the ocean was out of sight but within hearing distance. A gull soared overhead in the last of the evening's light and I watched its flight as I got out of the car, feeling as alone as that solitary bird.

There had once been other houses out here on the spit, summer homes owned by families who came back to them every year. What had happened to them?

No one came to investigate the sound of the car. Would inhabitants of the inn be able to hear it, over the covering murmur of the ocean?

I'd looked forward to getting here, and now I didn't want to walk up to the door. I took a few steps in that direction, then paused to look back across the bay. The lights of Bascom's Point glittered there, welcoming little beacons in contrast with the darkness of the inn. Maybe I should have stayed in the village and come out here in the daytime, although surely if the aunts were gone the old man would have known it. Aunt Stell said people in small towns knew everything about all their neighbors.

Disappointment washed over me in a sickening wave. Two weeks ago, I'd had everything. Now all I had was a half-interest in a tumbledown old inn that didn't look as if it were worth paying the taxes on.

Maudie had been right. I shouldn't have just started across the country this way, without knowing what I was getting into. I was on the verge of turning back to the village for the night when I saw the light appear in one of the windows.

Uncertainty held me. Did I really want to stay here, even if the aunts still operated the place? I'd run from Hampton, run like a child who can't face up to her troubles; although I'd had no real reason to think I'd find sanctuary here, I was crushingly disappointed not to have done so.

I didn't have time to come to a decision. The door opened and a round, pale face stared at me in the twilight and a voice demanded, "Who are you? What do you want?"

[4]

THE OLD lady was one of the aunts; I didn't know which one. She was so tiny I might have taken her for a child if she hadn't had blue-white hair. She peered at me nearsightedly.

"Are you wanting a room?"

"Well, yes, I suppose I am. I'm Brenna St. John."

She moved a little closer to the edge of the porch so that the boards creaked warningly beneath her meager weight. "Brenna? Arthur's daughter? Good heavens, what are you doing here?"

She didn't give me time to reply, however, but reached out a hand, drawing me up the steps and into the house. We were in a dark hallway, with a kitchen to one side of us; we'd obviously entered through the back door. I stumbled over something, but she didn't turn on a light, only urged me ahead of her toward a faint glow at the far end of the corridor.

"I'm Zell . . . Grazielle, you know, only nobody calls me that except when they're angry with me. Come in, come in, they'll be so surprised to see you!"

I stood on the threshold of the room, noting with rising dismay how shabby and ill-lit it was. There was a threadbare old rug, so dim I couldn't tell its colors, and a clutter of mending and knitting and newspapers. Here, too, were the other aunts, who looked up in a manner that was somewhat less than welcoming.

"We haven't got any spare rooms," one of the women said, not pausing in her rocking and knitting. She spoke not to me but to the little woman beside me.

27

"Oh, but it's little Brenna, you know, Arthur's daughter," Zell said. Her introduction made me feel odd. I was a foot and a half taller than Zell.

Callie . . . I remember now, the tall, thin one was Callie, the oldest of the three. She stopped rocking and leaned forward as if willing her eyes to see clearly in spite of the inadequate light.

"Brenna? Good God, what are you doing here?"

I shifted my weight uneasily, like a child caught in a misdeed. Why hadn't I called, or sent a telegram, or *something?* I'd thought that a half-ownership gave me the right to come, but maybe it didn't. They had lived here all their lives; no doubt they thought of the inn as exclusively their own. I cleared my throat, my discomfort increasing. "I hadn't anywhere else to go."

It wasn't quite true. I had some money and I could have found another job in Hampton, if I'd cared to stay there. It hadn't occurred to me that they'd be taken aback at my arrival on their doorstep.

They were staring at me, three pair of bright eyes in the weathered old faces. All three of them wore cotton print housedresses and bedroom slippers.

"Well, come in, come in," Callie said finally, when I'd begun to think I might as well turn around and leave. "We heard about Harold, getting himself into a mess. Always expected he would. The only surprise was he waited so long to get caught."

It was difficult to come up with an appropriate reply to that. Heaven knew I'd thought all sorts of bitter things myself about the Senator's behavior, but when someone else expressed similar thoughts I felt the need to defend him without actually being capable of doing so.

"Everything's gone," I said at last, wishing I'd never come. I ought to turn around and walk out at once, instead of standing here defending myself, making excuses. "All the property, the house Aunt Stell lived in. Everything except this, the inn. The lawyer said I had a half-interest in the inn."

For a moment no one said anything. I could hear the distant surf and the pounding of my own heart, almost as if I were frightened, which was absurd. What was there to be afraid of?

"Well, is that right?" Zell was examining me through the granny glasses she'd put on. "Is that right, young Brenna owns half the inn?" The idea seemed to please *her*; a grin was spreading across her small features.

Callie made a snorting sound. "Has for some time. Stella made out the papers several years ago. Sit down, sit down . . . don't expect me to get up, my feet are tired."

Relief nibbled faintly at me. At least that didn't come as a horrible

28

revelation to them. I sank into the indicated chair. "You know all about it then."

Callie made another of the snorting sounds. "Of course. You've owned a quarter interest ever since your father died and willed you his share. Didn't they tell you that? And then Stella added her interest to give you half. Not that it's much of an inheritance, considering what you must have been expecting."

My mouth felt dry. "I wasn't expecting anything."

"Nothing from the Senator?" She spoke the familiar title in a way my uncle would have resented had he heard it, her contempt scarcely concealed. "But he was a rich man, wasn't he? All kinds of interests. It's a good thing the inn wasn't where Harold could get his hands on it, or I suppose we'd have lost our share, too. I knew he was a crook even when he was a boy. I told Stella that, but she didn't listen."

I spoke around the unexpected ache in my throat. "She loved him."

The old eyes were suddenly perceptive as her hands stilled on the knitting in her lap. "And you loved her. Well, Stella was a good girl. Too bad it had to end the way it did. And you"—she scrutinized my face in the lamp-light—"you got hurt, too, didn't you? Weren't you planning to get married pretty soon?"

The ache deepened and I had to speak quickly before it was impossible to speak at all. "We've broken our engagement."

"Who broke it? You or him? No, that's none of my business, is it?" She turned to her sister, who had so far sat in silence. "We're just about to have a cup of tea. Egg's supposed to be getting it, but she's so slow. Would you like a cup of tea?"

"I'd love one," I said and, for some reason, had to blink against the tears.

Tiny Zell had taken her place in one of the rockers which were the primary furniture in the room except for a rather stiff and unused-looking sofa and a multitude of small tables mostly buried in odds and ends. Her feet barely touched the floor. "So you've come to stay with us, have you, Brenna?"

I hesitated. It had seemed so logical before I left Hampton . . . and so brash and thoughtless now that I was here. "I thought I might stay . . . for a little while. Only Aunt Callie said . . . there were no rooms."

"No rooms to rent," Eglantine corrected me. She, too, was short, but round and well padded whereas Zell was fine-boned and slim. "But it's half your house, so of course it's all right. Which room, Callie? There's only two empty, the corner one and the little middle one. The corner one's nicer."

"It also rents for more," Callie pointed out. "Twenty dollars a week

29

difference, and we promised a room to the man that Egg talked to."

"But it's part Brenna's house," Zell said. "Shouldn't you let her choose?"

I broke in quickly. "I'm sure the smaller one will do nicely. I'm sorry, I ought to have called. . . ."

Zell chuckled. "Can't call. No telephone. All the poles went down when the hurricane took out everything on the spit . . . everything but us. Company didn't want to go to the expense of putting them all back up again just for us, not when nobody else was rebuilding."

"Is that what happened?" I was momentarily diverted. "A hurricane? I thought I remembered other houses out here."

"Used to be plenty of 'em," Zell agreed. "All went down, two years ago. Freak storm, left us untouched or as good as, except for a bit of the roof." She rocked, picking up her own busywork, and a granny square of crocheting grew in her agile fingers.

"Nobody called us, anyway, to amount to anything." Callie grimaced at her younger sister. "Egg, get the tea and the cups. Don't forget, four cups."

Egg paused beside my chair to pat my hand. "Goodness, you're quite pretty, aren't you? Brown eyes like your father's, only his hair was much darker."

"No, it wasn't," Zell contradicted. "Arthur's hair was sort of brown with light streaks in it where the sun had bleached it. Just like hers."

"It was darker." Egg had lost her jolly look.

"I'd love a cup of that tea," I said, before it went any further. We sat in silence until Egg brought it; she must have had the water on to boil earlier because it didn't take her long. The beverage was served in lovely cups and saucers, all exquisite and all different. They were part of Egg's collection, she told me. She had them from all over the country.

"Not that I ever got to visit much, very far away. But people send them to me."

After the first rather chilly reception, they seemed to warm. I was glad they didn't ask me any of the details about recent events at home. Instead they chatted about minor domestic matters, and Egg asked if my sandals were Italian; gradually the tea made me feel better. It wasn't until I'd relaxed considerably that I noticed why the light was so dim and realized why Zell hadn't turned on a light in the hallway on our way in. They were using kerosene lamps.

"Isn't there any electricity either?" I asked into one of the lulls.

"Off and on," Zell told me. "It's been off for two days, since the last blow. They've been working on it. More than likely it'll be on again tomorrow. Until we get another storm. I think they'd like to cut us off, same as the phone company, but so far they haven't figured out a legal way to do it.'' She chuckled, as if that were a good joke on the power company.

Egg stood up and began to put the cups and saucers on a tray. ''It's your turn to wash, Zell.''

Zell's tiny face puckered like a child's in righteous indignation. ''It is not. Teacups are your responsibility, not mine. I only take turns with the dinner dishes. After all, I do *pay* for my room.''

''A *reduced* rate.''

''But I'm a *guest*. I don't own half the house, like you and Callie.'' She shot me a sly look. ''I'm only a cousin. I only rent a room, and I do dinner dishes every other day in order to get a reduced rate, but I don't have to wash teacups.''

''I'll be glad to do them,'' I offered just as the commotion began outside.

''What on earth is *that?*'' Callie put down her knitting and turned her head as if by so doing she could see out through the back wall of the house.

''It's a dog,'' Zell said.

''But we don't have a dog,'' Egg observed.

I sprang up in some consternation. I'd completely forgotten poor Rudy. ''I do . . . I forgot and left him in the car! I hope it's all right if I bring him in. . . .''

''It sounds as if he's eating someone. Better see who it is and call the dog off.'' Callie didn't sound as if she were a dog fancier, but she hadn't forbidden Rudy the house. All of us except Callie hurried back down the dark corridor, Zell leading the way.

''I'll bet it's the man who reserved a room. See, your dog won't let him out of his car.'' She stepped back when Rudy bounded toward me to lick eagerly at my hands. ''Goodness, I hope he won't bite.''

I hoped he wouldn't, too. I made vague sounds of apology, getting the Airedale by the collar and dragging him toward my car. He must have come out through a window. He sat obediently when I got out his dish and scooped a handful of dog food into it.

I didn't pay any attention to the newcomer who had driven in until the dog was busy gulping his food; when I turned toward the inn then, Egg was holding up a lamp and Zell held open the door while she explained that guests were usually received at the front, which he would have reached had he continued on around the loop of drive.

The guest was a man in his early forties and wearing a blue suit. Involuntarily my eyes went to his car, parked not far from my own. It wasn't white, however, but some dark color.

Still, I caught my breath because he looked so much like the man who had appeared to be following me from Hampton.

He vanished into the inn, the aunts following. I stood in the dark, waiting for Rudy to finish eating, hearing the quickened beat of the pulses in my ears. Surely I was mistaken; it couldn't be the same man. If it *were*, I couldn't swallow it as coincidence, that he'd stayed so close behind me and then come to the very inn where I was staying.

But, of course, it was nothing of the sort. A dark car, not a white one. He was simply another stocky man in a blue suit; there must be hundreds of men who would answer the same general description.

It was another ten minutes before I followed the others inside, for Rudy had been cooped up too long and wanted to romp. I allowed him to run, since he made no effort to go far, and my thoughts washed around me with the turbulence of the sea beyond the ridge.

How naïve I had been to think that returning to the scene of childish happiness would automatically wipe out the soul-searing events of the past few weeks! I might better have gone to some totally unknown place, for though I knew no one in Bascom's Point except the old aunts, the villagers undoubtedly knew who I was. The Senator's niece, of course, and everyone in the country knew about *him.*

However, I was here, and I might as well make the best of it for a few days. Once the dust had been allowed to settle, so to speak, there would be plenty of time to decide whether to stay on or to go. The bleak sensation aroused by thinking about going, to some unknown and equally unwelcoming town, made me only too aware of how vulnerable I was, for all my ideas about independence.

Egg met me in the back hall, having just washed out the teacups. She smiled tentatively at Rudy. "My, he's a big one, isn't he?"

"Yes. He's quite well behaved, though. I hope it's all right if I keep him in my room."

"So long as he doesn't bother anyone." She didn't sound very sure that he wouldn't. "I suppose he *is* house-trained?"

She was carrying a kerosene lamp, which seemed to cast more shadows than light as we moved through the ground floor. Rooms opened on both sides of the corridor, rooms filled with heavy dark furniture. We met Zell near the foot of the stairs that rose from the front of the house, out of what must be the main lobby.

32

"Shall I take Brenna up to her room?" she offered.

Egg informed her, with some dignity, that she would do it herself. It was, after all, *her* inn and her job.

Zell grinned at me. It was hard to believe, when she looked such a mischievous gamine, that she was seventy years old, the youngest of the three aunts.

"Let Egg run up and down the stairs. She needs the exercise more than I do, at that."

"Running up and down stairs won't affect my *metabolism*," Egg said, tight-lipped. I guessed that Egg and Zell often spoke in italics.

The stairs were narrow and uncarpeted, creaking under our weight. They turned several times, as if they'd been built helter-skelter, without planning; by the time we reached the second floor I had no idea which direction was which.

"I hope the little room will be all right," Egg said on a note of apology. "Once it gets cold, you'll like it better than the big one because it's easier to keep warm. If you're here that long, I mean. We don't have many young people; we're too isolated and they're used to reliable electricity and telephones and things like that. They don't like the quiet out here."

She paused at one of the identical doors that ringed the landing and stretched on down the narrow hall, giving me a chance to ask a question.

"But you keep most of the rooms rented most of the time?"

"We try to keep them rented. It's the only income we have, except for our trust funds. It was enough once, but the way prices keep going up I guess we'll have to die soon; it won't stretch."

She led the way into the room and I followed, at once relieved that the "little room" wasn't the horror I'd halfway anticipated. It was small by ordinary standards, I supposed, and had only twin dormers overlooking the end of the spit, although I didn't learn that until daylight. There was a bare wood floor, painted brown, and hand-hooked rag rugs at strategic places. The double bed had a crocheted granny squares spread in bright colors, and there was a small desk and a maple rocker with a cushion.

"There's a bathroom down the hall; it's got a sign. We've only got the two bathrooms up here and one downstairs. That's one reason we can't draw more customers. I guess people are used to private baths, although we got along without them well enough in the old days." She gave me a smile. "Come down when you're ready in the morning. Regular breakfast is at eight, but anyone who wants it earlier or later just shifts for himself.

33

Good night, Brenna. I'm glad you've come. It's good to see a young face. All these old people are depressing sometimes.''

I'd have to remember that, I thought when she was gone. Remember not to let my self-pity show so that *I* was depressing as well as depressed.

She had lit one of the kerosene lamps for me, and it gave the room a warm, cheerful glow. I looked around, comparing it with my room at Aunt Stell's. Ah, well, I'd had fourteen years of living in luxury; it was time to see how everyone else lived, and no doubt I'd be all the better for it.

Rudy made himself comfortable on the rug beside the bed, curling up there as if it were his appointed place. I scratched him behind the ears, grateful for his company.

I got ready for bed in a hurry, forgoing the usual amenities of washing and tooth brushing. After making sure there were matches beside the lamp, I turned down the wick and blew into the chimney to put it out. And then, because I was used to fresh air for sleeping, I raised one of the windows.

Althought it was only early September, there was a nip to the air. I liked the smell of it, fresh off the ocean this way, and for a few minutes I leaned on my elbows on the sill, kneeling on one of the rag rugs.

I heard the car coming long before it reached the inn. Was it coming here? There was nothing beyond us but sand dunes and beach grass and water, although the road did stretch on toward the tip of the spit.

Sure enough, the car stopped here. I heard the door slam, but it was out of sight on the other side of the building. I waited, but no sound of voices or knocking carried to me. Since they'd indicated all their rooms were filled, I assumed it was one of the guests.

A few minutes later Rudy lifted his head and emitted a low, rumbling growl. It wasn't intended to be intimidating, I decided, but was more a notice to me that someone was stirring. I heard the footsteps go past my door; I thought they entered the room next to mine.

I got into bed and lay in the darkness, resigning myself to the masochistic force that had enveloped me every night since the horror began; let it all roll over me, all the terrible scenes from the first incredible newscast to the final handful of dirt thrown onto matching caskets, and then I would be able to sleep.

For the first time I dozed off almost at once and even my dreams were untroubled.

[5]

I WOKE up hungry and was urged on by Rudy, who wanted to go out. I dressed quickly in slacks and a pullover and let us out into the hall.

The fragrance of coffee drifted up the stairs. I looked around to see if any fellow roomers were astir, but all the doors were closed, including the one I thought the latecomer had entered last night.

The aunts were in the kitchen, Eglantine and Grazielle squabbling over something. I stood in the doorway for a moment in uncertainty; there was a dining room, but it was empty. Instead, a man was eating hotcakes at a round table in the kitchen itself. He didn't notice me but went on chewing. He wore a large hearing aid in one ear, although he was not so very old—in his middle fifties, I guessed. He was sturdily built, and when Callie introduced us, he looked at me through very thick glasses that magnified and blurred his light-blue eyes.

"Donald Rossdaie, one of our guests," Callie said. "This is our niece, Brenna St. John."

Mr. Rossdale nodded and went immediately back to his hotcakes, his tongue pursuing a trickle of syrup at one corner of his mouth. I settled at the opposite side of the table to be served up my own breakfast by the aunts. Zell dropped into the chair next to mine for what was obviously an after-breakfast cup of coffee.

"I let my dog loose outside," I said. "I think he'll be all right. There's nothing to bother, is there?"

"Unless he bites a guest." She looked as if she might enjoy seeing such a

35

thing. "Only sand and water, no flowers or lawn to uproot. How did you sleep?"

I admitted to the best night's sleep in weeks, then regretted the oblique reference to the reasons for my poor sleeping habits, but Zell didn't follow up on that.

"We eat out here in the morning. Lunch and dinner in the main dining room. Callie says it isn't reasonable for a bunch of old women to try to maintain restaurant hours, so it's lunch between noon and one, and dinner between six and seven, and you have to arrange for dinner ahead of time or you're on your own. The kind of people who stay with us don't seem to mind."

I was mildly curious about the others, who came straggling down while I was eating. I began to feel quite out of place. Mr. Rossdale was the youngest, except for me. The others were all from their late sixties well up into the eighties. There was Mr. Darryl Montgomery, who reminded me somewhat of the Senator, with his thatch of carefully brushed white hair and his mod jacket and tie and two-toned blue shoes to match. Mr. Montgomery informed me that he was in real estate. He ate daintily but at some length.

There were the Avery sisters, Lulu and Clara. I didn't make out which was which; they were almost identical, wispy little old ladies in dresses made from the same bolt of pastel printed cotton. It sounded as if they had lived here in the same shared room for years.

There was Sherman Foster, an extraordinarily tall old gentleman in a seersucker suit such as I thought had been worn around the turn of the century, with a gold watch chain draped across his vest. He was smiling and polite, and both Zell and Egg were, to my astonished amusement, making eyes at him.

I didn't see the man who had arrived last night. "Is this everybody?" I asked Zell, under cover of the muted conversation around us.

"No, there are several more. One youngish fellow, he's already out on the beach, and the one who came last night."

"What's his name? The newest one?" It continued to linger, the faintest suspicion that he'd been a fellow traveler all the way from Hampton.

The name she gave me was not Charles Tolman, however.

"Bill Haden, I think it was. You're not going to find our guests very exciting, I'm afraid. Not unless that hairy fellow appeals to you. I used to have a gentleman friend with a mustache, oh, over fifty years ago. It was really very nice."

36

Egg, bearing a plate of scrambled eggs and toast for each of the Avery sisters, overheard the remark.

"I suppose you're trying to make us think Irving kissed you," she said. "*I* happen to know he *didn't*."

Zell's mouth contracted. "I don't know how you could *know* that."

"You were only seventeen, and he was a grown man and not interested in schoolgirls. I remember him very well."

"I didn't say whether he kissed me or whether he didn't. All I said was he was a gentleman friend, and he *did* like me. He said he liked *small* girls, not *fat* ones."

Egg's cheeks were pink, perhaps from her exertions over the stove. "I wasn't fat."

"Not so much," Zell conceded, "when you were nineteen. I think your dog is scratching to come in, Brenna. Will he need to be fed?"

"I have dog food, but if there are scraps I'm sure he'd love them."

I offered to help clear the tables, but I was brushed aside.

"Not on your first day here," Egg said. "You've had a rough time; you'll want a few days to rest and relax."

All eyes swung in my direction. Did they know why I'd had a rough time? I wished Egg hadn't mentioned it, but I forced a smile and told them to let me know if they wanted me to do anything, and then I went to care for Rudy.

Since the inn was so isolated and surrounded by sand and water, there seemed no reason why he couldn't be allowed to run free. It was still cool enough so that my pullover sweater felt good, but there was the promise of warmth in the sun. As they didn't need my help, I decided to go for a walk along the bay.

It turned out to be a long walk, along the curving pale crescent of sand that skirted the bay, then around the end of the spit and back up the ocean side of the finger of land. Though Rudy was obviously entranced with the waves and delighted at being allowed to run free, he never went far from me. A shout would bring him racing back in long, graceful strides.

We had the world to ourselves, except for a lone figure far up the beach on the ocean side, a man in a cranberry-colored sweater and jeans. I couldn't make out any more about him except that he moved like a young person; perhaps he was the "hairy" one Zell had mentioned. I had no wish to meet him yet. I had all I needed right here, the dog at my side and silence surrounding us, except for the surf and the gulls.

Balm to the soul, Aunt Stell had called it, and she was right. I could feel the healing atmosphere already. The magic of Bascom's Point was not just a fantasy of childhood; it was the reality of nature's own power to regenerate.

As the sun grew higher and warmer, a marvelous lethargy overtook me. Rudy came racing back to fling himself at my feet, panting. I looked down at him with a grin.

"That's what I need, too. A rest. Let's find a hollow in the sand, where we'll be out of the wind, and take a nap."

The sand was clean and warm and I slept. Perhaps I was making up for all the nights I hadn't slept; at any rate, when I was roused by Rudy's barking, the sun had worked its way from east to west.

Confused, still groggy, I sat up. I must have missed lunch altogether. It was a wonder the dog had stayed with me.

"Will he bite?"

The unexpected voice, deeply timbred, unquestionably male, brought me scrambling around on all fours. I felt awkward and at a disadvantage, crouched there at his feet.

It was the hairy one, all right. All six feet two of him, with hard muscles under the cranberry wool and the faded denim. The beard was red and there was a flourishing mustache to go with it. I stared up into the blue eyes . . . an odd shade of blue that was vaguely familiar.

"Will he bite?" The question was surely academic, since Rudy had stopped barking and was simply keeping a watchful eye on the situation.

I staggered to my feet, and the man put out a hand to pull me up . . . a large, strong hand with fine reddish fuzz across the back of it, a hand I surely knew.

He saw recognition, mingled with disbelief, flash across my face; the beard split in a grin revealing uneven but very white teeth.

"Hello, Brenna. I wasn't sure it was you, at first."

"Max?" I was stunned. I'd gotten over Max years ago, so I didn't understand why I had this hit-in-the-stomach sensation. He hadn't let go of my hand and I was too paralyzed to remove it.

"Good old Max. Remember me? Your ex-husband? Or almost-once-your-husband or whatever the hell it was."

He looked down at the hand he held, rubbing his thumb over the rather pale circle of skin around my third finger. "It wouldn't have been my ring you recently removed, so it must have been someone else's. As an old friend and lover, am I allowed to ask the current status?"

There was a pain in my chest. I put up my free hand to massage the area over my breastbone.

"Recently . . . un-engaged . . . if there is such a word."

He nodded as if he were pleased. "I saw you, from up the beach, walking the dog. Of course I couldn't tell who you were, but you didn't look like one of the old ladies. Around here anybody under seventy is an adolescent, but I thought you might be in my own league. I was going to walk up and ask if I hadn't met you somewhere, you know, a real original approach, and then all of a sudden you disappeared. I figured you'd gone to earth to avoid me, so I went on back to the inn for lunch. After a while they got to wondering out loud what had happened to you, and I volunteered to come to the rescue. Took me a while. I probably wouldn't have found you if it hadn't been for your dog. He took a dislike to me."

Rudy wasn't exactly menacing, but he didn't like Max touching me either.

"Shut up, Rudy. Sit," I said automatically. "What are you doing here? Did you say . . . are you staying at the inn?"

"Sure. It's cheap, even if it has few other virtues. Or did have few until you showed up and gave me a bonus."

"What are you doing here?"

"Recuperating. From pneumonia, of all the stupid things. And a beaut of a penicillin reaction, on top of that. The doctor said to get lots of rest and gradually work up to plenty of exercise and come back in a month, prepared to work less intensely. I've been here four . . . no, five days. So I have a little over three weeks yet to go." The oddly light blue eyes took on a remembered gleam. "It's going to be more interesting with you around."

I sounded breathless. "Why should you think that?"

"A pretty girl is always better than no pretty girl, I've always said. Remember how I always said that?"

"You're an idiot," I told him and watched the grin widen.

"Ah, and I remember how *you* always said *that*. Still, an idiot's better than no man at all, isn't he?"

"There's always Mr. Rossdale, with the hearing aid, or Mr. Foster," I said and heard myself giggle. God, how long had it been since I'd done that!

"Mr. Rossdale reads *True Crime* magazines and hears little or nothing of what goes on around him. He isn't interested in ladies unless they are mutilated corpses . . . you should see the illustrations in those magazines! And Mr. Foster is a real charmer, but he's already got both Zell and Egg working on him; I doubt he'd want to take on a third female, although you might have the edge, being slightly their junior."

"Max. Max, I can't believe it's really you."

He opened his mouth, a vast cavern in the midst of all that red hair. His finger indicated a back molar. "My gold tooth, see? It's me—Max. Want to see the scar on my. . . ."

"No," I said hastily. "I believe you. It's really you. Why all the facial growth?"

"Don't you like it? Lots of girls are very much turned on by red beards and mustaches."

"It will take some getting used to."

"Plenty of time. Three weeks anyway. *Are* you going to be here that long, too?"

"I don't know." Just remembering why I was here was enough to take a bit of the sparkle out of my voice. "I came because . . . because. . . ."

"Because there was nowhere else to go. Poor baby. I read the papers. It's been hell on wheels, hasn't it? So you came to the good old aunts to kiss you and make you well."

"Well, you see I haven't changed either. I always wanted someone to kiss me and make me well. Only now I know it doesn't really work."

"You sure about that? Maybe it depends on who does the kissing."

I shouldn't have been surprised when he pulled me into his arms. Max was still Max. But I'd been a long time away from him, and my initial response was automatic resistance.

Max, however, was a past master at overcoming resistance, if by no other method than brute force. We wrestled for a minute until I started to laugh, and he let me go.

"That's not how you're supposed to react when a man kisses you."

"It feels so funny. All that hair!"

"You're the first one who's ever complained about it."

"And there've been dozens, no doubt. I'm not really complaining . . . it's just odd."

"It grows on you."

"Not on me, it doesn't."

And we were off again, as if the years had fallen away and we were once more seventeen and nineteen; in the ensuing struggle, during which we fell laughing and breathless onto the sand, Rudy barked and jumped around us and finally put an end to the silliness by nipping Max on the behind.

"Damn!" He let me go and rubbed his posterior. "Call off your dog, lady, before he gets something more vital!"

"Rudy, down! Down, I said! Now stay! Did he hurt you?"

"Yes. Look and see if there's anything missing."

"Your pants aren't torn, so that doesn't seem likely. Oh, Max, Max, who'd ever have dreamed you'd come walking back into my life, wilder than ever? Where have you been? What have you been doing? Are you married? Is there a girl?"

"If I were married, would I be wrestling with you? Certainly there are girls, there have always been girls. But no special one. You know something, Brenna? There must have been a hundred girls in the past nine years, but not one of them was special. Not the way you were."

I'm not sure what that might have led to if he'd left it there for me to chew on and respond to. But he didn't. He got to his feet and jerked me along with him, which set Rudy off again. By the time we got the dog under control, which was to say prevented him from taking another nip, Max was talking about the food at the inn.

I was hungry, but I'd rather have talked about Max. I had often thought about him in the months following the annulment of our teen-age marriage, but that was so long ago. I'd never have dreamed we could meet and fall at once back into the old, easy ways.

Of course, I knew we hadn't really. Many things had happened to each of us. We'd both grown up for one thing. Max was a man, not a boy, and we'd have to get acquainted all over again. Yet it was lovely to race with him over the dunes toward the inn, Rudy barking beside us, and feel young again, young enough to be wild and silly and to laugh and enjoy the touch of a man's hand.

Lunch was long over, of course. All Callie said was that they'd wondered if I'd had a mishap of some kind and that I could rummage in the refrigerator.

Max insisted upon preparing lunch for me and embarked upon building a sandwich. "Building" was the proper word for Max's sandwiches. It had avocado, tuna fish, mayonnaise, lettuce, and cream cheese, and was topped off with two ripe olives. With it I got a glass of milk. He himself had a beer.

I raised my eyebrows. "Beer used to be strictly for evenings. What happened to milk?"

"Milk gives you kidney stones. Beer doesn't."

"Do you have kidney stones?"

"No, of course not. I stopped drinking milk." He wiped up a dollop of cream cheese and licked it off his finger.

"Cheese has calcium in it, too," I pointed out. "That's what makes the kidney stones, if anything does."

He shrugged. "You can't give up everything. Tell me about you, Brenna. Catch me up on nine years."

"All in one breath and while I'm eating? You first. What are you doing for a living, this job that you do too intensely?"

"I'm a hospital administrator. Don't laugh, it's true! I'm a very good hospital administrator."

"You can't be. You aren't dignified enough."

"What's dignity got to do with it? I have all the patients in stitches, and that's not all bad. Don't choke, drink some milk. I spent three years in the Marines as a medic, and then somehow I got promoted to something to do with running a field hospital, and then it seemed the logical area to go into when I got out of the service. Frankly, I didn't know anything about anything else."

"You wrote lovely poetry once. Do you still?"

"Certainly, but you can't make a living writing poetry. At least I can't. Administratoring pays very well. And that brings me up to date."

"Nine years worth? What about all those hundreds of girls?"

"They are not something I am going to discuss with you. Tell me about the guy who took his ring back."

I sighed. "I don't think I want to talk about him either. Not yet anyway."

The bantering note faded from his voice. "Did he call it off because of what happened to the Senator?"

Yes, he was the same old Max. I gave in. "As a matter of fact, he did. Not very flattering, is it?"

"The son of a bitch wasn't worth your little finger if he did that."

"He's a lawyer with political ambitions," I said, vaguely surprised to hear myself making excuses for Larry. "It would have been difficult. . . ."

Max said a sharp four-letter word. "A man would act like a man, and that ain't the way, honey. Listen, did you bring any fancy duds with you? Silver lamé, something with sequins?"

"Heavens, no! What would I want with something like that?"

"Let's go out to dinner. Old Callie's a great plain cook, but let's go where it's nice and cozy and private, where we have to dress to the teeth and wear our diamonds."

"Now? At two in the afternoon?"

"Well, I've got to run a few errands first, and it'll take an hour or so to get to the place I'm thinking of. Suppose you have a nice leisurely bubble bath, and comb your hair, and put on the gladdest rags you've got, and when I come back we'll get out of this place for the evening and catch up on old times."

He eyed me expectantly, and I found myself responding as I had always responded to Max.

"All right," I agreed. "Will you settle for garnets instead of diamonds, though? I'm fresh out of diamonds." I looked down at the pale circle on my third finger with far less regret than I'd have thought possible only a day or two ago.

"I'll settle for whatever you like. I'll get started, take care of my errands, and call you when I get back."

It was amazing how much my spirits had risen since I'd encountered Max. I finished my sandwich and made another, more conservative, one, giving the last of it to Rudy. The dog seemed perfectly content to lie beside the back steps while I unloaded my belongings from the trunk of the car and carried them inside. I didn't think he'd run off, not after his hubcap drinking dish had been left under a dripping faucet and he'd drunk at it. He'd tried seawater and found it not to his liking; he had sense enough to stay where he knew he'd find food and water, and I fancied he was becoming attached to me, too.

I met the newest guest on my way up the narrow stairs with a suitcase in each hand. I encountered him on one of the landings; I thought he was startled, but after the first glance he didn't look at me but squeezed against the wall so that I could pass.

When I hesitated, he plunged on down the steps without a word.

I paused, looking after him. He was wearing slacks and a sport shirt rather than a blue suit, yet my uneasiness was aroused again by the conviction that his bulk was familiar. Damn! *Was* he the man who'd been driving behind me? If so, what was he doing here, at this dilapidated old inn?

I brought his name out of memory, the name under which he'd registered, and called after him. "Mr. Haden?"

He must have heard, but he didn't stop. He disappeared around one of the turns in the staircase, leaving me banging my luggage against my knees.

Maybe Haden wasn't his name; maybe that's why he didn't answer to it. I made a sound of disgust with myself. There were plenty of stocky, middle-aged men, and I hadn't gotten that good a look at the man in the white car . . . and besides, this one hadn't arrived in a white car, it was dark blue, I'd noticed while I was watering Rudy.

I forgot Mr. Haden, or whoever he was, and I entered my room.

[6]

I DROPPED the suitcases, forgetting that one of them contained breakables, and closed the door behind me, staring around the little room.

I wasn't a perfect housekeeper, by any means, and normally I wouldn't have noticed items being slightly out of place. Only I hadn't brought in anything but a small overnight case, last night, and those belongings had been stowed in the closet and in one dresser drawer. There was nothing visible in the room to indicate that it was even occupied.

So why was the closet door ajar, the dresser drawers pushed in so hastily that they were not properly closed, and the corner of the crocheted spread flipped back as if someone had been looking under the bed or the mattress?

The aunts hadn't been in. There would have been no need for that because I'd made up the bed myself before I left, and there hadn't been any other cleaning or straightening to do.

Only in my newly suspicious state would these things have registered, but register they had and I didn't like it. There was a key in the lock on the inside; I hadn't bothered to turn it, thinking of this more as a home than a hotel, which was foolish of me.

I checked through the belongings in the drawers and the closet; nothing was missing so far as I could tell. Well, from now on, I'd keep the door locked.

It was at that point that I remembered the man on the stairs. Had *he* been interested in my belongings? My purse still stood on the dresser, open, with its contents freely inspectable. My wallet, with identification, driver's

44

license, and cash, was in the hip pocket of my jeans; thank heaven I'd had sense enough not to leave *that* lying around.

Since no damage was done, my mood of resentment soon passed. I unpacked and hung things up, shaking out wrinkles and debating over what to wear for my dinner date with Max. Nothing looked quite what he'd indicated he had in mind, but there were more things in the car.

Belatedly I realized I'd left the car unlocked when I came up with this load of goods. I went clattering on down the stairs, hoping whoever had inspected my room hadn't been into the car while I wasn't looking.

It seemed, though, that no one had bothered anything. Old Mr. Foster, coming in as I went out, nodded smilingly. "Quite a watchdog, that fellow of yours. He doesn't want anyone to walk anywhere near your car, although I explained to him that I didn't intend to touch anything. I had to walk right out around it."

"I hope he isn't going to be so intimidating that I'll have to tie him up. . . ."

"Oh, no, I shouldn't think so. He simply doesn't want anyone to molest your belongings, and you can't blame him for that." Mr. Foster held the screen door for me and then went on about his business.

I surveyed my self-appointed protector with mingled feelings. "I should have had you upstairs in my room, chum. *That's* where I needed a watchdog."

He wagged his stumpy tail with enthusiasm as I hauled out another load of belongings, obediently staying behind when I told him to. There was quite a bit to carry, although not so much really when you considered that, except for the books I would have shipped to me eventually, it was the accumulation of my lifetime.

In all fairness, I had to admit that it had been a good lifetime, up to a few weeks ago. My parents had been warm and loving; a good deal of the shock of their deaths was alleviated by the same warmth and love freely offered by Aunt Stell and the Senator when I went to live with them. The only time they'd ever been totally unable to see my side of anything was when I married Max.

While I carried and unpacked I thought about Max. About us, all those years ago when we were kids. I had been rather bitter, for a time, about the Senator's interference in what I felt was no one's business but my own. I'd cried and yelled at him and locked myself in my room and refused to eat for several days.

I could see now, that he'd been right, at least to some extent. We were too young to know what we were doing; we were totally unprepared to earn a living, for one thing, although Max had been quite confident of his ability to take care of me.

And when the marriage was annulled and Max didn't communicate with me in any way or try to see me, my life gradually returned to normal; there were other boys, and then young men, and I hadn't been all that unhappy.

What would happen now? Would Max be interested in me again? Could we revive what we'd once had between us? Or was that too much to expect?

I didn't care, I thought recklessly. For now it was enough to have a contemporary to talk to, to do things with, while the wounds healed. I couldn't think of anyone better than Max to do it with.

I was ready long before he knocked on my door. I let him stand in the doorway while I gathered up a jacket and a purse.

"Cozy little room. Mine faces the ocean and the wind blows in around the windows. Not too bad this time of year, but in the winter I'll bet it's colder than hell. Are they charging you for this, or are you a nonpaying guest?"

"I have no idea. I'm now half-owner of the place, but we haven't discussed finances yet. I couldn't find anything with sequins; will this do?"

Max had always had a bold, almost predatory way of running his gaze over a girl's figure; he softened this with a grin that split the beard and mustache. "You look gorgeous. Yellow was always one of your best colors."

"You've gotten more colorful since I knew you."

He fingered the lapel of his jacket. "You like the new threads? After a total of four years in uniform, I've decided to be fashionable. The patients at the hospital like this, too; my pale blue suit, worn with a blue-figured shirt and a blue and white tie, makes them forget about their postoperative gas pains. What are you doing—locking the door?"

"I am definitely locking the door." I dropped the key into my handbag. "Too late, of course, like after the horse is gone; better late than never."

"What's that mean? Somebody steal something from you?"

"Not a thing, so far as I can figure out. Somebody was in here, though, poking around while I was sleeping on the beach." I hesitated, then added in a voice that wouldn't carry beyond the two of us, "I've got a halfway hunch it might have been the newest guest . . . Mr. Haden he calls himself."

Max digested that for a moment, making no move toward the stairs. "The guy who came last night? Why do you think that? You know him?"

46

"No. But someone who looked a lot like him followed me a good deal of the way from Hampton, only that one was driving a white car and Haden is driving a blue one."

I told him about it. When I had finished, he was rather noncommittal. "I just got a glimpse of the guy myself. He didn't look like a sneak thief, but you never know. It can't hurt to keep the door locked."

We went on downstairs and I stopped in the kitchen, where Callie was already beginning dinner preparations, while Max brought his car around to the door. I wasn't wearing the right type of shoes to run around in the sand.

"I'm going out for dinner," I told her, "and I may be late getting back. I'll leave Rudy in the yard, unless you'd rather I tied him up to the car or something."

Callie sniffed, looking up from the greens she was cleaning. "Suit yourself. Long as he doesn't run off the guests."

Zell came in from the pantry carrying an assortment of flavoring bottles. "I'm going to frost some of my special cookies for dessert," she told me. And then, noting my change of costume, she said, "Aren't you going to be here?"

"No. I'm driving up the coast for dinner with Max. We're old friends," I said, forestalling any questions about that. I hesitated, and then felt compelled to add, "I think I ought to tell you. Someone got into my room and went through my things. Nothing's missing, so far as I can tell . . . I hadn't brought most of my stuff inside yet. Anyway, I've locked the door now, just in case."

There was a small shocked silence, both aunts staring at me. It was Callie who finally spoke. "We've never ever had any trouble with anyone stealing anything."

"Except when the Senator was here week before last," Zell reminded.

"He only said someone was in his room, didn't say they stole anything." Callie's mouth took on a twist that boded ill for any thief in *her* establishment.

My voice sounded odd, the way I felt. "The Senator was here, week before *last?* Do you mean Uncle Harold?"

"Had the same room you had," Zell chirped, setting out her vanilla and lemon and orange flavoring bottles on the counter. "He didn't like it much, but everything else was full. I suppose he's used to fancier quarters, but since he was here for only the one night it doesn't seem like it would have hurt him much."

"But week before last?"

"A week before he was shot." Callie said it in a voice like that of an Old Testament prophet.

"But why? He *never* came here."

"Not much, not for years. He and Stell came when Father died, came for the funeral, but didn't stay overnight, went right off to Washington on the afternoon plane. Always flying somewhere, the way other people walk or get in their automobiles."

"What did he want?" I wasn't sure why the Senator's visit had sinister implications, but it seemed to me that it had.

"Said he wanted a few hours to think, away from all those reporters. I guess he thought, but it didn't do him much good, did it?"

"Hey, are you standing me up?" Max demanded, and I spun around to meet him.

"No, I'm coming. We'll see you all for breakfast," I told the aunts, and went out into the late afternoon sunshine with Max.

Rudy wanted to go with us, or maybe I should say, with *me*. He definitely didn't like Max; I had to speak sharply to the dog to stop him trying to nip at Max's heels.

Max held the car door for me, not turning his back on Rudy. "Look old boy, fun's fun, but this is getting tiresome. You take another piece out of my anatomy and you're going to lose some teeth."

"I don't know what's the matter with him. Rudy, stop it! Stay! Stay right there until I come back!"

We headed toward town. Rudy was a forlorn figure sitting beside my car, but I had other things on my mind. "Max, did you know the Senator was here at the inn just a week before he was shot?"

He didn't take his eyes off the road. "No, was he? I thought he didn't like beaches or country places."

"He didn't. The aunts said he came to be able to get away from the reporters, to think."

"Sounds reasonable. Maybe the reporters don't like sand in their shoes, either."

"He had the same room I have."

He arched one thick red eyebrow at me. "You think that's significant?"

"Darned if I know what's significant. It just seems out of character. And sort of a wild coincidence . . . both you and the Senator coming here, of all places, after years of not seeing each other."

"I didn't see him. He was gone by the time I got here. Which is just as

48

well, no doubt." There was a hostile note in his tone that was impossible to overlook.

"Are you still bitter, because he broke us up and had the marriage annulled? I was, too, for a while, but now I can see that he was right in a way. I mean, we were too young."

"And like the God Almighty he always considered himself to be, Senator Harold McCaffey made that decision on our behalf. Personally, even though it's resulted in a few dents and bruises, I prefer to make my own decisions."

I turned to watch his profile against the smooth, pale waters of the bay. "You *are* bitter."

"I suppose he won you over by the trip to Europe and the little sports car and all the other goodies. Well, I didn't get any of those, love, and six months in jail seemed to me a rather stiff price to pay for wanting to be married to the girl I loved."

It was a few seconds before that really sank in. "What do you mean, six months in jail?"

He grinned, but there was little humor in it. "Uncle Senator set me up for a good one, honey. He didn't just want us separated; he wanted me to be made thoroughly aware of just how rough he was prepared to play if I came back into your sweet young life. Six months in a little Southern county jail, for drivin' and drinkin'. It was even worth smashing up a perfectly good car that he'd paid for, to see me tucked away. To be truthful, he scared the hell out of me, because the sentence was one year and I thought I was going to have to serve the entire thing. A year is a long time when you're nineteen years old."

"Max, give it to me straight. Don't . . . don't talk in innuendos and. . . ."

"I'm giving it to you straight, honey. After they took you back home to Hampton, a couple of thugs worked me over a bit, just to teach me a lesson about poor white trash messing with the Senator's niece, and then we went south to a place where the po-lice are mighty indebted to Senator McCaffey for somethin' or other. . . ."

"Max, damn it, stop using that corn-pone accent and just tell it." I was feeling ill, yet I had to hear the rest of it. I'd wondered why Max didn't try to contact me, not with a note or a phone call, nothing. I didn't want to believe what he was saying, but I did. Max was convincing.

"All right. I'm not poor white trash anymore, at least I've stopped thinking of myself that way. You want just the hard facts, here they are: the Senator hired men to beat me up, then doused me with liquor, poured enough of it down me to make sure I'd fail a blood-alcohol test, and smashed up me

49

and the car. I could have been hurt worse; I came out of it with no more than a fractured wrist and a laceration worth twenty stitches in my scalp. They had a 'trial' and they threw me in a cell and I sat there for six months. When I got out, there was a real tough fella met me at the bus station and told me what would happen if I didn't stay away from nice girls.''

"Oh, Max! I had no idea . . . why? Why should he go to all that trouble? I was underage; he could have kept me from marrying you again . . . it all sounds so brutal and so unnecessary!''

"Brutal it was. But necessary, from the Senator's point of view. He had to put me in my place, teach me a lesson. Well, he taught me one. I went in the Marines and got toughened up; I used to pretend it was him I was stabbing with the bayonet during basic training.''

I felt sick and shaken. My fingers trembled and I knotted them together in my lap. "I'm so confused. It's as if he were two different people, maybe more. He was very good to me, you know, when I was growing up. He provided for me as if I were his own. I never loved him quite the same way I did Aunt Stell, but I . . . I *liked* him, Max. Until the whole terrible mess in Washington, and then I resented him so badly; I said unkind things to him; I was more concerned with what was going to happen to Aunt Stell and me because of what he'd done than with what was going to happen to *him*. And then when he was shot it was so horrible . . . and I felt sorry for him again . . . and now this.''

We had passed through Bascom's Point and were heading for the main highway that ran north along the coast. I was scarcely aware of the flying scenery.

"Max, I lived with that man for fourteen years, and I didn't know him at all. He was a complete stranger to me. Aunt Stell would have staked her life that he wouldn't do anything dishonest or unethical, and she knew him better than anybody! And if anyone else'd told me a story like the one you just . . . I'd have said they were crazy, absolutely crazy!''

He took it for granted I believed him. "Everybody's at least two people,'' he said in a more gentle tone, the animosity fading. "You, me, the Senator, even your Aunt Stell . . . two different people. The one you see on the outside, and what they know themselves to be on the inside. The secret man . . . there's one in everybody. Sometimes he's good, and sometimes he's bad . . . and sometimes it's a relative thing, depending on your viewpoint. Most of us manage to justify a lot of the rotten things we do. Like I justified not coming back after you when I got out of jail. I was afraid, Brenna. It isn't pleasant to admit that, but I was still a bit shy of twenty and I wasn't a tough raised to settle his problems with a knife or a broken bottle. I was scared, so I told myself it was only good sense to stay away from you.''

I heard my own raspy breathing. Something sharp and acrid rose in my throat.

''He sent word they'd kill me if I showed my face around Hampton again. I believed him, honey. And even after I got out of the service and I wasn't really afraid anymore, I never got around to looking you up, although it's always sort of hung in the back of my mind that someday I would go home and find you again.''

''Why did he do it, Max? All the terrible things . . . you and then all that mess in Washington . . . he was an honored and respected man, he had money and position and power, but it wasn't enough. . . .''

'' 'Power corrupts—absolute power corrupts absolutely' . . . who knows why anybody does anything?'' He shot a look at me from those light-blue eyes. ''I take it you didn't have any doubt that he was guilty as charged.''

Wearily, I shook my head. ''No, not really. He as good as admitted it. Oh, no specifics, nothing like that. But he fully expected to be convicted and sentenced to a prison term; he was furious that the men he'd helped, the ones he felt owed him something, weren't coming to his aid and covering up for him. He never once denied to us that he was guilty. Aunt Stell couldn't take it; she took an overdose of sleeping pills, so at least she was spared seeing him shot down.''

''I know. I read about it. I think I might have come to find you then, if I hadn't been sick. That was about when I succumbed to the pneumonia. By the time I got better, the weakness had passed.'' His tone was lighter. ''I figured you'd forgotten about me years ago, and I might do more harm than good by stirring up old memories. Only when I found you sleeping in the sand dunes . . . I decided it was kismet. We were meant to run into each other again.''

Gradually, our conversation drifted into other, easier channels. The place Max had chosen to eat was on the beach, with soft lights and music and all kinds of atmosphere. We ate seafood and talked and danced a little and talked some more.

It was late when we returned to the inn. Max cut the engine and in the silence we listened to the surf. When he pulled me over against him, I made no protest. This time when he kissed me I didn't laugh about the beard and the mustache. I kissed him back.

[7]

I WOKE wondering why I felt so good, and then I remembered. Max. I had found Max again. There had been a time when I'd felt some resentment against him because he hadn't tried to get in touch with me, but I always knew the Senator was responsible for our separation. And so, with the romanticism of seventeen, I had decided that my uncle was intercepting the letters Max must be sending. Once I went so far as to search the Senator's desk, looking for them. Most of the resentment was reserved for *him*, not for Max. I smiled, remembering.

I was up and dressed in a hurry, almost as eager as Rudy to get out and around.

There was no sign of Max in the dining room, however, and Zell slyly anticipated my question by informing me that he'd driven off some half hour earlier.

Disappointed, I took my place among all the old ladies and gentlemen at the round kitchen tables.

One of the Avery sisters said, "Please pass the syrup," as I slid into my chair.

The syrup pitcher was directly in front of Mr. Rossdale, the man with the hearing aid. He went on eating, chewing methodically, until the lady raised her voice.

"Mr. Rossdale, if you please, may I have the syrup?"

He turned myopic eyes in her direction; the distortion of his thick glasses made him, for an instant, look like some gigantic, pop-eyed monster. Then

52

he responded appropriately and went back to eating, and he was simply a middle-aged man engrossed in his food.

I listened to the chatter around me, the conversation of people who have lived with one another for some period of time. They were making plans for the day. Lulu and Clara Avery were driving into town on a shopping trip. Zell was going along to look for some more knitting worsted of a particular shade of green. Egg was in earnest, low-voiced consultation with old Mr. Foster about something I didn't catch. I felt a bit as if I'd been trapped in an old folks' home.

Callie brought her own breakfast to the table and sank into the chair next to mine. Immediately, Mr. Montgomery, of the snowy white hair and the realtor's license, leaned toward her.

"It wouldn't hurt to talk about it, Miss Callie. You might find the offer more attractive than you think."

The old aunt ate with more grimness than pleasure. "I've already given you an answer, Mr. Montgomery."

"But how can you give me an answer when you haven't heard all of the question? You haven't, you know."

Zell spoke to me then, and I missed the rest of what sounded like a moderately interesting conversation. "Brenna, I almost forgot . . . Mr. Spadin was over this morning; he's our nearest neighbor, in that white house where you turn off onto North Spit Road. He'd been in to the post office and they gave him a telegram to bring out here . . . since it was addressed to a St. John they assumed you were here with us."

She dug into her apron pocket and brought out a folded and slightly crumpled envelope.

Egg and Mr. Foster came out of their private huddle to comment on the service. They thought it was disgraceful that a telegram should be allowed to lie in a post office box until someone got around to picking it up.

"Is it anything important, dear?" In Egg's life I'm sure telegrams were always important.

I ripped it open and read the brief message. "Brenna: If you've gone to Bascom's Point and you get this, please call me at once." A telephone number followed, and it was signed Maud Tremway.

Maudie. I felt a pang of guilt that I'd allowed her to worry about me. I should have called her, on my own, when I got here.

"Not bad news, I hope?"

I looked up at the circle of curious faces. Even Mr. Montgomery had

53

given up trying to persuade Callie of whatever it was, and was watching me. Everyone except Mr. Rossdale, who was stolidly working his way through the stack of pancakes and apparently hadn't heard enough to know I had a telegram.

"Just a request that I call an old friend," I said, and put the message into my pocket. "Maybe I'll go into town after breakfast . . . where do I find a telephone?"

They told me, and the moment was past. I'm sure I disappointed them, all those old people who had so little to brighten their lives; they'd hoped for a moment of excitement, however vicarious.

Chairs were pushed back, plates scraped and gathered up for Egg to wash. One of the last down, I was also one of the last to finish, so I was still there when Zell came back rather breathlessly. "Callie—he's gone. That Mr. Haden. His door was open and I was going to close it, but I could see his things were all missing. I looked in the closet and the dresser—there's not a thing left but the key on the inside of the door!"

Callie, the last bite of toast suspended in midair, fought unsuccessfully with a scowl. "But he hadn't paid his bill. He was here for two nights, and I fixed all his meals. . . ."

"Have you got the license number of his car?" Egg demanded. I could tell from their faces the seriousness of the situation when a guest left without paying.

"I've got the one he put on the registry card, but that's not saying it's the right one," Callie said slowly. "I didn't go and look at it myself."

"I didn't think he was that sort of man," Egg commented. "I mean, he wasn't very talkative or friendly, but he seemed very proper. Well brought up, you know."

"Are you going to stand around gabbing all day, or get the dishes done before it's time to fix lunch?"

Hurt, Egg withdrew. Zell continued to watch Callie's face. "Are you going to report him to the police?"

"Have to go into town to do it. And chances are they wouldn't catch up with him anyway. I'll send a bill to the address he gave, but the sort of people who go off without paying don't usually give you their right addresses."

Or their right names? I wondered with a resurgence of the uneasiness I had felt before regarding the man who called himself Bill Haden. Had he followed me here? Had he searched my room, then left when he found nothing of interest?

54

Why would he have followed me? Why would he think he'd find anything?

At any rate he was gone. Zell offered to go up and clean his room, and Callie assented as if her mind were elsewhere.

I decided to walk into town and give Rudy a run at the same time. It was another perfect September morning, crisp but not cold, with the sun sparkling on the waters of the bay. Rudy was eager for a romp, and I ran with him for a distance, enjoying the pull of unused muscles. I'd been too long without exercise.

I found the only public telephone booth the town offered, and called Maudie at her sister's. She came on the line, sounding tense until I'd assured her I was all right.

"I'm so glad you called, I've been thinking and thinking about you. I guessed you might go to Bascom's Point because the old aunts were there, but I wasn't sure. Look, dear, you're sounding much better. Are you?"

"Yes, I think so. Guess who I met here, Maudie."

"Who . . . I can't imagine."

"Max Von Rys."

"Max? Whatever is he doing in Bascom's Point?"

"Recuperating from a bout of pneumonia. I didn't recognize him at first; he has a mustache and a beard."

She was silent in the face of this stunning information. I never knew how Maudie really felt about Max. She'd always been perfectly pleasant to him, when he was coming around the house all those years ago. But she hadn't spoken a word in his defense or mine when the Senator had ended our marriage.

"It was good to meet an old friend," I said. "He's the only young one here . . . at the inn, I mean. The average age among the rest of them is about seventy. Would you believe it, I was going to sun myself out on the dunes yesterday and I fell asleep for more than four hours."

"It's all those nights of not being able to sleep properly. I'm glad for you, Brenna. And if Max is a help, well, I never thought he was quite so worthless as the Senator did. Look, dear, do you know anything about the Senator's keys?"

"The Senator's keys?"

"Yes. One set of his keys are missing. Nobody thought too much of it to begin with, but the strangest thing has happened, Brenna." Her voice altered perceptibly. "Has anyone asked you about the keys?"

55

Distracted by Rudy blowing noisily against the glass panes of the folding door of the booth, I opened it enough so that he could lick at my knee. "No, why? What's happened?"

"Well, last night someone got into the house and literally tore it apart. Mr. Sawyer, he's the one who's taken charge of the estate, you remember, he's fit to be tied. And the poor fellow they had guarding the place, he's in the hospital with a cracked head. He's conscious now, and he says he never heard anyone breaking in, but he did hear a noise in the study, and when he went in, someone bashed him with the poker from the fireplace!"

I muttered vaguely sympathetic words. "They figure whoever it was had the Senator's keys?"

"It seems that way, how else would they have got into a locked house? The thing is, they called me . . . one of those men who came and asked questions, the tall one named Hastings, the one with the scar, wanted to know where you were. That was late last night, and it scared me no end, and I told him I didn't know . . . it was all I could do to *think*, and I didn't know really, I only *guessed* you'd be at the inn. I don't know why they would want to talk to you again, I mean, you have your own keys, but you never had the Senator's, did you?"

"No, of course not." The sun was warm on my back, but I felt a chill, although I couldn't have said why. "They can't think *I* came back and ransacked the place, can they? Why would I? I had the run of the house for days after . . . I didn't need to *come back*."

"It worries me when I don't know what's going on. Brenna, I didn't want them to surprise you the way they did me, to upset you again. But I thought you ought to know what's happened since you left. Just a few hours after you went away two of the men were there again, the ones that worked with that Hastings, and they asked about tapes and if the Senator had another briefcase. I told them not that I knew of, and they went through his things looking for more tapes. I told them he did most all his dictating at his office, but they messed things up anyway. I stood outside the door because it didn't seem right to let them just . . . take over, so to speak, and I heard one of them say something about blank tapes, but I don't know why they'd want blank tapes, do you?"

"No. I'm sorry they're continuing to bother you, Maudie."

"Oh, I'm not letting them do it, not really. They wanted me to go back last night . . . after midnight, imagine! . . . and see if I could tell them if anything was missing, but I told them I can't leave now. My sister's sick and my place

56

is here. I don't see what difference it makes anyway. They never catch those thieves.''

"So long as they don't think it was you or I," I told her, "I'm not going to worry about it. It's someone else's problem. I never saw the Senator's keys, Maudie. He used to keep an extra set in the top drawer in the desk in the study, but they went through that the day after he was shot. I've just remembered what I do have, though, and that's a key to Addison's." That was the firm I'd worked for until I quit with the intention of getting married. I pulled out my key ring and looked at the assortment. "One of Mr. Addison's pet peeves is employees who leave without turning in their keys. Tell them I'll send it back first chance I get, will you?"

"Yes, all right. I'll call them. Brenna, take care, and keep in touch, will you, dear? Give my regards to Max.''

I hung up then and stepped out of the booth to where Rudy was impatiently waiting. I didn't see what it could have to do with me, but I didn't like the sound of it . . . someone filching the Senator's keys so they could gain entry to the house.

"Hey, why so pensive? They used to offer a penny for your thoughts, but surely they're worth more than that these days.''

Beside me Rudy rumbled a warning, which Max ignored. He had left behind the sartorial splendor of last night, reverting to jeans and the heavy dark-red sweater. He came toward us across the deserted street, smiling a welcome.

"I've just talked to Maudie. She sent her regards.''

"Good old Maudie. Did she give you bad news?''

"After what we've been through the past few weeks, I'm not sure what would qualify. I don't see how it has anything to do with me anyway. Someone apparently made off with the Senator's keys and ransacked the house last night. I was just wondering if there was any tie-in with somebody searching *my* room.''

He towered over me, a reassuringly normal male hulk. "Like what? I mean, I can see why they might go through the Senator's belongings. He left a lot of enemies, all those people he was threatening to drag down with him.''

"But what did they hope to accomplish by tearing the house apart?''

"Find the evidence, I suppose, whatever proof he had that he wasn't alone in his evil deeds.'' He put a hand on my arm, his eyes darkening as he watched my face. "I'm sorry. This is still a very painful thing, isn't it? But that's why he was shot, you know. To shut him up, to keep him from testifying to anything that would involve somebody who didn't want to be involved. You must have realized that.''

I leaned into him, ignoring Rudy's attempt to come between us, welcoming the arms that came around me even though we were standing in plain view of the half dozen villagers going about their business.

''No. I mean, I guess I did, subconsciously, only until now I hadn't heard it put into words and I suppose I didn't want to put it into words myself. When we saw him shot . . . it was so horrible I don't believe we thought beyond the fact that he was dead and that we'd have to deal with Aunt Stell. And then just a few minutes later we found her dead, too, and there was so much to do . . . so many arrangements to make, we didn't have time to think beyond the funerals. Afterward . . . I was so tired and so heartsick I didn't try to figure it out, that someone was . . . was shutting him up before he could talk.''

''He was a very angry man. I saw him on the newscasts when the reporters were hounding him for information. He didn't admit anything to them, of course, but when they got him cornered, he said he wasn't alone in this and he wasn't going to be the only one indicted.''

''I think he believed at first that some of them would come to his rescue,'' I said slowly. ''I remember he mentioned that Senator Carlson wouldn't even talk to him on the phone. He said he thought he had some friends, but they'd all crawled under the rug, forgotten the favors and canceled the debts. He said they'd thrown him to the wolves. Yes, he was very angry. But he wasn't a foolish man, Max. He wouldn't have been careless with whatever evidence he had.''

''No. If he'd been that, they wouldn't have had to kill him to get at it.''

The rough wool of his sweater scratched my face, but I didn't want to move away from him. ''Do you think they found what they were looking for?''

''Who knows? I don't suppose you had any idea what form the proof would have been in? Papers, anything like that?''

''No. He always carried a briefcase, he was carrying one when he died, but the authorities had that immediately. So far nobody's said what was in it, but who . . . whoever it was who . . . who shot him, who broke into the house, must have felt there was more, somewhere, than what was in the briefcase.''

''Well, let the authorities take care of it. That's what they're for. It hasn't anything to do with you," Max said, and let me go, tucking my hand under his arm as we began to walk toward his car.

"Can I be sure of that? I mean . . . well, somebody did search my room night before last. There wasn't any reason to think I had anything valuable."

"Sneak thieves often steal as little as a handful of silver. It could be no more than a coincidence."

I shivered. "But what if it isn't? What if someone thinks I have something that's important? Maudie guessed I'd come here, to Bascom's Point. Someone else might have guessed it, too, or that man . . . Haden, or whatever his name was, the one who might have followed me . . . Max, did you know he skipped out without paying for his room or his meals?"

"He did?" Max's eyes narrowed. Perhaps it was only because the sun was so bright. "That's interesting."

"It's frightening, is what it is. I'm not used to being mixed up in anything . . . anything sinister. It's so hard for me to take in . . . that all these people the Senator associated with all these years, some of them are really crooked, and at least one of them is a murderer. . . ."

"You knew a lot of them, didn't you?"

"At least to speak to, yes. They often came to the house for weekends or evening conferences, and sometimes I was with Aunt Stell and the Senator when we had dinner with them either in Washington or at home. They all seemed perfectly ordinary, decent people. . . ." I remembered what he'd said about the secret man, the one inside each of us, the one no one else knows.

"Who were his special cronies?"

"There were dozens of them, Max. You know what he was like, a very gregarious man, very social. . . ."

"When he wanted to be," Max agreed. "Well, I'm sure someone's looking into all this, and they'll know who the men were that he was closest to. I feel sort of sorry for the innocent ones; they'll all be scrutinized with a powerful lens, anyone who had anything to do with him. Including possibly you. I'm surprised they haven't had you in and put you through the mill."

"Why should they?" I protested. "I don't know anything about his business affairs. I don't know anything about anything."

"You were one of the few people near him, physically near him, the last few days of his life. He might have said something to you in a moment of fear or anger, something to give a clue to what he intended to do."

"He holed up in the study with the door closed most of the time, with a

59

bottle. His lawyer came several times, and I heard him talking in there, but I couldn't understand anything he said. He was very bitter and he said he wouldn't go down alone. That's all. I told them that."

We had reached the car, and when Max opened the door, Rudy sprang into the front seat, panting. Max wasn't looking at the dog. He was looking at me.

"You said he was in the study, and you heard him talking. Just to the lawyer or to someone else?"

"No one else came that I knew of."

"But was the lawyer there every time you heard him talking?"

"No. I don't think so. Some of the time I thought maybe he was on the telephone, trying to reach people who might have helped him."

Max stared down at me. It was hard to read the expression on a man's face when it was camouflaged with so much hair.

"Or speaking into a tape recorder?"

"Tapes . . . Maudie said the men who were searching through the desk said something about blank tapes. Well, he could have been making tapes, of course; he did have a little portable recorder he kept at home or carried with him. But he couldn't have done any more than say things, making up accusations, maybe, it wouldn't be proof . . . nothing they could use in court."

"Not in itself, no. But if he gave information, listed the deals various people had been involved in, for instance, names, dates, places, it would be possible for somebody to dig out the rest, the proof. And he might have recorded where the proof could be found. What do you think, Brenna? Was he holed up using a tape recorder?"

"Well, he could have been," I conceded. "All I heard was the voice, not what it said. But if he had, I'd think he'd have carried the tapes with him or hidden them very well indeed . . . not just left them lying around the house."

"He didn't know he was going to be shot in broad daylight with all those people around. He might have considered the house a safe place to leave evidence. If someone broke into the house, it seems to me the most likely reason would be to look for evidence. If they didn't find anything, all it proves is that they didn't look in the right place. They might even think you have it."

My outraged protest brought several heads around. The villagers of Bascom's Point stared at us curiously, until Max pushed me into the car and got in the other side. For a few minutes we struggled to get Rudy into the back seat, eventually overcoming his reluctance to obey.

"I don't have anything of the Senator's, and there's no reason for anyone to think I have! What would I want with the tapes, if I'd found any such thing?"

"They'd be extremely valuable. Valuable enough for anyone who was mentioned in them to pay a good price for them, I'd think. After all, anybody who'd kill a man to shut him up wouldn't stop at paying for the evidence."

I sat in a sort of numb horror as he put the car in gear. "Nobody could think I'd blackmail them . . . Max, you don't really believe they would!"

"If we're dealing with men who were scared enough to kill to protect themselves, they've done things worse than blackmail. So why wouldn't they believe it of someone else?"

I huddled on my own side of the seat, drawing no warmth from the sun that poured in the open window. "The Senator didn't know he was going to die, Max, and whatever his plans were, he expected to carry them out himself! Do you think whoever it was will give up, since they didn't find anything in my room?"

"Maybe. On the other hand, you still had a lot of stuff . . . most of it, in fact . . . in your car, even if it hadn't been locked. So, if you had anything, it could still be there in your belongings."

The car was eating up the sandy road, taking me back to the inn more quickly than I wanted to go.

"There's nothing in my belongings except what I packed myself. There couldn't be. I did it all after the Senator was dead. There was no reason why he'd have hidden anything in my stuff anyway. He wouldn't have taken a chance on my finding it; we didn't talk much, but I'm sure he knew how I felt about the things he was accused of doing. He'd never have considered me a suitable accomplice for whatever he planned."

"Just what did he say about his plans? You didn't have the impression he intended to give up fighting, did you?"

"He said very little. No, my impression was that if he went down he'd drag as many people with him as he could, since they weren't rallying around and helping him. Max, what am I going to do?"

We were approaching the inn, but he didn't slow; instead, we swept on past it toward the end of the spit. He drove with the casual ease that good male drivers have, as if the vehicle were an extension of himself. The road widened at the very end where other cars had turned around, but he didn't turn. Instead he stopped the car and turned off the ignition.

It was a good place for a private talk. Nobody could approach without being seen for half a mile, at least. Earlier I had felt that the placid

61

surroundings were therapeutic; now everything threatened me once more, as I had felt threatened those first days after the news broke.

Rudy began to bark, demanding to be let out, and Max leaned back to open a door for him. The dog looked questioningly at me, stumpy tail wagging an invitation; when I didn't respond, he took off on his own, up the ocean side of the point.

"Max . . . if they haven't found what they're looking for, do you think they'll be back?"

"It's a possibility, I suppose. But, as you say, there was no reason for anyone to think you were involved, that you'd know anything about his papers or his tapes, if he had any. I doubt if you've got anything to worry about, unless you have some sort of guilty knowledge."

"I haven't! I don't know a thing, I swear it!"

"Then there's nothing to worry about, is there?"

I stared at him in exasperation. "How can you say that? If someone *thinks* I know something, or *have* something, and they make another attempt to get whatever it is. . . ."

"You're staying here at the inn, with plenty of people around, including me. You've got one of the most damnably protective dogs I ever saw, and I'm perfectly willing to set myself up as watchdog, too. Just take it easy for a while, don't go anywhere on your own unless it's daylight, like now, and you can see anybody sneaking up on you. . . ."

"What good would it do to see them? Max, I'm scared!"

He was leaning against the door on his side of the car, overpoweringly large in the small space. "Honey, don't panic. There's no reason anyone would wish you any harm, so far as I can see. I'm willing to become a twenty-four-hour-a-day guardian, if you like."

For a moment that didn't register. Not until he leaned toward me and traced the curve of my jaw with one finger, his face so close to mine that I could have counted the hairs in his thick eyebrows.

"Nine years ago old Uncle Senator was around with his bloodhounds to track us down, and his connections to annul our marriage, and his goons to see that I was put out of commission for a long time. Today there isn't anybody to stop us if we want to play house again." And then, because the ambiguity of his final phrase must have struck him, or the lack of expression on my face showed that I needed clarification of it, he added, "I've suspected it all along, because of the way I kept thinking about you and the way all those hundreds of girls I was bragging about failed to turn me on, but I'm sure of it now."

62

His hands reached for mine, drawing me toward him. "I still love you, girl. What do you say? Let's get married again, Brenna."

I'm not sure what I'd have said because when our heads drew close together there was a low growl and Rudy, who had reentered the car unnoticed, thrust himself forcibly between us.

I drew back with a laugh. "In books, when the dog growls at a man you know he's the villain."

Max didn't reply to that, except to shove down on the door handle and get out of the car, pulling me with him. "I think we're safer away from your jealous dog, and I'm not finished with this conversation."

I allowed myself to be drawn out, welcoming the hard warmth of his hands, the urgency in his voice and manner. There was scarcely a tingle of the old pain that until only a short time ago had nearly incapacitated me.

I wasn't stupid enough to think there wouldn't be any more pain, but my life was taking a new and unexpected direction and it looked like a great improvement on the old one. I let him pull me into his arms, and it was quite a while before it even occurred to me that someone could be observing us from the inn.

When I did think of it, I didn't care.

[8]

MY EUPHORIA lasted for the time it took to get back to the inn. We had laughed and talked and kissed and walked along the sands holding hands. When Max pressed me for an answer, I told him it was too soon to make an irrevocable decision, but I left all the doors open for one in the near future.

We were amazed to find that we'd wasted an entire morning (although Max insisted that was the wrong word) and that it was lunchtime. In a buoyant mood, we marched into the dining room to find two newcomers in addition to the regulars.

One of them was a stranger, a lanky young man with too much brown hair that fell into his eyes, wearing the casual clothes of a beachcombing vacationer.

The other one stood as we entered, dark, well groomed, good-looking, and only too familiar.

The smile slid from my face as he came toward us, his eyes flicking at Max, dismissing him.

"I've been waiting for you, Brenna."

My response was polite, automatic. "I'm sorry. I didn't know you were coming."

"No, of course you didn't. I'd have called, but the operator insisted there was no telephone here." Larry smiled, somewhat incredulous. "I need to talk to you. Alone."

He glanced at Max again, but Max didn't courteously melt into the woodwork as Larry's eyes had suggested. He stood his ground, his voice as casually controlled as Larry's.

"Aren't you going to introduce us, Brenna?"

I sounded nervous and uncertain. "Yes, of course. Larry Engle, Max Von Rys."

This time Larry didn't dismiss him so quickly; the mutual scrutiny might have been funny under other circumstances, if my sense of humor hadn't been at such a low ebb. I'd never seen a cockfight, but I thought it must start somewhat this way, with the antagonists warily circling each other, looking for an opening.

That each of them recognized the other's name was unmistakable.

"We were about to have lunch," Max said. "How about the corner table, over there? Would you like to join us, Mr. Engle?"

That put Larry at a slight disadvantage, which he wasn't used to and didn't like; he had no intention of considering Max to be his host.

"I'd like to talk to Brenna . . . alone."

"Sure thing. Right after lunch, right? Let's fill our plates; it's all buffet style here at noon." Max touched my elbow, herding me toward the table Callie and Egg had set out, and I moved. I wasn't sure what I wanted: for Max to go away and let Larry say what he'd come to say or for Larry to simply leave without saying it.

I'd been dating Larry for a long time, had been engaged to him for six months, had planned to marry him. Somewhere, in that house back in Hampton, there was a stack of wedding invitations, beautifully engraved, setting the date: September 19 at eight o'clock in the evening in the church where I'd gone with Aunt Stell for the past fourteen years.

Yet staring at him now, when we'd filled our plates with something I didn't notice and were seated at one of the small tables, it was as if I'd never seen him before.

Larry was a very attractive man. Very neat. Expensive scent. Highly polished shoes. Prosperous-looking. Especially as opposed to Max, who wore jeans and a slightly ragged sweater and combat boots.

Yet Max didn't come off to any particular disadvantage; he emanated maleness and self-confidence, and I knew without knowing how I knew that Larry was just as aware of that aura of *machismo* as I was.

God only knows what I ate. To say that my thoughts were chaotic is an understatement. I sat between two men who had each, at one time, been very important to me. I had once been forcibly separated from Max, yet he had

65

not only come into my life again but wanted to become the most important person in it.

And Larry . . . our parting had been his idea, not mine; resentment lingered at the memory of our last meeting. Why had he come here? What did he want?

And more important than that, how did I feel about him now?

You'd think a girl could tell how she felt about a man, but at the moment I had no idea. I was uncomfortable with the two of them, politely asking for the salt and not bothering to make conversation other than that. Max had brought a can of beer to the table and I suspected he'd done it deliberately to emphasize further the contrast between them.

The other diners were watching us, some surreptitiously, some, like Zell, openly and with great interest. As for me, I couldn't find a place to rest my own eyes, and twice I saw that the latest guest was watching me like the others, although when I looked his way he pretended he hadn't been.

Max chose to prolong the agony by having dessert, which he could easily have done without, to my way of thinking.

"There's rhubarb pie, and Miss Callie makes superb pie. Or tapioca pudding, if you're less venturesome. I'm for pie," Max stated. "What'll you have, Brenna?"

"Nothing, thank you."

"Mr. Engle?"

"Nothing, thank you." Larry drained his coffee cup and gave Max a look that would have driven a lesser man off.

Not Max, however. No, Max brought back his pie, complete with a scoop of ice cream, and a final cup of coffee, and he ate it in a leisurely fashion while I silently willed him to hurry up, and Larry, I suspect, ground his teeth. Not that Larry showed anything; he was too well trained to do that.

Since we'd been the last to arrive, we were naturally the last to finish eating. I could see that some of the others were reluctant to leave without viewing the second act of our drama, whatever it was to be.

Zell's eyes, when she passed, were bright with amusement and delight. I wished I could share her enthusiasm for the situation.

At last Max forked the final bite of pie between mustache and beard and sighed with the satisfaction of a well-fed man. "Well. I'll go on about my business and let you take care of yours, Mr. Engle. Nice to have met you. I'll be on the beach, Brenna, when you're free."

Nice. Neat. Cutting Larry off within a short time, making it clear that he and I were getting together again as soon as Larry had said his piece.

We were finally alone, except that Egg was clearing the tables, and in the kitchen beyond, we could hear Callie bustling around. No one could hear what we said, however.

I looked Larry full in the face. "How did you know where I was?"

He chose not to answer that. "You didn't waste much time getting in touch with *him*, did you?"

Irritation made my voice sharp. "I didn't get in touch with him, as you put it. He was here when I arrived. I suppose Maudie told you. She had no right to do it; I didn't want anyone to follow me."

"What's he want? He acts as if he owns you."

"He's asked me to marry him." I was sorry I'd said that as soon as the words were out of my mouth, although there was no reason why it should be a secret.

One of Larry's eyebrows rose higher than the other one. "Has he? Well, that didn't take long, did it?"

"Larry, what do you want? You must have come here for something, and you didn't know Max was here, so it couldn't have been to make snide remarks about him. So what is it?"

His gaze was calm, almost paternal. "You're still angry with me, aren't you?"

"No. Although, if you don't stop fencing, I may work up to it. I take it you didn't come to ask me to kiss and make up."

A faint spot of color appeared in each cheek. "Brenna, you're making this rather difficult."

"Am I? I'm sorry, I thought it was you who was being difficult. What is it you want of me?"

For a few moments he simply sat and looked at me. "You're changed somehow. You're . . . harder, I guess that's it."

"Yes, well, you toughen up as life gets rougher or you don't survive. A week or two ago I hardly cared; now I've decided I do care, and I'm going to make it."

Unexpectedly, Larry smiled. I'd forgotten what a warm and lovely thing it was, his smile. "I'm glad. Brenna, believe me, I am sincerely glad. I'm really very sorry about . . . us, that it didn't work out. And I'll always be concerned for your welfare." He looked toward the door through which Max had left, as if the other man were still standing there. "I can't help wondering about your friend, Max. If he's right for you. If he is, then I wish you all happiness. I hope you aren't rushing into anything, though . . . no rebound stuff, nothing like that. You're too nice a girl for that."

67

He sounded so friendly, so sincere. Yet only a few weeks ago we had said we loved each other, we'd planned to be married. . . . Yes, I thought, Larry, too, had a secret man inside, one I never reached, never touched, didn't know anything about.

How could he talk to me this way? Had our positions been reversed I never could have done it. Yet it wasn't as painful as I might have expected it to be; perhaps I hadn't been as much in love with him as I thought, for I wasn't let down at the realization that he hadn't come to "kiss and make up." I only wanted him to get to the point and then leave. Max was waiting for me on the beach.

Larry leaned toward me across the small table, his expression earnest. "Brenna, it's been a long time since you've seen this Von Rys. What do you know about him?"

"You didn't come here to talk about Max surely."

"Don't put me off, please. I'm only concerned about you." Sincerity radiated from him, and I could see why he'd chosen to be a lawyer. "You said he was here before you were. Are you positive of that?"

I felt the frown forming. "Certainly I'm sure of it; he'd been here for four or five days when I came."

Larry frowned slightly, too. "Well, Maudie guessed you'd come here, so I suppose he could have, too, and anticipated meeting you. It would certainly look better if he got here ahead of you."

I made an exasperated sound. "Larry, for God's sake, will you stop this beating around the bush, making silly noises about Max, and tell me what you came to say? Max had no way of knowing I'd be here, no inkling that I'd be interested in him; he simply came here because he needed a rest and he knew Bascom's Point is a dead little backwater town where nothing happens and resting's the order of the day."

"Where's he from? What's he do?"

"He's the administrator of a hospital in some small town in Pennsylvania. What difference does that make to anything?"

"I don't know for sure. Except that it's a damned peculiar coincidence that he should show up at the same time you do, after all those years. You hadn't seen or heard from each other in all that time, had you? But now, though you've just barely arrived, he's already proposed . . . doesn't that seem odd to you?"

"No, what's odd about it? We loved each other once. Granted, we've both grown up since then. But we still hit it off; we still laugh at the same things, we have. . . ." I caught myself. "I have no intention of going into all

68

this with you. What has Max to do with anything of interest to you?"

Larry sighed, glancing around as if to be sure we could not be overheard. "Brenna, in spite of everything that's happened between us . . . and I do see how you could feel very bitter toward me and my family . . . I'm sorry that you were hurt. And I don't want to see you hurt any further . . . by this Von Rys or anyone else. There's at least a strong possibility that he didn't 'just happen' to be here. If it's true that he works as a hospital administrator, then I assume he wouldn't be acting on his own, but he might very well have been recruited by someone else who guessed, as Maudie and I did, that you'd come here. You spent some happy times here as a child, and your only remaining relatives are here, so it wouldn't take too much deduction. . . ."

I had taken off my sweater while we ate; now I was feeling chilly and shrugged back into it. "Recruited by whom? And for what?"

"Maudie told you the Senator's home had been broken into."

"Yes."

"Did you guess what for? I mean, what the thieves were looking for?"

I spoke without thinking. "Max says maybe someone wanted the evidence the Senator had that other people besides himself were involved in the scandal. Papers . . . or tapes."

I couldn't interpret the expression that crossed Larry's face. His tone was soft but vibrant. "Max said that? Well, well . . . how very interesting. Very perceptive of him. Because that's what the authorities think, too, that there was evidence that hasn't turned up yet. They've been through everything in his office and in the safe at home . . . and, of course, through the briefcase he was carrying when he was shot. Did you know that case held nothing but blank tapes? That made everyone wonder if he'd picked up the wrong ones by accident, although it doesn't seem likely to me he'd be careless with the real ones. Nothing's been found to implicate anyone else in anything that could result in an indictment. But everyone's sure there is evidence, somewhere, and we're certain it . . . or part of it . . . is in the form of tapes because he told his lawyer he'd made them. Isn't it intriguing that Von Rys came up with that idea?"

"I'd undoubtedly have come up with it myself if I hadn't been so upset. But I don't see how you figure Max has a personal interest in any of this."

"Don't you? Brenna, those tapes . . . or papers, or both . . . are potential dynamite. There are people who want them destroyed. There are other people who would find them a gold mine . . . quite literally . . . because the men they implicate would pay anything for them. Whoever finds them is going to be in a terrific bargaining position."

69

I felt the sickness spreading through my midsection and wished I hadn't eaten lunch. "And you think . . . any number of people apparently think . . . that *I* know something about them."

"Do you?"

The question hung between us for long moments. I could feel the warmth recede from my face, then rush back as anger kindled. "Do you think I'd have done anything but turn them over to the authorities if I'd found them?"

"You might not. I think anyone could understand that you'd hate to have any more scandal made public about your uncle. You might feel any evidence was better off being destroyed."

"Larry, I'll go along with the supposition that the Senator had papers or tapes and that they're potentially valuable or dangerous, depending on who they relate to. But I never saw them and don't know anything about them. And I'm curious to know why you're interested enough to come all this distance to ask me about them. That *is* why you came, isn't it?"

"Yes." He admitted that readily enough. "I've been retained by . . . by someone I'm not at liberty to name . . . who thought I might cooperate in helping turn up the missing evidence. I thought the reasonable way to begin was to approach you directly and simply ask."

"All right. You've asked. I don't know anything about anything."

"Maybe you only think you don't."

I pushed back my chair and stood up. "This is where I came in. I'm afraid your trip's been a waste of time if you hoped to learn anything from me."

Larry stood up, too, but he hadn't given up yet. "How about letting me go through your belongings to see if I can find anything suspicious?"

"Someone's already gone through my things and unless they found what they wanted and took it with them, there wasn't anything there. I packed all my belongings myself, after the Senator was dead, and there was absolutely no way he could have hidden his papers or tapes in my luggage. So forget it."

"Someone . . . what happened?"

I told him as succinctly as possible; I wanted to end this scene and walk away.

"Where was your friend Von Rys when your room was searched?"

"With me," I said, which was a lie, or at least partially a lie, since he certainly hadn't been with me the entire time I'd been away from my room. I only wanted to be rid of Larry and not drag this out any longer.

But I hadn't convinced him. He spoke slowly and thoughtfully. "That could be why he's here . . . to keep you busy while someone else looks for the tapes. After all, it would be easier for an old friend to do that than for a stranger to strike up an acquaintance."

At that point I said something rather rude and walked out of the dining room.

Larry kept pace with me, still plodding along with the same ideas, only trying to find a slightly different twist. "Your uncle was here a few days before he was shot, did you know that? Was Von Rys here then, too? Could they have met?"

I spluttered a bit, laughing. "Now that's one thing you'll never convince me of, that Max and the Senator were in any scheme together! They hated each other, and that's not too strong a word to use. Larry, forget it. Go home and tell your friend, or employer, or whatever he is, that the whole idea was a fizzle. The Senator didn't slip me anything, he didn't plant anything on me; if he hid something, he hid it elsewhere and I don't know any more than you do about where it was. Max being in Bascom's Point is only a coincidence, in spite of what you think, and he wasn't here when the Seantor was here, and they wouldn't have spoken a civil word to each other if he had been."

We nearly ran over Callie and Mr. Montgomery, the realtor with the snowy hair; they were in a sort of huddle in the main corridor, in urgent conversation. Callie said something sharp and moved away from him as we left the dining room, plunging back to her kitchen chores; Mr. Montgomery smiled faintly at me and went on toward the lobby.

"Brenna, wait, there are several things I want to. . . ."

"No, thanks. Max is waiting for me, and I have a dog to exercise. Good-bye, Larry."

I left him there and went out into the sunshine, eager to get away from him as quickly as I could. My escape was slowed, however, by the fact that one of my damp tennis shoes was missing from the steps where I'd left them earlier. The probable culprit wagged his tail and licked affectionately at my ear while I retrieved the shoe from under the porch and changed shoes.

I knew Larry was watching me from behind the screened door, but I didn't turn for a final wave. It was a relief to be free of him.

Yet I couldn't be free of the things he'd said, and some of them stayed with me as I whistled to Rudy and set out across the dunes to where Max was waiting.

[9]

WE WEREN'T alone on the beach this time; the newcomer, the young man who'd checked in just before lunch, was walking there, too. He passed within a few yards of Max as I topped the dunes with the beach grass scratching at my legs.

Rudy barked and set off after him; I yelled and the dog came back, tongue lolling, to run in circles around me.

Max swung in my direction but didn't come to meet me, waiting with his hands in his pockets. There was nothing nonchalant about his eyes, though, as he examined my face.

"Did he say anything to you?" I asked.

"Who?"

"The new guest. The one who just walked past you."

"Oh. No. Has your friend gone?"

"I hope so. I walked off and left him standing there."

Max reached for my hand. "So long as you didn't go off with him."

"Did you think I would? No. Whatever we had is all over. It's funny, now, I'm not even sure what it was. I thought I was very much in love with him, and I was happy with the idea of marrying him . . . and then when . . . then I realized I didn't know him at all."

"Nobody ever really knows anybody . . . fully, I mean. My parents have been married for thirty-two years," he informed me, "and they still surprise each other. Of course, my mother says it's because he doesn't really listen to what she says, and *he* says it's because she doesn't say what she means. What did Engle want?"

"The same thing the mysterious searcher wanted, I guess. The missing tapes or papers or whatever." I had no intention of repeating everything Larry had said, but that much of an admission seemed in order. "He said the Senator told Graden he'd made tapes implicating other people, but they haven't been able to find them. Apparently the ones he was carrying when he died were blanks. I told him I didn't know anything and he left."

Max's eyes narrowed. "It took you long enough, to say no more than that."

"Oh, we said more, but that's the gist of it."

"He hadn't changed his mind about jilting you."

"Would it bother you if he had?"

"Only if you considered listening to him." Apparently he read in my face that I hadn't. "What's his interest in the missing tapes?"

"He said he's working for someone whose name he isn't at liberty to divulge. He's a lawyer, you know."

Max stared toward the inn as if to determine what Larry was doing, but we could see only the top floors of the inn, not the grounds or the cars. "The Engles wouldn't be mixed up in it, would they? All the construction scandals, the bribes, the contracts bought and sold?"

I stopped walking, shocked. "Of course not!"

"How can you be sure? I never knew them, they were way out of my class when I lived in Hampton, but I knew *of* them. The Engles are a big-money family, prominent legal firm, all that jazz, right? People with money often want to earn more, and sometimes they aren't too particular about how they do it."

"Engles and Lawford is a very staid firm. The Engles have had money since before the Civil War; Mr. Lawford, senior, is a judge now and both sons are attorneys. They're all very respectable."

Max nodded, scratching his chin through the thick red beard. "Right. Just the kind of firm that wouldn't want it known if they got into anything a bit off-color. Suppose the Senator offered them a deal, a chance to pick up a little cash . . . not unnatural, considering that you were going to marry their only son."

"But their only son . . . and Mama . . . were very quick to reconsider that as soon as the scandal broke. If they were in it too . . . and that's an absurd supposition, I assure you . . . they'd have come to his aid in order to protect themselves, if nothing else."

"Not if it was too late to pull the Senator's chestnuts out of the fire, and it was. Harold McCaffey was nailed to the cross, honey. They had him dead to rights, and anybody who rushed in to support him ran the very grave risk of being sucked under with him. I'm mixing a lot of metaphors, but you get the picture. Here was the proof the man was a crook, and anybody who tried to defend him would be equally suspect. That's why none of them, even the ones with a lot to lose, came to his rescue. They were trying like mad to cover their own tracks, and they hoped to stop him before he implicated *them*."

He kicked a stone, then bent to scoop it up and pitch it far out over the water. "No, I don't buy it. Engle didn't just come here on behalf of a client. The only client who'd want the tapes for legitimate reasons would be the legal authorities, and there's no reason they'd bring in a junior partner from a firm like his. They have their own men. No, there's more to his coming than what he told you."

I jerked my hand away from his. "You sound as bad as Larry does . . . neither of you has any reason to think the other's anything but what he says he is, yet you both. . . ." I stopped. I hadn't intended to repeat Larry's words to Max, not all of them.

Max made a small sound of triumph. "Ahhh, I thought so. What did he say about me?"

"It was so ridiculous I don't want to think about it. No, Max, I mean it. It's upsetting to me to talk about all this, and I don't see any point to it."

"No point to it? Brenna, use your head! If he's throwing out red herrings about me, I have a right to know what they are!"

I wasn't sure whether he did or not, and we argued about it for a while, with me getting weaker. Max had always done that to me; for one thing, he could think faster than I could, and he had a very persuasive way about him. It usually didn't seem like bullying at the time, but afterward I would realize he'd steamrollered me.

I had to give him something, so with genuine reluctance I offered what I thought the most innocuous of Larry's accusations.

"He thinks you met the Senator here, just before he died, and that you're in some sort of cahoots, or were. He intimated that you're looking for the tapes, too, but for a less honorable reason."

Max gave a bark of laughter at that. "Oh, little does he know of our great mutual liking and respect, the Senator and I! What else did your little lawyer think about me?"

I wasn't about to go into further detail. "He doesn't like you, so he thinks your're a suspicious character. I'm beginning to think you're as big an idiot as he is, you're both so childish."

He swung around on me, a dangerous gleam in his eye. "You think I'm childish, do you?"

By the time he'd finished proving to his own satisfaction that childish was one thing he *wasn't*, we were in a different and better humor. We didn't talk about Larry again until we were on our way back to the inn and saw his car leaving as we topped the dunes.

"What the hell's he been doing here all this time?" Max scowled after the vanishing vehicle.

"Who knows? Or cares. Oh, damn!"

"What?"

"When I talked to Maudie, she said she'd call Addison's and tell them I'd send them the key I have of theirs. That's the firm I used to work for, I accidentally carried the key away with me, and I could have returned it by Larry if I'd thought of it. Mr. Addison really has a thing about employees walking off with keys, and I promised I'd return it. Who knows, I might want to work for him again someday."

He obviously considered this less than earthshaking. "Stick it in an envelope and mail it."

"Yes, I guess so. I'll have to get some envelopes. Actually, there are several keys on my ring I might as well get rid of; do you think I ought to send the house keys to the authorities, too? I never thought of turning them in."

He shrugged. "I can't see what difference it makes. After all, anybody can copy a key, so if they need more they can duplicate the ones they have. As long as you aren't going to use yours again, you could just throw them away. What are they going to do with the house?"

"I don't know. Maudie thought they'd eventually sell it, but it will probably be years before they decide who's entitled to what, since the Senator evidently got so much of what he had by . . . by illegal manipulations. I'm sorry I brought it up. I don't want to think about it."

"Don't, then. Use willpower," Max advised, and offered to race me the rest of the way.

Use willpower. He'd said it so easily, as if one could turn thoughts off or on simply by wanting to.

It wasn't that simple. I was disturbed by the things both Max and Larry had suggested about each other, and I couldn't help thinking about them.

And Max didn't let it drop. He asked Zell, point-blank, what Larry had been doing for an hour after I'd left him.

"Oh, he was just looking around. He said the inn was very nice and asked if we had any rooms available. We didn't, of course; that young Mr. Crane took the room Mr. Haden had, so we're full again, except for the storage room. We used to rent *that*. Oh, that reminds me, Brenna, if you want to store your suitcases there, so you'll have more room in your closet, it's the door opposite the bathroom, on your side of the hall.''

I murmured some acknowledgment, still busy with the idea that Larry had asked about accommodations here. He wouldn't have thought the inn was ''very nice''; I knew perfectly well the sort of accommodations he usually demanded, and he'd have had nothing but contempt for this rustic place. It disturbed me that he'd asked and I didn't quite know why.

''Where did he look?'' Max asked.

''Oh, he just wandered around and talked to a few of the guests.''

''Upstairs, too?'' Was Max's voice a bit sharp?

''Yes, I think he went upstairs. I didn't pay any special attention. I was trying to hear what all Callie and Mr. Montgomery were up to,'' Zell admitted with some frankness. ''He has a client who's interested in buying the inn, and so far she's refused to discuss it, but the way things are going, I don't know. And if she decides to do anything . . . well, I'd want to know.'' Her small face was worried until she turned to me; then it gradually brightened as the idea occurred to her. ''But, of course, she can't sell it, I mean, she can't decide to do that all by herself, can she? It's half yours!''

''Why would she want to sell it?''

''Well, mostly because they don't really make any money here, and the building's so old and needs repairs, you know. I expect if they sold it Egg and Callie would be able to get along in a rest home or something, or maybe they'd rent a little cottage in town because they'd have the proceeds from the sale. But all I have is my little pension, and it wouldn't support me anywhere else unless I could work for part of my keep, you see.''

Her birdlike eyes peered up at me. ''She'd have to talk to you before she could do anything, get your agreement. You'd tell me before any final decision was made, wouldn't you?''

''Yes, of course,'' I assured her, and she patted my arm, smiled, and trotted off about her business.

''I think I'll run into town,'' Max said when I turned back to him. ''I'll see you at dinnertime, OK? Table for two?''

He was gone, scarcely pausing for a reply. He hadn't even asked me if I'd like to go with him.

Not that I had any need to go. I went upstairs, unexpectedly tired, and stretched out on the bed, staring at the papered ceiling.

Max and Larry had made so many accusations against each other. Was there anything to any of them, or were they simply a normal reaction between two men who were, or had been, interested in the same girl?

I dismissed fairly readily the idea that Larry and his father were in any way involved with my uncle. I'd never heard the slightest hint of any business dealings between them. The Engles were old, solid money. I couldn't believe Larry's father would run any risks to increase the family fortunes when he already had everything a man could want.

Larry's suggestions about Max, however, were more difficult to laugh off. Oh, not the one about Max and the Senator having conspired together; I didn't for a moment doubt Max's genuine dislike, even hatred, for my uncle.

But was there anything to the idea that it was more than a coincidence that Max had been here when I arrived? He'd never vacationed here before, never come here with me. And it was true that anyone might have guessed this was where I would come when I fled from Hampton, so if he'd wanted to encounter me, coming to Bascom's Point wasn't a bad way to do it.

Larry had even seemed skeptical of Max's very ordinary background and his supposed reason for being here. I'd put it down to purely masculine jealousy except for the fact that it didn't make sense to be jealous if Larry no longer wanted me himself.

Max hadn't made any secret about where he'd been or what he'd been doing for the past years. And it would be so simple to check that lying about it would be pointless.

So simple to check.

I lay there, counting the rosebuds on the wallpaper, and the idea kept growing: *So simple to check.*

Max was gone; he'd scarcely be back in less than half an hour even if he'd only gone into town to buy a pack of gum. I knew the aunts liked to rest in their rooms or put their feet up in their private sitting room for a few hours before they fixed dinner.

I sat up and put on my shoes and went out of my room and downstairs. Sure enough, the lobby and the registration desk were deserted. I could see Mr. Rossdale rocking on the front porch, and there were voices somewhere out of sight as others beyond him carried on a desultory conversation. There was no one to pay any attention to me.

Feeling guilty enough to make my pulses race, I moved behind the high counter and reached for the box of current registration cards.

Max's was right there, made out in his bold dark hand. I noted the name of the town and the hospital he'd listed as his employer, committing it to memory. Maybe next time I was in town I'd call and see if he really worked there, if he'd only been gone as long as he said he had.

It was a sneaky thing to do. Maybe I wouldn't have nerve enough; I felt uncomfortable just contemplating doing it.

I knew with a sudden bleak clarity that for all my rise in spirits since I'd come here I was extremely vulnerable; I had come through a very difficut time and another such crisis would be even more crushing. I didn't really want to do anything to spoil the relationship that was building between Max and me . . . but I didn't want to commit myself only to get hurt again, either.

I'm not sure why I looked over the other cards. Someone could have come in at any minute and demanded to know why I was snooping around, and I wouldn't have had a good enough answer.

Yet I stood there, flicking through the registration cards, which weren't in any sort of order but were jumbled together. Perhaps in such a small place, and with a number of apparently permanent guests, the aunts didn't see the need for an alphabetical file.

The Avery sisters' card was dated eleven years earlier. Old Mr. Foster had been here for eight, and Mr. Rossdale had been here for nearly seven years. Certainly none of them had been recruited by anybody to come here and lie in wait for me. Even Mr. Montgomery, the realtor, was a resident of some two years' standing.

Bill Haden's card was still there, even though he was gone. No doubt if he'd checked out in the normal way, Callie would have removed the card. I glanced over the spaces where he'd filled in the requested information and stopped.

He listed his home address as Georgetown, D.C.

The man who had been driving a white car, who stayed at the same motel I did on the trip from Hampton, had also been from Georgetown, D.C.

A creaking board brought my head up so sharply that something snapped in my neck. I rubbed at the painful area, realizing that it was only someone walking along the front porch; he wasn't coming inside.

I drew a sharp breath, let it go, and returned to the registration card in my hand. Bill Haden, Charles Tolman . . . no similarity in names. They said when a person takes an assumed name he usually uses the same initials, but that had always seemed incredibly foolish to me. *I* wouldn't have done it had I been trying to conceal my identity.

If Haden and Tolman were the same man, would he have listed his correct hometown at both places? But, of course, he had no way of knowing I would be checking his registration information at either place, let alone both of them.

If Haden-Tolman had been following me, had been the one to search my room, had he finished with me when he found nothing? And who had sent him? Legal authorities, who wanted not only to solve the Senator's murder but to determine who else was involved in his illegal deals? Or the men who wanted those deals kept quiet?

The flimsy cardboard rectangle did nothing to answer any of those questions. I replaced it in the box and went on to the next one. There was one for Zell, written in a spidery but legible hand. Hometown, Bascom's Point. She'd been living at the inn for seventeen years.

The last card was the newest one, for the man who had just arrived. Tom Crane. Occupation: salesman. Employer: a pharmaceutical house in Michigan. Home address: a town in Pennsylvania.

Pennsylvania. The same as Max. Another coincidence?

I replaced the box on the shelf under the counter and walked around into the lobby. I remembered seeing a set of encyclopedias there in the bookcase, and maybe there would be an atlas.

There was. It was dated 1912, but the map of Pennsylvania showed both towns, the one where Max lived, and the one Tom Crane listed as his home address.

They were four miles apart.

I stared in frustration at the brittle old map with curling edges. Chances were nobody'd had the book out of the bookcase in fifty years, and I put down an impulse to tear out the map and take it with me. I didn't because reason told me the page had already revealed all that it could.

So two men here at the inn had come from towns only four miles apart in Pennsylvania. We weren't all that far from Pennsylvania; no doubt other guests occasionally came from there, as well as from Georgetown. It needn't mean anything at all. Certainly Max hadn't paid any attention to the latest guest, and there was no reason to think there was anything sinister about it even if they knew each other. Was there?

I hadn't learned anything that was of any help to me, only enough to increase my uneasiness.

I went back upstairs, and then, because I was too restless to sit still, I unpacked the remaining boxes I'd left sitting in a corner and put the things away. I didn't know how long I'd be staying here, but Aunt Stell had trained me too well to allow me to live with a stack of untidy boxes for any period of time.

That left the problem of what to do with the empty cartons. I didn't want to dispose of them, in case I wanted to repack everything eventually. Zell had said there was a storeroom down the hall, so, boxes in hand, I went looking for it.

There it was, across from the bathroom. The door stuck, and for a moment I thought it was locked, but it gave under pressure. I could see why they'd given up renting it out; it couldn't possibly have held anything bigger than a single bed and would have given a canary claustrophobia.

It was nearly full of boxes and luggage, stacked high enough to prevent my seeing out the one small window. If I were going to allow room for the door to be opened inward, I'd have to stack my own cartons on top of some of those already there.

I swung them up onto a suitcase already over my head and, in so doing, overbalanced the entire stack; I ducked in time to avoid being pelted with debris, but the top case had broken open when it hit the floor, spewing its contents all over the limited space.

Suppressing the words that rose to my lips, I bent to gather up the clothes.

The first thing that struck me was that these were someone's good clothes, several shirts folded as if from a laundry, and then a plastic bag filled with dirty laundry . . . I could smell the socks.

Odd, that anybody would put unwashed clothes away here. I propped up the top of the suitcase and began to pack the items back into it, and stopped again.

There was a blue suit neatly packed into the top compartment, a suit that looked familiar.

It was warm in the little room and dusty. I could still smell those dirty socks. It was almost as if I . . . the *real* me . . . watched from a distance, as my hands stopped putting clothes in and started taking them back out, inspecting each piece for some clue to its owner.

The tags, the ones encased in plastic provided for the purpose of identification, were tucked into one of the shirred side pockets. I stared down at them with the sensation of having my throat close so that it was an effort to breathe.

Bill Haden, 12 Glendon Court, Georgetown, D.C.

If Bill Haden had left without paying his bill, why was his suitcase here in this dusty room?

I wasn't at all sure what it meant, except that it wasn't good. I didn't find

80

anything else of interest in the bag, and I replaced it where I'd found it.

So far as I could see, there were only two possibilities. Either Haden had, indeed, skipped without paying his bill or something had happened to him and someone else had emptied the room of his belongings.

In light of the other things that had been happening recently, I hated to think what the "something" might be that could have happened to the man.

[10]

I WALKED into the aunts' private sitting room in the midst of an animated conversation between the two junior ladies, who were facing each other in the middle of the room as if they might come to fisticuffs at any moment.

"It's none of your business one way or the other," Egg was saying with some force when I paused in the doorway. "*You* don't have any interest in the inn."

"I've lived in it long enough so you owe me the courtesy of telling me if it's going to be sold out from under me," Zell countered.

"If and when any such thing is settled, you'll be told along with everybody else."

"I don't think Callie's told *you* anything either. I think you're just as much in the dark as *I* am."

They saw me then. Egg flushed a little, I thought, although she was always rather rosy-faced. Zell turned to me with a petulant expression.

"They're at it again, Callie and Mr. Montgomery. But Callie can't sell the inn without *your* say-so, can she, Brenna?"

"I wouldn't think so."

Egg turned to me with curiosity written across her round countenance. "Would you want to sell your share if the offer was good enough?"

"I don't know. I haven't thought about it. I suppose the money would be of more use to me than half an interest in an inn that doesn't really support the rest of you. I mean, it's obvious that you don't need my help on the staff and you couldn't afford to split the profits with another person."

"Oh, it isn't all that bad," Egg assured me. "Mostly we get by just fine.

It's only when someone skips out without paying or steals something . . . that's what hurts.''

That brought me back to what was really on my mind. "About the man who skipped out without paying—Mr. Haden?''

Zell's smile blossomed. "Oh, did you hear about him? Wasn't that nice? Callie felt much better about it. He wasn't a very *friendly* man, you know, never said half a dozen words to anybody, did he, Egg? But at least he wasn't a crook.''

My words sounded hollow. "How do you know that?''

"Why, isn't that what you were talking about? The money order Callie got from him this morning? He didn't write a note of explanation or anything like that, but Callie said probably he just didn't have the right change and he wanted to go before we were all up, or something. Anyway, he stopped in the next town and got a money order to pay his bill. In fact, I think he overpaid it by two dollars, Callie said.''

"The next town? Why wouldn't he have gotten change in Bascom's Point, if that was the problem?''

"Why, because nothing was open when he left, I expect. By the time he drove over to Jordon's Hill, the post office must have been open. Our little office here, they don't usually have much money on hand either. Next to impossible to cash a government check there, for instance if you want to buy a money order and need some change. Mr. Perkins hardly ever has more than fifty dollars on hand at one time.'' She went on about the local post office; I scarcely heard what she said. So Mr. Haden had sent the money to cover his debt. Or had someone else done it so that no one else would try too hard to find the man who had vanished during the night?

I spoke without realizing that I was interrupting Zell. "Do you know there's a suitcase belonging to Mr. Haden up in the storage room? Who put it there?''

There was a silence while both women looked at me.

"Are you sure, dear?'' They exchanged dubious glances.

"It has identification tags with his name on them, and the blue suit he was wearing the first time I saw him. . . .'' Not when he arrived here, I suddenly realized, but when he was following me, driving a white car. I was just as suddenly convinced that Haden and Tolman were one and the same and that he'd somehow changed cars in order to keep me from becoming suspicious.

It was too late for that. I was so suspicious of everyone that it was frightening.

"Maybe . . . maybe he's going to send for it,'' Egg suggested uncertainly.

I thought that highly unlikely. Why wouldn't he have taken it when he left? Assuming that he left under his own steam and in control of himself and his belongings. Was it completely wild to feel that I couldn't assume any such thing?

"Who put his luggage in the storage room?"

They looked at each other. "I didn't see any luggage," Egg said slowly. "It must be the way Zell says, he'll send for it. Maybe he doesn't know where he's going to be or something."

The man had a car, with room for the suitcase, so it wouldn't matter whether or not he knew where he was going to be, I thought. But I didn't say that.

Callie spoke sharply from the doorway behind us. "I thought you were going to do the salad greens, Eglantine."

I could tell, both by her tone and Egg's face, that use of the full name indicated displeasure. Egg flushed a deeper pink and brushed back a stray strand of white hair.

"Zell's going to do it for me. I . . . have an engagement."

"Well, whoever's going to do them had better get at it. I won't have time."

Egg sort of sidled out of the room, past her thinner sister. Zell stared after her. "I swear, the way she makes up to Mr. Foster is disgusting in a woman her age."

Callie allowed her eyebrows to rise. "Is that who her engagement is with?"

"She wouldn't put on her pink dress just to fix vegetables, would she? You know, she was very bold when she was a girl and she still is! My father always said boldness wasn't attractive in a female."

"Maybe not," Callie agreed. "But it's the bold ones seem to end up getting the men. You'll be here for dinner, Brenna?"

"Yes." Max hadn't suggested anything else, and in the state of mind I was in maybe it was just as well. "Is there anything I can do to help?"

"No, thank you. You coming, Zell?"

"I suppose so. But if Egg thinks she's going to talk Sherman Foster into proposing, she's got another think coming. He admires willowy females—he told me so—and Egg certainly doesn't qualify for that!"

I might have found time to be amused if I hadn't been so alarmed about so many other things. Haden-Tolman had frightened me when he was around, but his disappearance didn't make me feel any better. It felt wrong, no matter how I looked at it.

Another thing that seemed wrong was the fact that the Senator had visited Bascom's Point only a few days before the scandal broke. The more I thought about it the more strongly I was convinced that he'd come here for a definite purpose.

He didn't like the beach; he barely tolerated the old aunts (possibly because of a rather thinly veiled contempt for him, on their part); and at a time in his life when I knew he must have been frantically busy trying to stave off the full-scale investigation that would lead to his indictment, I could not believe he had simply come to this place he disliked for any sort of rest.

Why then? To hide something, the something for which people now seemed to be looking?

It seemed an unlikely spot for that, either the little town or the inn. There must have been dozens of safer and more practical places to hide tapes or papers, places close to home and easily reached. I didn't think he'd have wanted anything valuable beyond his immediate reach.

And so I came back to the same question. Why? Had he come here to meet someone?

I thought over the guest list at the inn, although of course anyone in the village might also have been a possibility. There were mostly old men or women without either money or influence; I couldn't imagine how any of them could have been of any value to Harold McCaffey.

In spite of myself I remembered what Larry had suggested, that my uncle had come here to meet Max. I still rejected the idea, for according to the registration card Max hadn't arrived until after the Senator's death. And unless I questioned the truth of Max's statement about what had happened to him at the hands of the Senator's hired thugs, it was impossible to believe he and my uncle would ever have conspired together or even spoken to each other.

Why then did I continue to have this nagging uneasiness about Max? Or was it only guilt on my own part? Guilt because I was so ready to listen to Larry's suggestions and accusations, because I sneaked around and looked at the registration cards to verify the fact that Max had arrived when he'd said he had.

The aunts had left me to go on about their own business, and I moved restlessly around the lower floor of the inn. The permanent guests had evidently established routines that included walking on the beaches in the nicest weather, but mostly meant playing cards or reading or visiting with one another on the front porch or in the lobby.

85

Dear Lord, what a dull way to give in!

"Brenna! What are you daydreaming about? You were looking right through me."

I blinked before my eyes focused on Max. He was grinning in the old amiable way, and for some reason that made me uncomfortable.

"I'm sorry. I didn't hear you come back. I was thinking about them"—I waved a hand toward the porch—"sitting around doing nothing all day. I don't know how they stand it. I hope I don't end up that way."

"No reason why you should. Marry me and live it up for the rest of your life . . . or at least when we get to be seventy we can sit together and rock and hold hands."

He bent to brush his lips across mine, then drew back to look at me more soberly. "What's the matter? Did that Engle creep get you upset?"

"Yes, I guess he did. There are so many things I don't know about, and something horrible's going on . . . wouldn't you be upset?"

"No, I don't think so. Concerned, maybe, but not to the point where I'd let it spoil my own life. Let's go get a little sunshine. There may not be many more days like this; they're predicting a storm, and then we'll be stuck inside like the old-timers."

We spent another day on the beach, and it was lovely. I let myself forget Larry and the doubts he'd aroused. We walked, holding hands, beside the water's edge. Or we lay on the sun-warmed sand and talked or dozed.

We talked and talked and talked . . . of all the things we'd done and seen and felt and thought during the nine years we'd been apart. And gradually my confidence in Max was rebuilt; he spoke easily and spontaneously and, I was convinced, truthfully about himself.

I didn't pour out my inner feelings quite so readily, but Max had always had a way of drawing me out, even on subjects I'd intended to keep to myself.

When we returned for dinner, we separated to change clothes. The inn wasn't quite as informal as our present attire would have suggested; the other guests were too much older to appreciate wet sandy jeans in their dining room.

I had left my room locked, as had become my custom, but the moment I entered it I realized someone else had also used a key. I didn't at first know what the intangible difference was, but the hair prickled on the back of my neck as I stood there on the multicolored rag rug.

And then I did know. The faint scent of tobacco . . . someone had been smoking in here since I was gone.

I suppose a smoker doesn't realize how powerful the scent of tobacco is, to a nonsmoker, in a room where no smoking has previously been done for some time. The Senator sometimes indulged in rather large black cigars, but he'd been careful to confine them to his own quarters, where Maudie claimed the stench was enough to turn one's stomach. Certainly it clung to drapes and other fabrics long after the smoker had gone.

And so it was here. I found a faint feathering of ash near the wastebasket, although no cigarette butts remained and the ashtray provided by the aunts was pristinely untouched.

Someone had been here and long enough to have smoked at least one cigarette. It seemed to me that every nerve end tingled as my gaze roamed the small room, looking for any other indication that it had been invaded.

Foolishly believing the room to be secure because the door was locked, I hadn't thought to set up any of the TV-type traps used to determine whether or not one has had unwelcome visitors. Still, I'd been here such a short time and only recently transferred my belongings to the dresser drawers so that they were in good order. I thought it worth a check to see if my things had been disturbed.

They had been looked through and left neatly . . . but not quite so neatly as *I* had left them. Inside the closet the smell of tobacco was even stronger, for it had been trapped there when the door was closed.

Who in the hotel smoked? I wondered. It had to be a guest, didn't it? Anyone else would certainly have been noticed wandering around.

Max didn't smoke. And Max had been with me on the beach nearly all day.

Unwanted, the memory returned, of Larry saying, "That could be why he's here, to keep you busy while someone else looks for the tapes."

But there was no reason why he should have done that. He already knew someone had searched my room before and that I was convinced there was no way my uncle could possibly have planted his tapes in my belongings.

The invasion of my privacy both angered and frightened me.

When the knock sounded behind me, I jumped and spun around, heart thumping audibly, to open the door.

It was only Callie, her hair escaping its usual neat bun, her print cotton covered with a voluminous apron in bright colors that seemed at odds with her personality and her present facial expression.

"Zell and Egg are watching things in the kitchen. I thought I might talk to you for a minute," she said, without noticing anything amiss in my own face.

"Certainly. Come on in." I closed the door behind her and indicated the rocking chair. I didn't wait until I'd sunk onto a corner of the bed before I took the initiative. "Callie, do any of you smoke? You or Zell or Egg?"

"Smoke?" Her gnarled fingers settled on the arms of the chair, her eyes blank.

"Cigarettes," I prompted. "Do you?"

She made a grimace of distaste. "Can't stand the filthy habit. I think Egg tried it once or twice when she was a girl, but my parents would never have allowed such a thing and she was only doing it to be daring. She didn't like it either. Good thing. Couldn't any of the three of us have afforded to do it the past few years." There was a grim note of reality in her voice.

"Who does? Of the people who stay here?"

"Does what? Smoke?" She made a visible effort to be responsive to a question she obviously thought of little interest. "Mr. Montgomery smokes an occasional cigar, I believe. So does Mr. Foster, if someone offers him one. He can't afford to buy them either. Why on earth do you want to know?"

"Because someone was smoking in here while I was out today. Can't you smell it?"

She tipped her head, cautiously sniffing. "Why, yes, now that you mention it. Cigarettes, not cigars, I'd say."

"Yes. Have you ever seen any of the others smoking?"

"No. I got a no-smoking sign up in the lobby and in the dining room, both. Lulu Avery is allergic to tobacco smoke, and I don't like it much either. If they want to smoke, let them live somewhere else. I can't think why anybody'd come into your room to smoke, but if I were you I'd keep the door locked from now on."

"I've been keeping it locked. Someone used a key. I assume there is another one besides the one I have."

"Two keys to a room, plus the house key," Callie affirmed. "But nobody would. . . ."

"Somebody did. Where are the extra keys kept?"

"On the board behind the desk. They didn't steal anything, did they?"

"Not that I can tell. But the keys are right there where anybody could walk up and take one, and there isn't anyone around to watch them most of the day, right?"

"Never had any trouble before, and I've lived here all my life; my father ran the inn when I was a little girl, and the keys have always hung right there on the board, handy-like."

Handy-like. Yes, indeed. Very handy. "Then it won't do me much good to keep my room locked, will it, if there are other keys available to anybody who wants one?" But who was I to complain of their system? I had walked around the desk and looked at the registration records I had no right to see.

"Well, I could put the other keys to your room away, on my own chain, I guess." Having disposed of my little problem, Callie went on to her reason for coming. "I suppose you've heard that Mr. Montgomery is trying to get me to talk about selling the inn."

She looked far more perturbed over this prospect than over my report of breaking and entering.

"Yes, Zell mentioned it. She's concerned over what will happen to her if you sell. Are you considering it?"

Her mouth took on pinched lines that were so natural I decided she must be having more than her share of problems lately.

"Since you're half-owner, I couldn't do anything without your say-so."

"Is Mr. Montgomery's client offering you a good price?"

She plucked at a string on her apron. "Not particularly, but it's the best offer we're likely to get. It's an old building, and it hasn't been maintained the way it should have been, simply because we haven't had the money to do it. It's a sort of vicious circle: We haven't the guests to pay for the repairs that would attract more guests. Bank financing is out of the question for us; we're too old, and we'd have to convince a banker we could make enough money to repay any loans. Frankly, I doubt if we could."

"Then you think you ought to sell?" I wasn't sure how I felt about it; I didn't have the emotional ties with the place that they did, but it had belonged to my father's family for a hundred years and it was rather sad to think about it being lost to us.

"No. If I can, I think I ought to hang on until we all die." She said this quite matter-of-factly. "So long as we can make ends meet, we're better off here than we would be trying to stretch our pensions anywhere else. Egg and I wouldn't be quite so bad off as the rest of them; we'd have our share of the money from the sale besides the pensions, and maybe we could make it last long enough. But Zell has nothing; her pension wouldn't support a kitten, let alone a human being, if she couldn't do little odds and ends to pay for part of her keep. The rest of them aren't much better; everybody here lives on an income designed to support them at the prices twenty years ago. This may not be a luxury hotel, but it's better for most of them than they could get anywhere else, you see?"

I saw. I nodded. "I wish I had the money to help you fix up the place,

Callie. But I haven't a thing except a small bank account that probably isn't much more than enough to keep me until I can find another job."

She made a negative gesture, surprisingly forceful, with an arthritic hand. "That's not why I came up here to talk to you. I know you're not rich, any more than we are. The thing is, you do own half the inn, and we've never paid you any of the income from it. There's no sense beating around the bush about it—we can't. We'd have to sell, unless you can let us go on the way we are. When we're gone it'll all be yours and you might get a few thousand out of it. But I've got to know what you want to do, so I can make my own plans."

I stared into the lined face, struck by the thought that she might have been lying awake nights trying to figure a way out of her dilemma. On impulse, I leaned forward and covered one of her hands with my own.

"Callie, you've got more right to the inn than I have. You do what you feel is best for you and Egg and Zell. I'm ashamed to even be here, taking up space you could be renting out to guests. When Max leaves...."I hesitated because I wasn't yet ready to make *that* decision. "Well, I won't be here long. I'm feeling so much better already. I'll have to find another town, a place where I can work. As long as you can hang onto the inn and keep all of you living here, you do it, and don't worry about my interest in the place."

Her eyes searched mine for a moment, as if to verify my sincerity there. "You're sure?"

"I'm sure."

She stayed a few minutes longer, talking about all the years this place had seen; she and Egg had both been born in one of the rooms up on the unused third floor. They'd had to close off those rooms because they were no longer fit to rent, and there were no funds for paint and wallpaper and updated plumbing. But if they could keep the other rooms filled, they'd make do, Callie said. It was actually perceptible, the way the tension was oozing out of her; it softened her face and her voice as well.

She made me feel guilty because I wasn't being all that generous or altruistic. Certinly I didn't want to live for any length of time in the atmosphere of a pleasant but dowdy old boardinghouse, with pleasant but doddering old people. I couldn't even stay in Bascom's Point; there was no way to earn my living there. The inn meant far more to Callie than it could ever mean to me, yet she acted as if I'd just given up my share in something very valuable.

After she had gone I changed into a presentable-looking dress and brushed out my hair. I considered makeup but decided the sun and the wind had given me enough color . . . or was Max responsible for that?

I opened the door and started out, then turned back for my small handbag. I had to have that in order to carry my keys and my money; I certainly couldn't leave them in the room. I was standing near the dresser when I heard their voices.

"Nothing. Not a goddamned thing."

It was a man, not a voice I recognized. But I recognized the second one, all right, and was transfixed in the act of transferring my wallet to the small purse from a larger one.

"Hell. Well, all right. You can't win 'em all."

Max went by my door, pausing to pull it shut without seeing me behind it. I heard them on the stairs, two pair of male feet making no effort to be quiet.

I knew who the first speaker was, now, by logical deduction. The voice was one I hadn't heard before, so it could only be the newest guest, what was his name? Tom Crane.

Tom Crane, who came from a town only four miles from where Max lived in Pennsylvania.

I wasn't quite ready to grapple with the implications of these few words exchanged between them. I closed the door behind me and descended the stairs with the strong feeling that the second floor was empty except for myself. It probably was; Callie had been in my room longer than I'd thought, and I was late for dinner.

Max was waiting for me in the dining room, relaxed and holding what looked like a scotch on the rocks. He was talking to Tom Crane, who held a matching glass.

They turned toward me, Max's smile widening in appreciation, Crane pleasantly expectant. My feet moved as if of their own volition while I tried to get my brain in gear, to begin to think clearly.

"You're gorgeous in pink, just the way I remembered you," Max said, putting an arm around my shoulders and drawing me close to him. I must have been as responsive as a stick of driftwood, but he didn't seem to notice. "This is my girl . . . I'm trying to talk her into being more than that, and I think she's weakening. Brenna, this is Tom Crane."

Tom Crane was about Max's age, only much taller and thinner. His nondescript hair kept falling forward into his eyes and he kept pushing it back, which seemed a boyish gesture. His eyes, however, didn't strike me as being boyish at all. They were sharp and mature and rather cold.

His lips stretched in a smile that would have been very friendly if I hadn't been looking into his eyes. "I'm happy to meet you, Miss St. John. I understand you're related to the ladies who run this place."

"You want a drink, Brenna?" Max gestured dangerously with his glass. "The ladies St. John don't furnish booze, but I brought a supply of my own. They do let me use their ice. We've got about five minutes before dinner, I think; there was some sort of crisis over burned beans or something, and they had to start over. Shall I get you a scotch?"

I started to lick my numb lips and forced myself to stop. "No, thank you. You and Mr. Crane are old friends, are you?"

Both men denied it instantly, Crane with a shake of the head, Max in words. "Oh, no, never saw each other before we met coming downstairs a few minutes ago. But it turns out we're both from Pennsylvania, even live not too far apart. Isn't that a coincidence?"

It certainly was. I might have accepted it as only that if I hadn't heard those few words in the upper hall.

"Where did you get to anyway? I heard you leave your room a few minutes ahead of me, but when I got downstairs I couldn't find you."

So that was why he thought himself safe to speak to Tom Crane and now deny they'd met before; he heard Callie going and thought it was me. I couldn't think up a reply that would sound genuine; I turned in relief when Egg bustled toward us, waving us to a table.

"We've fixed some more green beans, and the roast is ready to go. Sit, sit, we'll be right with you."

I heard Crane murmur something about leaving us alone, to which Max didn't protest, and allowed myself to be seated at one of the small tables. My brain was functioning again and I almost wished it wouldn't.

I could not for the life of me put an innocent connotation on those brief sentences I had mistakenly overheard.

I had no doubt at all that Max was lying to me about knowing Crane and I wanted to scream at him.

"Why?"

[11]

WE ATE, Max hungrily, I with great effort because every swallow threatened to choke me. When Max said anything, I murmured some sort of reply, sometimes totally unaware of what I replied to.

I kept hearing Tom Crane's voice, saying, "Nothing. Not a goddamned thing," and Max responding, "Hell. Well, all right. You can't win 'em all."

And Larry saying, "That could be why he's here . . . to keep you busy while someone else looks for the tapes. . . ." *God.*

"Brenna?" I suddenly found that Max was staring at me, a faint frown showing amid all that red hair. "What's the matter?"

"Matter?" The echo was inane. *My* face wasn't covered with hair, and it had always been easily read by those who knew me. What did he see there now?

"You made sort of a . . . a moaning sound. Aren't you feeling well?"

I took refuge in the shelter he offered. "I guess not . . . I have a vicious headache." It wasn't even untrue; the things I'd been thinking had tightened my muscles until I actually was feeling the pain of them. I pushed my plate away. "I can't eat. I think . . . I need to lie down."

He stood at once, although he hadn't completed his own meal either. "I'm sorry . . . I knew you weren't quite yourself. Come on."

"Please, don't come with me. There's nothing you can do, and I just want. . . ." I couldn't tell him what I wanted; I couldn't so much as form the words.

He paid no attention to my protest, moving around the table to pull out my chair. I knew eyes were on us as we rose, but nobody said anything. Max insisted on taking me upstairs, and then he didn't leave but settled me on the bed, found a light blanket in the closet to put over me, and went down the hall to the bathroom for a wet cloth to put over my eyes.

"Take it easy for a while. I've got some aspirin if you want them."

I swallowed two of the white tablets and accepted the cold cloth, which did feel good. "Thank you, Max. Now go on back and finish your dinner."

"I can eat anytime. I'll sit here for a while and keep an eye on you."

"I'm not dying, Max, I just have a headache. Please go."

He didn't answer and I didn't hear the door open or close; instead there came the faint creak of the rocking chair as it took his weight.

I gave up. My thoughts were boiling inside me, incoherent but compelling, and I surrendered to them, letting them go where they would.

Max, Larry, the Senator, Mr. Engle . . . Max had suggested that Lawrence Engle might somehow have been involved in the Senator's schemes. I hadn't seriously considered the idea at the time, but now it intruded again and I didn't have what it took to beat it off.

I didn't know Lawrence Engle at all well, considering the fact that I'd been engaged to his son. In a way he was like the Senator, in that he was completely absorbed in business matters and had little time for his family; he was used to the best of everything and took it for granted that his wife and his son and his servants would put his wishes first at all times. He was austere and dignified, where the Senator had been almost professionally gregarious, though I understood he was powerfully dynamic in the courtroom. He'd certainly always been very pleasant to me. He had seemed pleased when we announced our engagement, even to the point of giving me a bit of jewelry that had belonged to his mother as an engagement present. Not valuable particularly, he told me, but it was beautiful and he valued it for sentimental reasons and he wanted me to have it.

I had sent it back after Larry broke our engagement.

It was all a kaleidoscopic nightmare. I twisted uneasily on the bed, as if it were possible to move physically away from my thoughts, and Max put out a hand to cover mine.

"Maybe I ought to see if I can get a doctor."

"Oh, don't be an idiot! For a headache?" The words came out with so natural an irritation that he was reassured.

"Do you think you can go to sleep if I keep still? Or would you like me to read to you? You used to like it when I read poetry to you. I notice you have a little volume here."

Maybe hearing the poetry would take my mind off myself and off all the things I didn't want to talk about.

I listened for a time without registering the words. Max had a good, deep, masculine voice, and he read well. I remembered the nights I had lain within the circle of his arms, those nights before the Senator's men found us; I remembered as if it were only a few days ago, his breath on my cheek, his voice and the love words he spoke, the poetry he had composed especially for me.

Gradually I started to hear again, and the pain in my head began to recede.

> Like water I came;
> Like water I am . . .
> In shallows, spreading thin;
> In borrowed depths, quiet,
> Holding in shimmering crystal
> The mystery of life,
> The wonderment of what and why.
>
> In restlessness I run,
> The rapids are wild and churning and roar
> As I fling myself on the rocks below.

As I listened to the familiar words, the turbulent thoughts subsided; the poetry and Max's low voice drew me away from one pain, but nearer to another.

> Now I am discarded,
> My tears fall as rain;
> I am moody as an April day.
> I dance, I sing, I pray;
> I am the mirage in the desert;
> I am the Cup in His name.

The Max I remembered would never have done anything to hurt me. He had loved me, all those years ago when we were not yet grown. Could he have changed so much that he would deliberately hurt me now? Changed so much that he would lead me to believe he wanted me again only to satisfy his own selfish and ulterior motives?

I wished, with a sudden desperate intensity that was childish in everything except the pain it caused, that it were possible to see into the people around me. I hadn't seen into the Senator, or Larry, or even Aunt Stell; no more could I read what lay behind the façade that Max presented to me and the world.

I didn't hear the end of the poem. Only when he paused some time later, belatedly realizing what he was reading, did my mind backtrack and pick up the sense of it.

"Go on," I told him quietly.

> I shall come into your room
> As if yesterday were today,
> And we shall talk together
> As if you had not gone away.
>
> We shall not speak of parting—
> This day will be too bright for grief—
> We shall guard each short minute,
> Knowing Time is a clever thief.
>
> I shall feel your angel touch
> (Your quick, glad clasp) become real
> And I shall dream happily,
> With memories Time cannot steal.
>
> And though I may not follow
> Your gentle wandering through the spheres,
> Alone, I shall remember,
> Remember through tomorrow's years.

Ever since my mother died, Aunt Stell had been there when I needed her. To talk to, to offer comfort. I thought of her as Max read, and the tears began to slide down my cheeks under the wet cloth that was no longer cold enough to be refreshing. I couldn't have said whether they were tears for Aunt Stell or for myself, but I could feel the pressure building within my chest and I knew I couldn't subdue it.

"Brenna! Darling, I shouldn't have read that; I didn't know how it was going to be . . . Brenna, Brenna!"

Max was out of the chair and beside me, drawing me into his arms, using the sodden washcloth to wipe my eyes. He held me as if I were a child, and I cried.

I hadn't wanted or expected to cry, and yet it was strangely therapeutic, relieving tensions and inhibitions as well. How could I doubt Max when he knew how I felt, when he responded so fully to my need?

I gave a final hiccuping sob and drew myself away, feeling vaguely ashamed of myself but better for it all the same.

"I suppose you and Stell read that book together," Max said quietly.

"She gave it to me. The author's a friend of hers, a charming little old lady who's survived every pain there is, I guess, in her eighty years . . . no, don't feel badly about it, Max, I needed that. I'm only sorry you had to be subjected to it."

"Brenna . . . I love you. You know that? I love you, and I don't want to miss being subjected to whatever you're going through."

Considering just what I had been going through and the way Max himself fitted into it, I had to laugh. For a minute he thought I was getting hysterical, I guess. I shook my head.

"No, I'm not going off the deep end. That *was* funny, but you'll have to take my word for it; I can't explain it to you. Max, do you think I ought to get in touch with whoever's in charge of the investigation of the Senator's death? There was a man who came to the house . . . well, there were half a dozen of them, but the one in charge was a man named Hastings. At least he's the one who asked the most questions. It was all so horrible, and I was so upset I don't remember much of what was said, but I think he was with the Justice Department. Would that be right?"

"Probably. Or the FBI. I'm sure they're in on it anyway. Why?"

"How would I get in touch with them? Hastings, for instance?"

There was a small silence while he looked at me. Although it was still daylight outside, it was getting quite dim in the room, but neither of us moved to turn on a light.

"Have you thought of something that might be evidence, to tell them?"

"No, not really. But whoever it is who's poking around . . . whether he's trying to scare me or only doing it incidentally . . . is going too far. I wonder if it's time I was in contact with the authorities."

His expression didn't change. "Has something else happened?"

I told him about the smoker-searcher of the afternoon.

He exhaled quietly. "It's not much to tell."

"I know. But it has to have something to do with the Senator's death,

97

doesn't it, or with the missing evidence? Why else would anyone pick on me? There's nothing to make anyone think I'd have valuables or money lying around. It's so little, someone going through my drawers and poking into my closet . . . and I don't see how they'd be able to tell who it was. But maybe they ought to know someone seems to be interested in me or my belongings."

What did I hope, that he would say, "I am one of them," and show me something to prove it? I don't know. He stood up and walked toward the window to look out toward the end of the spit.

"Is that all you have to tell them, that somebody's searched your room a couple of times?"

I thought of the mysteriously vanishing Haden-Tolman, the money order which had fortuitously arrived to pay his bill and at the same time abort any search for him, his luggage tucked away in the storage room, the conversation I had overheard in the hall just before dinner, the things both Max and Larry had suggested.

"I think that's enough," I said, and managed not to sound evasive.

"Well, it's a bit of a pain, I'll admit. Especially since you'd left the door locked. I don't like that, that someone can get in anyway. You forgot to lock it before supper incidentally."

"Callie says she'll remove the keys from the board and keep them where they aren't available to anyone else."

He turned back to me, silhouetted against the window so that all I could see was the dark bulk of him. "Brenna, let's. . . ."

I didn't get to hear what he was going to propose, for there was a sharp, firm rap on the door.

I opened it to find the realtor, Mr. Montgomery, standing there in the dimly lighted hall. He peered into my gloomy room.

"Oh, I'm sorry, were you lying down?"

I reached for the light switch. "It doesn't matter. Is there something you wanted?"

"Well, yes, I'd like to talk to you if I may." He stepped into the room, stopping short when he saw Max. "Oh, I say, I *am* sorry. . . ."

I couldn't be bothered with what he thought, finding the two of us in an unlighted room together. One look at my tear-stained face ought to have convinced anyone he hadn't stumbled into a love nest, but I didn't care one way or the other.

Mr. Montgomery smoothed back his luxuriant white crest in a gesture much like the one my uncle had employed. "I . . . ah, wanted to talk to Miss St. John. In a business way, you understand."

Max didn't move from his position by the window. It looked darker outside now that we'd turned on a light. "Don't let me stop you. We don't have any secrets from each other, do we, Brenna?"

I didn't dare dwell on that. "Please sit down, Mr. Montgomery. What is it you wanted?"

"Well, it's about the inn. I don't suppose Miss Callie has told you. . . ." He paused with some delicacy.

"She told me you have a client who's made her an offer for the inn. She also said she wasn't interested in selling it."

He cleared his throat. "Yes. Well, that's true, I haven't been able to persuade her to seriously consider the offer. That's why I decided to come to you. I didn't realize until today that you're a part owner."

"Half," I confirmed. "However, the place has been Callie and Egg's home all their lives. I certainly don't intend to be at cross-purposes with them about it. If they don't want to sell, that's all there is to it."

He leaned toward me, touching his tongue to lips that seemed too pink. I supposed the avid expression denoted his interest in the commission to be received should he talk anyone into such a sale.

"May I take it that you would have no objection to selling if Miss Callie thought it advisable from her standpoint?"

"She can do as she likes; I've already told her she doesn't have to consider me."

"Ah! Very good, very good. It *would* be the wise thing to do, you know. I have a client who has made an offer, a good firm one. It isn't likely there'll be many more such offers for this place, considering the condition it's in, you know. It needs all sorts of costly repairs that Miss Callie is in no position to handle. And she's an old woman . . . they're all old, the three of them; they belong in some nice comfortable cottage with their feet up, not trying to run an inconvenient old inn that can't do much more than provide them a subsistence."

"They seem to think that's preferable to sitting with their feet up, as you put it, and trying to exist on their pensions." I was already tired of the subject; I wished he would go.

"But if they sold the inn they'd have a little cash to supplement those pensions, plenty to last them to the end of their days." His eyes were guileless, supplicating.

99

"Zell wouldn't share in that cash, and neither would any of their other tenants. Callie's concerned about them all, where they'd go, how they'd manage if they were forced to leave here.''

"Well. . . .'' He smiled as if to suggest that we shared an amused tolerance for the foibles of the aged. "It's herself and her sister Miss Callie should be concerned about. After all, we can't any of us take on the cares of the whole world, can we?'' He shrugged. "If she wants to share her cash with the others, that's her business, I guess. After you've collected *your* half, of course. Cash money for property in these days isn't to be sneezed at, you know. We have to grasp our opportunities when they arrive.''

"Callie doesn't consider this an opportunity. And she's quite capable of making her own decisions about her best interests; she's certainly not senile. I'm afraid you're wasting your time, Mr. Montgomery. I have no intention of trying to influence her one way or the other.''

The smile slid off his face. "My client is prepared to pay cash tomorrow, upon agreement to vacate as soon as possible. A building as old as this one, needing repairs . . . you aren't likely to see another offer like that.''

For the first time Max spoke lazily from his spot at the window. "What's the offer?''

Montgomery hesitated; when I didn't object to the question, he answered it by naming a figure that was apparently supposed to impress us. Knowing nothing of real estate values, I looked to Max for an opinion.

"It doesn't sound like such a great offer to me. The property alone, right on the beach this way, ought to be worth half that.''

Color began to work its way up Mr. Montgomery's neck and face and into his snowy hair. "As you say, the beach property is valuable. But the building itself is falling apart.''

"Why does your client want it then? I mean, there's a big barn of a place on the other side of the bay that's for sale. I don't know what the asking price is, but it's obviously in much better repair than this one.''

The color deepened. "I don't ask my clients why they want a particular piece of property, Mr.—Von Rys, is it?''

Max was not at all put out at the testy note in the man's voice; in fact, he smiled.

"Do you ask them their names?''

For a moment Montgomery didn't respond, as if he hadn't understood the question, so Max rephrased it.

"Who is this client who wants to pay this exorbitantly generous price for a falling-down old inn? What's his name?''

Montgomery stared at him, then replied with dignity. "I am not at liberty to reveal that at this time."

Max's shaggy red eyebrows rose. "Oh? Why's that?"

I noticed a faint tremor in the realtor's hand where it rested on a pinstriped knee. Had it been there before or had it been precipitated by Max's words?

"I don't question a client when he desires anonymity, Mr. Von Rys. There are many reasons. . . ." His voice trailed off and he stood up. "I see that I haven't made any progress here, Miss St. John, and I'm genuinely sorry." His glance toward Max suggested that he might have done better without Max's interference. "You leave me no choice but to report to my client that I've failed to negotiate an agreement."

Max sounded so amiable he had to be putting it on a bit. "You do that, Mr. Montgomery. Seems sensible, under the circumstances."

When the man had gone, Max closed the door and stood with his hand on the knob. His face was thoughtful if I correctly interpreted what I could see of it.

"I'd like to know the name of that client."

"Does it matter? Callie doesn't want to sell, and there's no reason why she should do it against her will. He can't do any more than ask her to, can he?"

"No, I wouldn't think so. Listen, how are you feeling? Headache better?"

I'd forgotten my self-induced headache. "Yes, I guess so. I'd better go down and feed Rudy; I forgot about him."

"I think I'll run into town and replenish my supply of booze. I'm about out. Why don't you take a warm bath and go to bed and let those aspirins work? I'll see you in the morning."

I felt somewhat let down at the idea that he was going to run off to the village, probably to sit in a tavern and talk to the locals (Max had always been great at talking to the locals, wherever he went) while I stayed here. Which was silly, of course, because a short time ago I'd wanted nothing more than to be left alone.

We walked downstairs together. I could see that Max was already off on the evening he had planned with whatever males he could round up. Well, I'd wanted time to sort out my thoughts and impressions; it looked as if I had it.

I waited until he'd driven away before I called Rudy. Usually I didn't have to call him; he stayed fairly close to the back porch, especially when a meal was due.

Puzzled when he didn't come, I walked a short distance toward the road, calling again. Maybe Egg or Zell had fed him, knowing that I'd gone upstairs without finishing my dinner. Still, he'd never failed to be there before when I came out.

Rudy didn't come. After a while I got a jacket, for the evening was growing cold, and I walked all the way out to the end of the spit, calling him over and over.

He didn't come galloping up to leap on me with his oversized feet. The night wasn't so black but that I'd have seen his dark shape against the paleness of the sand had he been anywhere nearby, I thought. The rising moon sent a path of glinting light across the waters of the bay and made the road quite clear, but there was no sign of Rudy.

He didn't come home at all that night.

[12]

I'M NOT sure when I began to be really frightened.

I was mildly concerned, at first, because none of the aunts had fed Rudy or had remembered seeing him since midafternoon. Though I hadn't had him long, the pattern of behavior had been well established: He ate at regular times, and he'd always been available the minute I stepped out of the house to go for a walk.

I kept thinking Max would show up soon and help me hunt for him, but the hours wore away and Max didn't come either. If I'd known where to look for him, I'd have driven into town, although at that stage of things I was still feeling that it was probably silly to get excited about a dog failing to come home. Rudy might have chased a bird too far up the beach and been too tired to run back. It didn't seem likely that anything very serious had happened to him.

Everyone in the inn knew he was missing. I went around the big, gloomy lobby, which was lit by electric lights now since the power had been restored, asking each of the guests if they'd seen Rudy.

The aunts didn't believe in strong lights, or they felt the higher-watt bulbs were too expensive; at any rate, the light wasn't much better than when we'd been using kerosene lamps. Egg and Zell and Mr. Foster and one of the Avery sisters were playing some card game. They all looked up at me with serious but unhelpful faces and negative replies.

The other Avery sister—Lulu?—was reading a romantic novel. She thought Rudy had been on the back steps shortly before she had dinner; she hadn't been around the back since then. Mr. Montgomery had gone out, probably to take a client to see a property, she thought, although how they'd examine it in the dark she didn't know. He often saw clients at night, though. He set up appointments at his office during the day. She'd often wondered why he lived way out here where there wasn't even a telephone; she thought it must be inconvenient for a realtor, although he didn't seem to mind, and, of course, the accommodations were inexpensive.

I paused, diverted momentarily from my search for Rudy. "Doesn't Mr. Montgomery do well in the real estate business?" Now that she'd mentioned it, the inn didn't seem a likely place for a prosperous businessman to live.

"Oh, I really don't know." Lulu—or Clara, whichever she was —blushed. "His office is over in Jordon's Hill, you know, not here in Bascom's Point, so I haven't seen it. No doubt it's just that this is pleasant for a person with no family. We're kind of like a family, all sort of friendly." She offered me a timid smile.

I said something I hoped sounded amiable and moved on to the final occupant of the shabby old room. Mr. Rossdale apparently had exclusive use of a big leather chair in a corner where he was engrossed in a *True Detective* magazine.

I spoke twice before he lifted his head, blinking at me as if he had to strain to remember who I was.

"My dog. He's missing. Do you remember seeing him?"

He had an odd sort of voice, as if he weren't used to talking. Or perhaps he was deaf enough so that he didn't hear much of other people's voices anymore, and that affected his own speech. I noticed that he looked straight into my face as I spoke, so maybe he was reading lips as much as he was hearing.

He shook his head when he understood the problem. "No, I haven't seen him."

That exhausted the possibilities, since Tom Crane wasn't around. I had a sudden vision of Crane sitting with Max in some dark, cozy little bar, spending the evening together getting acquainted—or reacquainted—while I tried to find Rudy alone.

That brought me back to something I'd been working around the way one does around a sore spot . . . that conversation between Max and Tom Crane earlier in the evening, just before they denied they'd ever met previously.

I kept thinking about it when I went back outside to make the rounds one more time, calling for Rudy. I couldn't imagine any explanation for the words they'd used that would verify their claim to being strangers to each other.

The sky was clouding up, blotting out the moon from time to time, and the wind was rising. The promised storm was moving in off the ocean. I called again, facing into that wind; no shaggy-dog shape came bounding over the dunes to meet me.

Could Rudy possibly have followed Max's car toward town? I wondered. He didn't like Max, but he might have thought I was in the car, and if he followed it too far before being left behind, he could have been lost.

I decided to get in my own car and drive into town for a look. I drove slowly, with the window open, stopping several times to call; I heard nothing except the increasingly heavy sound of surf.

The village of Bascom's Point was even less lively at night than during the day. A few of the houses showed lights, most of them no more than the unearthly glow denoting television viewing in progress. It didn't take long to check out the entire town by driving the length of the main street and back; there were two taverns open, and Max's car wasn't at either of them. I drove around the one that had a small parking area in the rear, to make sure.

Well, if he'd wanted to replenish his supply of drinkables, he might have had to go to a bigger town to get them. Still, I was very much disappointed. I'd have felt better with Max helping me look.

By the time I got back to the inn the wind was howling audibly around the corners and whipped my hair into my face with an alarming force. I called again, hoping Rudy might have returned while I was gone. Nothing.

The other guests were straggling up to bed when I went in. Zell met me as she came out of the kitchen carrying a tray bearing teapot and cups.

"Oh, Brenna! Did you find your dog?"

I shook my head. "No. No sign of him. Is there enough of that so I could have a cup?"

"Certainly, dear. Come along into the sitting room. We're a little late tonight; we've been fastening shutters after we heard the storm warnings."

"Shutters?" My eyes went to the window. It was impossible to see anything through the curtains. Egg and Callie were rocking and working with their bright-colored yarns. I wondered who would wear the socks Egg was making in an argyle pattern of green, purple, and lavender.

"Winds of gale force, they're predicting," Callie said, sounding grim. "The shape our roof's in, wouldn't surprise me if we lost half of it. Then

105

we'd have to take Mr. Montgomery's offer whether we wanted to or not.''

"Just got the power on," Egg observed, putting aside the socks to pour tea. "And now it'll probably be out again before morning. Be sure your lamp is filled and that you have matches, Brenna."

"There's no shutters on the upstairs windows," Callie told me, sipping from a delicate gold-trimmed cup. "We can't get at them. The panes are small and not so likely to blow out, but without shutters we used to lose the big windows across the front."

We drank our tea and talked for a few minutes before we all went to bed. I checked outside one more time, increasingly concerned about Rudy. Would a storm be dangerous for him?

There seemed nothing to do except to go to bed when the others did. I took a hot bath in the old-fashioned tub and then, wrapped in a warm robe and in slippered feet, I knocked on Max's door on the way back to my own room. I was fighting all sorts of suspicions and doubts, yet I trusted he'd help me decide what to do about my missing dog.

There was no answer. Max hadn't come back yet.

I started to turn away, and then for some reason I couldn't have explained I turned the knob. The door wasn't locked; it swung inward at my touch. Maybe I could find something to write on and leave him a note, so that when he came home he'd know how worried I was.

There was a magazine lying on the dresser, with a pencil beside it, as if made to order. I saw when I reached for it that he'd been doing a crossword puzzle.

And I saw something else that brought me to a halt with a lump in my throat.

There was a bottle of scotch on the end of the dresser, and it was three-quarters full.

So why had he really gone into town?

The idea of writing him a note was forgotten. I turned off the light and withdrew, fighting tears. Something was wrong, very wrong. Max was lying to me, misleading me, and I didn't know why.

I returned to my room. I didn't want to go to bed. I wondered if I'd be able to sleep at all. I heard the first spatter of rain against the windows and I stood there, irresolute, wishing I'd thought to get something to read. All I'd brought with me of my own books was the slim volume of poetry by Aunt Stell's friend. It wasn't the sort of thing I needed tonight.

I sat in the rocker with one small lamp burning, listening for footsteps signaling Max's return. Maybe I'd even approach Tom Crane, if I heard him come in, to see if he'd help me make one more search for Rudy before the worst of the storm hit.

But nobody came. The house creaked and moaned in protest against the rising winds, and I could hear the surf even above the gale.

I must have dozed, for I suddenly jerked wide awake with a crick in my neck. My watch showed that it was nearly one o'clock. I stood up, massaging the sore muscles, and opened the door into the hallway. Could Max have come in while I was asleep?

The hallway wasn't carpeted and Max was wearing those heavy boots, so I doubted that he could have passed without my hearing him. A small night-light burned and the doors were all closed. Behind one of them, someone was snoring.

I tightened the belt of my robe and stepped out into the corridor. If Rudy had come back he'd be hungry. I might as well go down and see.

The house seemed alive around me. I knew it had stood for a hundred years, undoubtedly through many such storms, yet it made me uneasy to hear groaning timbers. Somewhere far off something was banging an erratic rhythm; one of the shutters must not have been securely fastened.

I went down the stairs and into the back corridor. There were no night-lights left down here except one rosy frosted bulb over the desk in the lobby; little of the light penetrated to where I was, and I turned on lights as I went, grateful that the electricity was still working.

The wind was sweeping in off the Atlantic, and the door I opened was on the opposite side of the building. Nevertheless, the wind whipped the screen out of my hand and slammed it against the house. It was raining, not hard, although the strength of the wind made the drops sting when they struck my face.

"Rudy? Here, Rudy!"

There was no response. Indeed, with the racket the elements were making I wondered if he'd even hear if he'd taken shelter under the porch. I hesitated to get soaking wet to look there, yet knew I'd feel better if I did it.

Wait a minute. Weren't there some raincoats hanging in the little closet space off the kitchen? I retraced my steps and found just what I needed, a complete collection of slickers with hats and everything. I struggled into one of the heavy garments, fastening it over my robe, and then opened a likely-looking drawer in search of a flashlight. In a house where the power was frequently interrupted, they would surely have flashlights.

I found one on the third try, a long one that cut a bright swath ahead of me. I blessed Callie for keeping it filled with fresh batteries.

I was nearly blown off the steps and had to grab for a railing to keep from falling. There was no sign of a moon now; the night was totally black. Maneuvering around so that the worst of the storm came at my back, I got down and aimed the flashlight under the porch.

Rudy had been there, all right, at some time since our arrival. There was a well-gnawed beef bone lying in the sand, and another tennis shoe he must have found somewhere after I'd retrieved mine.

There was no dog. Swallowing hard against disappointment, I started to withdraw when I saw the other small object, dark against the light sand.

It was stiff to the touch, fabric of some kind. I drew it out, but that was no place to examine it, not with the rain and the wind tearing at me. I stumbled up the steps and into the house, fighting to get the screen closed and latched behind me.

Once inside, I replaced the flashlight in its drawer and reached for the light switch. Callie's pathetic little forty-watt bulbs weren't enough to enable me to look at anything.

It was then that I smelled it.

My head came up sharply. Smoke?

I forgot the object I intended to examine; I forgot to turn on the kitchen light. I moved back into the hallway, sniffing, and there was no doubt about it. Something was burning.

Oh, God, no, not a fire, I remember thinking, and about that time I realized that the rosy glow I was seeing was coming from the aunts' sitting room, not the bulb over the registration desk.

I stood for a paralyzed instant on the threshold of the room, seeing the flames shooting up the curtains and dancing across the back of the chintz-covered sofa.

The following few minutes were a bit of a blur. I know I screamed and started pounding on the closed doors. The aunts all slept on the first floor, but I wasn't sure who was where or even which of the doors opening off the small side corridor were bedrooms.

Zell appeared in an incredible nightcap and sprigged flannel gown; for a minute I didn't realize why she looked so grotesque until she squealed, "My teeth!" and ran back for them.

Egg and Callie spilled out of adjoining rooms and I babbled that the sitting room was on fire. To their credit, nobody panicked; Zell was dispatched to rouse the sleepers above, and the rest of us dashed back to the scene of the fire. Callie and Egg grabbed fire extinguishers from the kitchen and shouted to me to get the one behind the desk; I found it and tugged it free of its restraining clips with fingers so cold they had trouble functioning.

I had no idea how to work the extinguishers, but Callie and Egg did. By the time the others came pouring down the stairway we pretty well had it under control. The Avery sisters were as astonishingly dressed as Zell in her cap: They wore matching baby doll pajamas with lace trim in a rather sheer fabric, one of them pink and one blue.

Callie continued to spray the smoking sofa long after there were no flames left. The curtains were destroyed and the wallpaper blackened. The colorful argyles Egg had been knitting had melted into a gooey mess.

Mr. Rossdale's hearing aid dangled from his ear; when someone spoke to him, he reached up and pushed it into place. "Where's the other two, those young ones?" he wanted to know.

"Doesn't matter now, does it?" Mr. Foster asked. He was the only one who'd pulled a robe over his nightclothes. "Fire's out. What in heaven's name happened?"

"Looks like somebody upset a lamp." Mr. Rossdale poked at the charred and cracked chimney of a kerosene lamp that had stood on the table at the end of the sofa. It now lay on the end of an equally blackened sofa.

"Egg put out the lights," Zell said into the comparative silence. I was once more becoming aware of the elements that battered the house.

Egg put down her fire extinguisher with a squawk of protest. "I turned off the *electric* lights. We didn't have any *lamps* lit."

There was a little squabbling over that and how it could have happened. Callie put an end to it. "Well, it's out now. The sofa's ruined; maybe if you gentlemen would take hold of it you could pitch it out the back door, so we can be sure there's no fire left down inside it. We won't be able to fix it anyway."

That accomplished, Zell was dispatched to put on water for tea to calm the nerves of those who felt a hot drink was needed before they could sleep.

I passed up the tea. I knew I wasn't going to sleep no matter what I drank. I let myself into the small room and locked the door behind me, shaking in a delayed reaction. I realized only now that I was still wearing the slicker, and I took it off and dropped it over a chair.

It was several minutes later, when I was brushing my hair before the mirror, that I remembered the object I'd found under the porch.

What had I done with it? Could I have jammed it into a pocket when I smelled the fire?

109

That was exactly what I had done. I held it under the light and stared at it for a long time.

It was a man's handkerchief, and it was torn on one corner, perhaps where Rudy had pulled on it. There were no convenient initials as a clue to its owner, but there was something else.

It had dried in a stiff, unnatural shape, and I knew at once what it had been soaked in to give it that starched finish.

Blood, I thought, and my cozy little room seemed very cold and I was afraid.

[13]

I WENT to bed at last, in sheer exhaustion and suffering from the cold, for there was no heat in the room and the wind worked its way in around the windows.

I didn't sleep, not for a long time.

If I hadn't gone down to check one final time for Rudy, we all might have been burned in our beds. The sitting room was right near the stairs; that avenue of escape cut off, there was only a narrow enclosed staircase to the upper floors, which rose from the kitchen area. I had enough imagination to picture how it could have been, trapped on the second floor of a burning building.

The bloody handkerchief lay on the dresser, mute but speaking. Someone had lost a lot of blood. It could have been only a man with a bloody nose, but in that case would the owner of the handkerchief have thrown the item away where a dog could pick it up? If it had been anyone at the inn, I couldn't believe he'd have bled that much without the rest of us knowing about it.

Where was Rudy?

And where was Max?

Neither Max nor Tom Crane had been in the place when the fire started.

After a pause I added the obvious mental note. *Why not say "after the fire was started"? You know perfectly well Egg didn't spill any lamp onto the sofa and start that fire. No kerosene lamps were lit last night; there was no need for them. And from the way the flames were moving I'd say some of the kerosene was deliberately spilled out along the back of the sofa to make sure it burned quickly.*

111

There was an ache in my chest that made breathing painful. *Max would never have set fire to a building and left people to die in it. Never.*

But where was he? Why hadn't he come back?

It was well after two when I heard male feet on the stairs. I had left my lights on (I couldn't bring myself to turn them off) and I sat upright, reaching for the robe across the foot of the bed. Surely if Max saw my light he would stop. I had no idea what I would say to him; I was totally confused about how I felt regarding him, but I wanted to talk to him.

I was still feeling for my slippers when my small light went out.

In the hall outside my door I heard a man swear. Not Max. Tom Crane.

"What the hell's going on?"

"Power's off again." I hadn't heard Mr. Foster moving around and his voice startled me.

"There were lights all over the place when I drove up. Something wrong?"

"Had a fire a bit ago," Mr. Foster said. "Lucky the girl smelled the smoke before it got any worse. I expect we're all sort of nervous about going to sleep now. I've been down the back stairs a time or two, just checking to see nothing's flamed up again."

Crane's voice was sharp. "I thought I smelled something, but figured you'd had fires in the fireplaces. How did it start?"

"Seems like Egg must have knocked over a lamp in the sitting room so the kerosene ran over the sofa somehow. We're all getting old, and sometimes we're careless. Good thing the girl was up and around. I don't fancy being roasted alive. Could have used you and that other one, Von Rys. Had to carry the furniture outside and let the rain finish putting out the fire."

"Isn't Max here?"

"No. Neither one of you nor Mr. Montgomery. We checked, to make sure nobody was still sleeping in case we couldn't put the fire out. Callie remembers the bad fire when she was a child, though; she keeps plenty of fire extinguishers around, and she's had to use 'em a time or two. I was going to make another check downstairs, I don't suppose you noticed anything amiss when you came in."

"No, but let's get a lamp and I'll go with you. We sure as hell don't want any more fire in this wind; are you sure the house won't just blow away?"

"Well," Mr. Foster said, his voice dry as they moved away, "never has yet, and it's weathered a few hurricanes in its time. Watch your step there."

So Crane didn't know where Max was either. Or said he didn't.

112

I got back into bed, the bathrobe spread over me for additional warmth. I wished someone would activate the furnace.

I heard the men come back upstairs and go into their rooms. I dozed, off and on, but real sleep was impossible. I could actually feel the house moving under the impact of the wind, and the sound of it was terrifying.

At dawn I got up and dressed, knowing I wasn't going to get any more rest anyway. If Max had returned, I hadn't heard him. I put on jeans and tennis shoes, old things that wouldn't be damaged by the wet, and a thick sweater to wear under the borrowed slicker.

Evidently I wasn't the only one to give up on sleeping. Everyone but Mr. Rossdale was down before I'd fastened myself inside the voluminous rubberized garment. Callie had the coffee pot on, and Mr. Foster was trying to get a weather report on the radio, although, as Callie pointed out, we could see and hear what it was doing.

Crane was dressed just as he'd been last night, and I wondered if he'd bothered to go to bed. He certainly hadn't gotten around to shaving yet. He eyed my preparations with interest.

"You're taking your usual morning walk in this, are you?"

"My dog's missing." I decided not to mention the bloody handkerchief. "I'm going to look for him."

"How long's he been gone?"

"Nobody's seen him since before dinner last night."

"Give me a chance to get a cup of coffee into me, and I'll help if you like."

"Any offers gratefully accepted," I told him. I was suspicious of him, but I needed all the help I could get. Certainly the old people weren't going to tangle with the elements today.

I was unprepared for the violence of the wind when I stepped out the back door. This time the screen was not only pulled out of my hands but off its hinges; I watched it go sailing toward the bay, tumbling end over end.

I checked under the porch, just to make sure Rudy hadn't returned in the hours before dawn; there was no sign of him.

Calling was useless. I doubted that he could have heard me from a dozen yards away. I braced myself and plunged out of the relatively sheltered area behind the building and nearly went the way of the screen door.

I found, however, that by leaning into the wind it was possible to walk. Progress would be slow and exhausting, with most of my energies directed toward staying on my feet.

I had no particular plan, but since I could see a good deal of the territory toward the end of the spit, it seemed sensible to go the other way. I had thought to follow the ridge of the dunes with the idea of looking down on each side. Between the fact of the rain and the fact that I could hardly hold my eyes open against the wind, however, I had trouble seeing much of anything.

I kept on going, cold and wet in spite of the slicker because the rain worked its way down my neck and up my sleeves and drenched the legs of my jeans and my feet.

After a while I had to admit that I couldn't go on this way indefinitely; I turned and cut over toward the bay side of the dunes, preparatory to returning to the inn.

I was watching the upper part of the inn, using it as a guidepost, when I tripped and fell over something, sprawling on the wet sand. I lost my breath and felt pain in my left ankle. I managed to sit up and pushed up a pant-leg for a look at a purplish weal forming there.

What the devil had I hit? I'd never noticed any rocks on the beach before; it was pure sand up here away from the water's edge. My groping hands encountered rock though . . . no, it was cement blocks.

While I rubbed gingerly around the injured area, I figured it out. This was the remains of the foundation of one of those houses that had once kept the inn company here on the spit. There had been no basements, of course, in an area where a hole only inches deep would immediately fill with water; they'd built this house, at least, on concrete blocks.

I got up, trying to ignore the painful ankle, and continued on my way, being more careful to avoid the rest of the foundation.

When I saw the dark spot on the sand ahead, I thought at first it was a bit of driftwood, perhaps a burned one because it was black. And then I saw that the black was a saddle on an otherwise sand-colored dog.

With a cry I dropped beside him, horror replacing the relief I'd hoped for upon finding Rudy. His body was motionless, on its side; his eyes were closed.

He was dead. But he wouldn't just have died for no reason, I thought, in a paroxysm of grief and anger. A young, healthy dog, he wouldn't have simply laid down and died! It wasn't the storm that had killed him, it hadn't even begun at the time I discovered he was missing. And then I saw that the sandy head was covered with blood on one side—diluted by the rain, yet unmistakable.

I put a hand on the cold body. Did I imagine it or was there the slightest rise and fall of the massive chest?

"Rudy? Rudy?" I knelt over him, achieving no response, but my own hope rose a bit, only a bit. I put my cheek firmly against the wet fur, ignoring the cold, determined to hear a heartbeat if there was one.

It wasn't easy to hear anything; I covered my other ear with my hand to reduce the extraneous sounds of surf and gale. Tears blurred my vision, indistinguishable from the rain on my face.

"There's a heartbeat. I know there is! I'll have to get help, I can't possibly carry you myself. . . ." I talked to him, touched him, reassuring him, although I knew he wasn't aware of me.

I stood, looking around to get my bearings, to make sure I could find my way back to this spot. I was a good quarter-mile from the inn. I wished there was some way to erect a marker, but nothing would have stayed where I put it. I could only estimate distance and direction in relation to the inn and to the village across the bay.

I began to run—an awkward, difficult thing in the sand. My lungs were aching and my heart pounding painfully before I'd covered half the distance.

I didn't see it until I was almost there; Max's car was back. He came out onto the back steps, with Tom Crane behind him, about the time I got within shouting distance. They were shrugging into raincoats, and it was Max who saw me.

"Brenna! Did you find him?"

I was too winded to speak, but I gestured, falling against him when his arms came out for me.

"Is he hurt?"

I nodded, struggling for speech. ". . . Bad. Help me. . . ."

Max turned swiftly to the other man. "You've got four-wheel drive, haven't you? It'll take the dunes all right?"

"Easy," Crane said, and they were bundling me into the Scout with no effort on my part, which was fine because I was ready to drop.

We jounced out over the sand, the vehicle rocking as each new gust hit it. Once I thought we were going over; somehow we didn't. I'd forgotten Max's defection of the previous night; I'd forgotten the bloody handkerchief and the fire. All I knew was that I needed help to get Rudy to a vet and that the hard strength of Max's arm around me was most welcome.

The men got out, leaving me to scramble after them. Both knelt beside the unconscious animal. I heard Max say, "Jesus, he's dead," and then in a

115

different one, "He's been shot! Look at the crease in his scalp, poor devil!"

I had my voice back now. "He's not dead; I put my ear against his chest and I heard a heartbeat! I did, Max, he's alive!"

"OK. Let's get him in the back of the car. We ought to have something to put him on . . . how about my slicker?"

For a few moments Max stood over us, trying to retain a grip on the coat while he took it off, his red hair and beard writhing wildly around his head. And then they were lifting Rudy, ever so gently, and putting him into the Scout.

An unguarded and meaningful look passed between the two men. I didn't know what it signified, except agreement between them. That Rudy was dead in spite of what I thought I'd heard? A thought regarding the way Rudy had been hurt? Or something else?

There was no time to puzzle over it. We got back into the vehicle and Crane swung it around, passing over the spot where the blood-soaked sand was already being washed clean by the storm.

"I don't suppose there's a vet in Bascom's Point," Crane said.

"No. There must be one in a town the size of Jordon's Hill, though. Let's go."

I could smell the wet wool of Max's sweater and tobacco (Crane?), and I wanted to cry and lean into the powerful shoulder for comfort. I wanted to say again, "He's not dead," as if that would make it so. Nobody looked back at the injured dog on our reckless ride to the next town; this confirmed my suspicion that neither of them believed the dog was alive.

We located the veterinarian by stopping the first pedestrian we met who was brave enough to be out in the storm. The doctor was a small semi-bald man in a white jacket who took one look at Rudy and hustled us back into surgery. He made disapproving noises throughout his examination, which we watched in silence.

He made a grunt of satisfaction, however, when he put away his stethoscope. "Well, we'll see what we can do. I can't make any promises, you understand. He's lost a lot of blood, I'd say, but his heart and lungs are still functioning, so maybe we've got a chance. We'll do what we can."

"Was he shot?" I demanded. "Is that what happened to him?"

"Not much doubt of that." He took in our bedraggled appearances. "This is going to take some time. You can wait if you like, but there isn't much to be gained by it. I'd suggest you check by phone this afternoon . . . give me four or five hours anyway."

I would have stayed, only Max wouldn't let me. With the knowledge that

116

Rudy had a chance, however slim, the horror receded until the anger that filled me took up all the space there was.

"Why would anybody try to kill him? He couldn't hurt anything out there on the point . . . there was nothing to damage, and he didn't bother anyone unless they got near my car."

Neither of them said anything. Tom Crane drove as if the Scout required his complete attention. I looked at Max, who was concentrating on the road almost as thoroughly as Crane.

"Where were you last night? I kept hoping you'd come back and help me look for him. He'd have had a much better chance if we'd found him when I first realized he was missing." I hadn't meant to sound so accusatory, but that's how it came out.

"I'm sorry about that. I got held up," Max said.

"In Bascom's Point all night?" I sounded like a shrew, as if I had a right to know where Max was and what he was doing. Maybe I said it to give him a chance either to make a reasonable explanation or to tell another lie. *Don't forget, he's already lied to you*, I told myself.

"No, I went further afield than that. I was trying to run down some information," Max said, "only it was a waste of time. I'll have to try again later. Brenna. . . ."

He said my name in a way so heavy with meaning that Crane looked at him, then quickly away.

Max saw it. "I'm sorry, Crane, for injecting a personal note into a public conversation, but I've got something to say to my girl that needs to be said right now."

Crane murmured something that we took for assent, but Max hadn't waited for it. He was already speaking to me.

"Brenna, I don't want you to go back to the inn. I have to, but I could pick up all our things and bring them away."

I pulled back so that I could look into his face more easily. "What are you talking about? Of course I'm going back to the inn." I wasn't so keen on the things that had been happening there, but I wasn't prepared to take off on any sort of jaunt with Max either.

"You didn't give me an answer when I suggested we start over. So I'm asking you a second time. Let's get married . . . if we cross the state line there isn't even a waiting period . . . and we won't bother to go back to the inn at all. . . ."

I think there was more, but I didn't hear it. Alarm bells were ringing in all directions. That kaleidoscope was turning again, only this time it was a giant

117

one and I was inside it. I was trying to get out, only I couldn't, because it kept turning and the bits and pieces kept shifting and moving around me.

Why didn't he want me to go back to the inn? Where did he want to take me and why? Rudy shot . . . the bloody handkerchief . . . the fire . . . the missing tapes . . . Larry's accusations . . . Max's accusations . . . lies, lies. . . .

He stopped talking. He was looking at me, waiting for an answer. "Well, how about it?"

I said what I was thinking, although it wasn't what I intended to say at all. "Why do you want to get married?"

Max swore, very quietly. "That's what I've just been telling you. Weren't you listening?"

"I heard the first part anyway. About not going back to the inn at all. What's the hurry about getting married, and why on earth shouldn't we go back to the inn to pick up our things . . . if we wanted to leave, that is?"

Max sent another inexplicable glance toward our driver, who was staring through the rain-blurred windshield as if he were alone in the car. I had the sudden realization of how helpless I was, if these two men were in some sort of conspiracy together, if they decided to take me somewhere I didn't want to go.

It wasn't so much intimidating or frightening as it was anger-provoking.

"The whole idea is absurd. I have no intention of getting married on the spur of the moment, and I'm certainly going back to the inn. What would my aunts think if I didn't?"

"You could send them a note with an explanation."

"What explanation? That I'd suddenly lost my mind?" Would the aunts accept a note, with whatever excuse it offered, if someone else sent one in my name?

Max didn't answer. Instead, he spoke across me to Crane. "Didn't you say you had to stop to buy cigarettes?"

"Yeah, that's right. Is that drugstore open, the one up ahead?"

They decided it was, and Crane eased the Scout to the curb and got out, closing the door behind him with an effort. The wind this far inland wasn't as violent, but it was still a force to be reckoned with.

Max's hand closed on my shoulder, swinging me around. "Brenna, listen to me. I don't want you to go back to the inn because I don't think it's safe. I don't know what the devil all went on there last night, but from what Crane said that fire could well have been set. And somebody sure as hell shot your dog . . . maybe he'll get around to shooting people, too. I'd feel a lot better if you didn't go back there. I don't even want to go back myself. I want to take you away where I can keep you safe.''

I looked into his face, a face I had once loved, a man I had once trusted. How could I trust him now? If I'd been certain he wasn't involved in any of the peculiar happenings, if he hadn't lied to me, would I have wanted to marry him?

I didn't know. I only knew I couldn't be sure of his motives, I couldn't be sure of anything. And until I could, I thought I was better off making no decisions at all.

"Brenna, I love you. I thought . . . damn it, let me help you!''

"I'm sorry, Max, but I have no intention of running off and getting married. I'm not seventeen now. When I do get married, it will have to be for the right reasons and not a spur-of-the-moment affair.''

"Isn't being in love the right reason? I've got an additional reason—I think you're in danger in that damned place, and I want you out of there! The best way for me to protect you is to marry you and take you home with me . . . away from whatever the hell is cooking because of the Senator's indiscretions and stupidities!''

I turned my head and looked away. "I can't, Max.''

His mouth was a flat, pale line, but our driver was coming back and there wasn't time for more unless he wanted to say it in front of Crane. Crane got in, tearing open the pack of cigarettes, lighting one without offering them around, as if he knew we didn't smoke.

I sat rigidly between them, thinking the smoke seemed the same as I'd smelled in my room. I was crammed up against Max—there wasn't any other way to sit—and I could feel his muscles, taut and hard, anger and frustration in every line of his body.

We sped along the highway, and after a time I realized they weren't kidnapping me—they were taking me back to the inn. The knowledge did nothing to make me feel any better.

Like the men, I stared ahead between the slashing blades that tried and failed to give us decent visibility. I wondered if anything was ever going to make me feel any better.

[14]

MAX INSISTED on walking upstairs with me and unlocking my door himself. Not content with that, he preceded me into the room and looked around; I presumed it was to make sure nobody had planted any bombs while we were away.

"If you won't go with *me*, then go by yourself," he said. It was the first time he'd addressed me directly in some time, and the anger still showed for all that he was trying to control it. "Get on a bus or a plane and buy a ticket for somewhere way the hell away from here. Use an assumed name for a while and don't tell anybody who you are."

I didn't bother to answer that. Getting away did have a certain appeal . . . more than a little . . . only I didn't see how I would be any less vulnerable anywhere else than I was here. If someone could follow me to Bascom's Point, he could follow me anywhere else I chose to go. And the aunts, at least, I trusted.

Max swore and turned to leave . . . and stopped. "What's that?"

I turned slowly and saw the bloody handkerchief, stiffened into rusty peaks on the dresser top. I'd forgotten about it; I'd certainly had no intention of telling Max about it.

When I didn't answer, he picked it up to examine it at close range; I could tell that he'd made the same evaluation of its meaning as I had.

He shoved the door shut and held the handkerchief under my nose. "Where'd you get this?"

I hesitated, since I hadn't prepared myself for this eventuality; he must

120

have thought I didn't intend to answer at all because his left hand came up to grip my shoulder.

"Brenna, haven't you got it through your head that this is no *game?* Somebody is playing for keeps; he's desperate—or *they* are—there must be more than one of them. This is blood . . . a lot of blood. Where did it come from?"

"I found it under the porch when I was looking for Rudy. It wasn't there when I crawled under looking for my shoes, so it can't have been there very long." The words came out reluctantly and yet with a sort of relief. How willingly I would have told him everything I knew if I'd had some assurance that Max himself wasn't involved!

He let go of me, turning to go to the window for a better examination of the handkerchief. I didn't think it told him any more than it had told me.

"Rudy found it, say sometime yesterday afternoon, and brought it home, tucked it under the porch with his bones," Max said slowly, more to himself than to me. "And then maybe he went back to where he got it from, looking for. . . ."

I couldn't control the prickling sensation up the back of my neck. "Looking for what?"

"For more of whatever smelled the same as this. Only somebody saw him and shot him because they didn't want him digging around. Brenna, you're smart enough to realize what this could mean. Somebody could have died, soaking that handkerchief. Did you ever get those envelopes to mail your keys in?"

I blinked, not following his swift change of subject. "No. Why?"

"I need something to put it in. I'm going to get it to the authorities."

"No!" I put out a hand, but I knew he wasn't going to give it back to me.

"Why *no?* What did you intend to do with it?"

"I . . . don't know, but it's evidence of some sort, and I found it, so I ought to be the one. . . ."

"All right. Come along with me."

There was a challenge in his voice and face. The trouble was, I didn't know just what it entailed.

Max had turned away from me and was opening dresser drawers, poking around in my underwear, ignoring my squawk of indignation. He pulled out a quilted plastic envelope that I used for hose, dumping its contents back into the drawer. "Here, this will do, it's waterproof, isn't it?"

"Max, you have no right. . . ."

He looked at me, really looked at me then. For a moment he was quite still, reading my face. The anger and frustration seemed to fade out of his own face.

"That's it, isn't it? You're scared, as scared as I am, but you don't trust me. You're afraid I'm part of what you're scared of."

There was no way to keep the admission out of my expression. I didn't have that kind of control.

"*Are* you, Max?"

"No." His voice was gentle, the old, sweet Max I remembered from those almost-forgotten nights of years ago. "I wouldn't hurt you for the world. Can you picture me shooting your dog or setting fire to a house full of people?"

I could picture him lying to me about going to town for a supply of booze, when he had a bottle of scotch in his room, and not coming back until the next morning. I knew he'd done *that*.

"I can't picture the old Max doing any of those things," I said, and was amazed at the steadiness of my voice. "But I don't know you, Max. Not the real, inner you. I have no idea what you're capable of."

"I'm the same as I always was, Brenna."

I shook my head. "No, you aren't. Nobody is. I loved a boy. You're a man, a man I don't know at all."

A gust of wind rattled the windows. He didn't look around. He kept looking at me.

"What could I do to convince you? I want to protect you, but I can't if you won't let me." He spread his hands in a gesture of resignation. "Tell me what I can do?"

"You could try telling the truth," I suggested. It wasn't said lightly; on the contrary, I'm sure my face conveyed how serious I was. "About why you're here, everything."

He sighed. "Everything. That covers a lot of territory."

I indicated the rocking chair. "We have plenty of time."

"I'm not sure we do, but maybe we'd better take it anyway." He rejected the rocker in favor of a corner of the bed; he'd have liked me there beside him, only I felt better where he couldn't touch me.

"You were here waiting for me, weren't you, just the way Larry said."

"Good old Larry. Yes, I was. I wanted to tell you the truth from the beginning, but my bosses weren't sure you could be trusted. When I insisted that I knew you, inside and out, and that everything would be safer and easier if we leveled with you, they said the same thing you just did. I hadn't seen you in nine years; there was no way I could possibly know what sort of woman you'd grown up to be."

"Maybe that's the starting point: Who are your bosses?"

"The names probably wouldn't mean much to you. Maybe your Mr. Hastings is one of them, although I never met him and nobody mentioned him to me. The one who contacted me is a fellow by the name of Miller; he's part of the official investigating team. They want the man who shot the Senator, naturally. There's a good chance he was a professional killer, and if that's the case, they also want the man who hired him. They want the tapes and papers the Senator left behind—it was a real shock when the tapes he was carrying turned out to be blanks. Maybe he was using them for bait, to lure someone into coming after them, because it seems he didn't make any secret of the fact that he'd dictated a lot of damaging information about a lot of people onto *some* tapes somewhere. Maybe he just thought if he carried something everyone would take it for granted they were *the* tapes and not look for the genuine ones, wherever he hid them. Anyway, the authorities want the men those tapes accuse. With the dope the Senator had on them, it should be possible to unravel a pretty large fabric of corruption and graft that needs to be exposed."

"And they think I'm hiding the tapes? Holding them to blackmail somebody or what? The whole idea is ludicrous."

"That's what I told them. They said you were a big girl now, and big girls don't always reason the same way they did when they were children."

"You searched my room anyway." I said it with a trace of bitterness.

"Not personally. Bill Haden searched it the first time. You still had a lot of your stuff locked in your car, so that was hardly conclusive."

"So he was a government agent, too?" I wasn't sure, at this stage, whether I could believe him or not, much as I wanted to.

"Yes. He was to follow you when you left Hampton. I was sent down here ahead of time, in case this was where you ran to. They figured there was a good chance you'd show up here, and if you did, it would look better if I were here first. So I took a leave of absence from my job and came."

"How nice that they happened to find you, the one person who might expect to get through to me." The bitterness was still there, just under the surface.

"They worked at that, they didn't just 'happen' to find me. Within minutes of the time your uncle was shot there were agents crawling all over the place checking into the background of everyone around him. His sec-

123

retary, his typist, his friends, and his family. Including you. They didn't find anything to indicate that you were involved in any sort of conspiracy, but they did dig up the fact that you'd once been married to me. It took them two days to locate me, which wasn't bad, considering the amount of moving around I'd done in that nine years.''

"And you drove right down here to wait for me, in case I *was* involved in something dirty."

Max gave me a level look. "I drove right down here after I'd argued for four hours that I wasn't going to do any such a damned thing. At this stage of things I suppose it's too much to hope you'll believe why I did it.''

There was a painful ache in my throat. "Well, go on, tell me. You always did have an inventive mind, so tell me.''

Something jumped in his eyes, something that might have been anger. "I came, my love, because I remembered you with affection and I thought that by coming I might be able to protect you. They were sure as hell going to send someone, and after listening to those guys for a while I decided maybe it had better be me. It wasn't so much that the authorities think you're knowingly involved in the mess, although there's one guy who considered it a possibility. But they thought you might be involved quite innocently, and if the cops can think of that, so can the robbers. You were simply one of the people they put a tail on, one of the people through whom they might learn something. They figured if you didn't hate me you might be more responsive to me than to a stranger, and if you did know anything I'd have a better chance than Haden of gaining your confidence. That's why I came, to find the tapes for Miller if I could and to see that you didn't get hurt along the way, no matter what else happened.''

"But I told you over and over I don't have the tapes and don't know anything about them. They couldn't possibly have been hidden in my things, unless the Senator came back and did it after he was buried!"

"I believe you. Only they're still missing, and nobody's discovered yet what the old devil did with them. He wasn't a stupid man, not *that* stupid, to have them just lying around where anybody could get their hands on them easily. He took some sort of precautions, and we have to figure out what they were. I'm sorry you were scared; I thought all along this was a stupid way to do it, but I had my orders. Which I'm now breaking. Of course, I'm only borrowed for this operation so they can't fire me . . . and I don't think they can order up a firing squad either." Amusement touched his mouth, but I wasn't ready to be amused. Not yet.

"What about Tom Crane, whom you didn't know?"

124

Max tugged absently at his mustache. "Tom's a friend. Not a professional investigator. I called and asked him to join me here without letting anyone know he was anything except a tourist. For one thing we needed to go through your belongings again, after they were all inside, while I distracted your attention. I know, you don't think it's possible the tapes are with you, but damn it, they aren't in the house in Hampton either or in the Senator's office or in any of the other logical places. We're positive there *are* tapes, and every indication is that the bad guys don't have them yet. I felt I needed a back-up man here, somebody who'd keep an eye out for you when I couldn't be around as well as someone to help with the things the department wants me to do."

"You're both doing a fine job of guarding me, if that's part of the plan. If Rudy hadn't disappeared, so that I was downstairs looking for him in the middle of the night, that fire would have eliminated me and a dozen innocent people *and* the tapes, if they're here."

Max swore. "That was a foul-up we hadn't anticipated. I mean, we didn't expect anybody to burn the place down with you in it, you understand, and we did think we had the bases covered. Only we got our wires crossed. I was supposed to be back by mid-evening, and I didn't make it. I didn't worry too much because I thought Tom would be here. He, in turn, thought I'd come back as planned and he sat in his Scout at the main turn-off and made sure nobody we didn't know came visiting during the night."

For a moment the significance of that escaped me. "But that means . . . if the fire was set, it was done by someone who lives here in the inn!"

Max nodded. "It would seem that way."

"But nobody is going to burn down a building with himself in it! And I was the only one up and around; I roused all the others! They were sound asleep!"

"It isn't hard to pretend you've been wakened out of a sound sleep. Whoever was responsible was undoubtedly ready to make his own escape when the time came. But you see what else it means, don't you? Somebody here, somebody living here, is on the wrong side of the law. Probably the same someone the Senator came here to meet."

"I assumed my uncle came here for some good reason. If it was to meet someone, why not assume that *he* has the tapes?"

"Because the Senator came here before he let go of them. He came *before* the word was out that he'd been indicted. If we're right, he made the tapes after the charges were made public, during those days you say he holed up in the library at the house in Hampton. So far as we've been able to find out, his only contacts were with his lawyers, who swear they don't have the tapes, and the people in his own household. Stell was in a state of shock, and nobody thinks it likely she'd have had anything to do with concealing evidence; even if she had, the stuff would have been found after she died. Maudie? Again, not likely. She was a close friend of Stell's, but she was still a servant, and she wasn't fond enough of the Senator to risk her own neck for him. Which is how we come to you, by logical deduction.''

"I wouldn't have risked my own neck and my own integrity for him either . . . at least I don't think I would have. You'll have to logically deduce something else, I'm afraid.''

"We have.'' He was looking at me intently. "We figure the Senator somehow used you, without your knowing you were being used. Nobody thinks you're involved in this in any way but innocently . . . anyway, I don't . . . but we're almost positive you *are* involved.''

I made a sound of exasperation. "And I'm *absolutely* positive I'm not. The Senator didn't know he was going to be killed. Why would he have depended on me when he knew I wouldn't have approved of what he'd done?''

"He had to do something with the tapes, and he couldn't very well walk around carrying all of them every minute. He also wouldn't have wanted to leave them anywhere they could be discovered by the men they will incriminate. Ergo, he hid them somewhere safe, somewhere you could get them for him, for instance, if he couldn't get them himself.''

We were talking in circles. We finally gave up trying to convince each other of anything and went on to my next sore point.

"You told me you were going to buy booze last night. What did you actually do?''

Max used a different four-letter-word from the previous one. "I was watching Montgomery's office, which was a total waste of time. How the hell did I know he had a cot in the back room and that he sometimes stays there overnight instead of driving back out here?''

I rubbed at my temples, wondering if my brain was softening. "What's Mr. Montgomery got to do with anything?''

"He's doing his damnedest to buy this place, for a figure that's not spectacular, but it's reasonably substantial and is being offered by a client who's willing to pay cash and wants everybody out immediately. Doesn't that strike you as being somewhat unusual? It's too early to say what this unknown client has in mind, but the inn isn't all that much of a bargain, and I think there's at least a chance the deal is somehow tied in with the Senator's affairs, althought I'll be damned if I know how."

"Watching Mr. Montgomery's office doesn't sound like a very profitable way to spend an evening."

"It wasn't. He decided to spend the night there, which I didn't realize until half the night was gone."

"But how did you think watching the place would be helpful?"

"I was waiting for him to leave." He spoke with exaggerated patience. "It's sort of a crummy little building; I didn't figure I'd have any trouble getting inside, once he left. Only he didn't leave."

"You were going to . . . break in?"

"Whatever. I wanted a look at those records. I figured the end justified the means."

"But if you're working for the Justice Department. . . ." Beginning to be convinced, I was backsliding now.

"Getting a search warrant takes time. And you have to show probable cause, which I'm not sure I could do. It wouldn't be up to me anyway, and you wouldn't believe how stiff-necked some of these official types are. They haven't listened to anything else I've suggested; why should I think they'd believe my hunch is right? That the potential buyer Montgomery has lined up has anything to do with the case at hand?"

He leaned toward me, and instinctively I withdrew so that he didn't make the physical contact he intended. "Brenna, I'm worried about you. I want this mess wound up so we don't have to keep looking over our shoulders all the time. I want it even more now; the next time somebody gets shot it may be a person rather than a dog. And that brings us to this." He tapped a finger on the plastic envelope holding the bloody handkerchief. "If you found it under the porch, chances are Rudy put it there. It hasn't been lying around for very long. So whose is it—whose blood is on it?"

I weighed, ever so briefly, the pros and cons of telling him what I knew. If he was working for the wrong side, he probably already knew it, so I wouldn't be revealing anything damaging to my own interests, would I? And if he was telling the truth, if the Justice Department was behind him, the sooner they knew everything I knew, the better.

"I think," I said slowly, "that it belongs to Haden, or Tolman, or whatever his name is. Didn't it strike you as strange that he just disappeared? Didn't check out, but sent an anonymous money order from another town, a town big enough so nobody'd possibly remember what the buyer looked

127

like. It might be interesting to know if he ever got back to Georgetown."

"So you looked at the registration cards, did you?" I thought there was a faint note of approval in his words.

"Is he missing? The man who followed me here?"

"Damned if I know. I never actually made any contact with him; I wasn't supposed to. I just knew they had somebody tailing you in case you didn't come here. I thought probably they'd called him off when you did show up here because they didn't see the need for two men in one spot."

A board creaked in the hallway and we both looked that way, but it wasn't repeated. I lowered my voice anyway so that it wouldn't carry beyond this room.

"There's one of his suitcases in the storage room down the hall. Full of dirty clothes and the blue suit he was wearing when I first saw him."

Max was suddenly alert. "Are you sure of that?"

"Yes. It seemed a funny thing to do with his luggage if he left voluntarily. He had a car . . . what happened to his car?"

Max was off the bed, prowling the small room in a way that reminded me of a caged tiger I'd seen as a child. "And if the handkerchief is Haden's . . . where the hell did Rudy find it? He was shot out there on the dunes . . . my God, there are miles of dunes. If there's a body, it could be anywhere."

I remembered something. "I tripped over some cement blocks . . . the foundation of a building that's no longer there. It wasn't far beyond where I found Rudy. Do you think . . . surely he couldn't have run very far after he was shot. . . ?"

"No, I wouldn't think so. Where's this storage room? I want to see that suitcase of Haden's."

There was no one about when we went down the corridor. I felt very conspicuous, for our feet sounded on the worn, uncarpeted boards, though I knew the storm was making enough racket to cover the sounds we made.

Max opened the door and peered into the grimy little room. "Ye gods, what a mess. Which is Haden's luggage?"

I stared at the stack of cartons where I had placed my own.

The suitcase was gone.

[15]

I FINALLY ate breakfast, at almost noon, by myself in the kitchen. Max had gone, with a promise of seeking out the authorities who had sent him here. He wasn't surprised at the disappearance of the luggage belonging to the man who had followed me. It had probably, he observed, been stashed there only as an emergency measure, until a better way could be found to dispose of it permanently. I took that to mean he assumed that the owner of the luggage had been disposed of, also permanently; this did nothing to reassure me regarding my own safety.

A car wouldn't be so easily hidden, and no doubt the police would turn it up before long if they looked for it. However, Max didn't feel that he could go directly to the local authorities; he must report our findings to the department that had sent him here, and he didn't want to do it from the pay phone in the village because it went through a switchboard.

He promised to check with the vet on Rudy's condition. "Be careful," he advised before he left. "And don't forget, Tom Crane is around and you can trust him to look out for you."

It had sounded so reassuring, until after he'd gone. Then the doubts began to creep back again.

There was little to do. The power was off once more so that the small black-and-white television at the end of the lobby was inoperative. Chances were it wouldn't have had watchable reception anyway.

The reading material available was almost as ancient as the encyclopedia I'd consulted. Not that I was in the mood for reading. For lack of anything else to do, I went back up to my room and went through my belongings, thread by thread, just in case everybody else was right and I was wrong. I found nothing to indicate that the Senator or anyone else had planted anything in my effects.

And then, remembering that my uncle had spent a night in this same room, I went over *that*, testing for loose boards (there were none), inspecting the back of the closet, pulling out dresser drawers, looking into all the places people in mystery stories hide small valuable objects. I didn't turn up a thing.

By late afternoon Max still hadn't come back. I was so tense that when Mr. Rossdale asked me if I'd seen his *True Detective*, I almost shrieked. I hadn't heard him coming up behind me, which was not surprising. The storm was so noisy we could hear it over the tinny music of the old-fashioned Victrola the Avery sisters were playing in the lobby.

Tom Crane, my supposed protector, had borrowed a slicker and a hat and had gone outside. I watched him setting off across the dunes and guessed that he was going to look around in the area where we'd found Rudy.

A body, I thought with the sensation of being caught in some mad dream, he was looking for a body to go with that blood-soaked handkerchief.

Zell paused beside me to peer after Crane also. "My goodness, what's he doing out in this weather? Tourists are the strangest people, aren't they? One of them got blown right into the bay once, two years ago. It was a wonder he wasn't drowned." She looked up into my face. "He's going out there where you found your dog, isn't he? Was he . . . nobody told me, how was the dog hurt?"

"He'd been shot."

Concern twisted her little face. "Oh, my, what a shame! Who would do such a thing way out here? But why's Mr. Crane going back there? There wouldn't be anything left now, surely, to show who shot him!"

"I don't know." I felt chilled and uncomfortable; even the thick sweater I wore indoors didn't seem to help. There were several fireplaces, and wood had been hauled in and fires built in all the ground-floor ones; this didn't help any more than the sweater, probably because the chill was internal, emotional.

By now there would be some word of Rudy . . . either he'd have survived surgery or he wouldn't have. I wished the inn had a telephone. Max had promised to bring back a report . . . only Max didn't return.

Neither did Crane. When I looked for him, after a time, there was no one out there on the dunes, no figure leaning into the wind. His Scout was sitting

130

in the side drive, so he hadn't left in that. Where was he then? What was he doing?

My own room overlooked the spit in the opposite direction. The bathroom, I thought, might give a view of the area where I'd found Rudy. As I went up the stairs, I thought of Max's warning to be careful.

Well, there was no way to get to my room without leaving the people. I climbed, listening to the creaking boards under my feet and an occasional protesting sound from the house as if the structure were being pulled apart by the storm. It didn't seem likely that nails could actually be drawn by the wind, but I remembered that there had once been many other homes on the spit and my uneasiness increased.

There seemed to be no one else on the second floor as I made my way along the passage to the bathroom. There, however, I was brought up short by frosted glass in the window thirty feet off the ground.

Momentarily frustrated, I muttered a few words under my breath. And in one of those freakish moments that sometimes come during a storm, when all sound is suddenly suspended, I heard a door close nearby.

I was chagrined at the way my pulses pounded in alarm. For all of Max's words of caution, I didn't really think anyone was going to attack me in broad daylight, not with all the inhabitants of the inn moving unpredictably about. So why should a closing door trigger such alarm?

I turned away from the bathroom. There were rooms whose windows would give me a good view of the landward end of the spit, but they were all rented to guests.

The third floor, I thought then. I'd been told that since there had been a lot of water damage up there and no money to put things to rights they'd had to stop using the rooms; there was the stairway, though, continuing on from the head of the lower flight, and there was nothing intimidating about it.

Nevertheless, I paused to look around me before starting up those stairs, to make sure no one was watching me. The hallway was empty, the rooms silent behind closed doors.

The creaking of the stairs wouldn't have been heard, I decided, over the sounds of the latest assault by the storm. As I reached the first landing and started up the final stretch of stairs I could hear the dripping of water somewhere above me.

There was a different smell up here, an odor of mildew and dust and possibly mice. The window on the top landing was so begrimed that little light penetrated the upper hallway; I paused in the dim pseudo twilight to get my bearings. That way was the end of the spit, so . . . over there I would look for a window.

The room I entered contained its original furniture, the veneer peeling, and wallpaper hanging in a grotesque mockery of the crepe-paper festoons used at children's parties.

I paid no attention to the disrepair but made my way to the window to look out over the sands. And that's all there was, pale and darkened by the rain, and the coarse beach grass whipped low by the wind. Nothing to mark the place where Rudy had been shot down, no sign of Tom Crane.

Belatedly I realized I was standing in water. I stared down at the puddle, wondering how long the lower floors would be inhabitable if they didn't do something about the roof. Did Callie know it was leaking again now?

I lifted my gaze to the ceiling, seeking out the source of the moisture. Strangely enough, the area directly above the window wasn't wet at all; in fact, it was the only part of the ceiling where the wallpaper was still intact.

Puzzled, I glanced back down again. There was a considerable amount of water on the painted wooden floor; where had it come from?

The answer came almost before the question was formed, for I saw now that there was water on the windowsill as well. A closer inspection confirmed my conclusion: The window had been opened, and very recently, for there were smudges in the dust across the sash where fingers had pressed while the window was pushed upward.

I stood quite still for a moment, speculating on the significance of that. It was impossible to determine the size of the fingers that had made the impression, the area had been smeared too much for that, perhaps with a sleeve or the side of a hand.

Without conscious thought, I put my own hands against the sash and pushed upward. The window rasped but moved easily enough, and the wind and rain whipped the old lace curtains and dampened my front. Yes, the water could well have come in that way, I thought, and stared again out across the dunes, seeking a tall figure in a slicker. There was nothing moving but the beach grass.

Woodenly, with a racing heart, I closed the window.

Someone else had stood here, had looked out across the dunes, perhaps watching Tom Crane's progress. Someone, I thought, could have stood at this window with a rifle and fired at Rudy.

The more I thought about it, the more sure I became that this was exactly what had happened. How else could the dog have been shot without the culprit taking a good deal of risk? Anyone walking the beach with a gun would have been seen and remarked upon.

But the water here on the floor had gotten there today, not when Rudy was shot. Today . . . while Tom Crame was out there looking for clues.

I felt as if I were smothering. *What if Tom had been shot?* What if he, too, were lying out there bleeding into the sand? Dear God, what should I do? If only Max would come back we could go looking for Crane . . . if only there were a telephone, so I could call the police . . . if only, if only. . . .

I could see the road to town and there was no car along its length. Max wasn't coming, not right away. There was no telephone.

Was there anyone in the house I could trust? The aunts, I thought. I refused to believe the aunts were involved in anything crooked, anything involving guns or killing. Yet the spriteliest of them was seventy years old and weighed less than a hundred pounds. How could I ask any of the aunts for help?

I withdrew from the room and retraced my footsteps to the lower floor. The compulsion to go out there and look for Crane was strong; fear was stronger. If I'd been seen going up to the third floor, if the person with the rifle realized what I'd guessed, I would be no safer out there on the dunes than Rudy had been.

Egg came through the corridor from the kitchen, tying the strings of her flowered apron. "Oh, there you are, Brenna. Callie wants to know, are Mr. Von Rys and Mr. Crane going to be here for dinner, do you know?"

My lips were stiff, as if I hadn't used them in a long time. "I don't know for sure. They should be. It's an hour or so, isn't it, to dinner?"

"More like an hour and a half. It's lamb chops, and we don't like to cook more than we're going to need, not with the price of lamb chops. If they don't show up until the last minute, though, and we don't have anything cooked for them. . . ."

"Why don't you go ahead and plan on them? I'm sure they'll pay for dinner anyway," I said. "Listen, I'm going to run into town and make a phone call, see about my dog. I'll be back for dinner, though, and if Max asks about me, tell him I'll be right back, will you?"

Egg nodded dubiously. "With that wind, you're apt to get blown off the road. Be careful."

"I will." Already I felt better, to have decided on some positive course of action, however slight. I borrowed one of the slickers and went out into the storm.

133

Egg was right about the wind; it buffeted the small car in a frightening fashion. I held it to the road with hands that cramped in the effort, watching the dunes as I went, hoping to catch sight of Tom Crane. There was nothing.

It appeared that the villagers had withdrawn to their firesides, for I saw no one on the streets. The boats had already been battened down against the gale, and the waterfront was deserted. I eased the car to the curb in front of the telephone booth from which I'd called before and fought my way into the cubicle.

A quarter in the slot elicited no responsive dial tone. The phone was dead. I swore under my breath. Were all the phone lines down then?

Across the street a wooden sign was flapping in the wind so that I couldn't read it, but I knew what it said, for I'd read it before: ROOMS FOR GUESTS, and below that, in fine letters, HAZEL EDMONDS, PROP.

I wasn't about to give up easily, not having come this far. I crossed the street, the heavy slicker billowing out behind me, and climbed to Mrs. Edmonds' front porch.

The woman who opened the door was younger than the aunts and had a relaxed, friendly attitude. She knew who I was, too; it startled me when she called me Miss St. John.

I was a bit breathless. "The pay phone seems to be out of order. I need to make a call to Jordon's Hill, and I wondered. . . ."

She smiled, opening the door wider so that I might step into her front hallway. "Mine was working half an hour ago; let me give it a try. It's always a problem in a storm. One of these days maybe they'll get the rest of the wires underground where they'll be safe. Let me try."

The telephone was there on a small table just inside her living room. I knew by her face before she told me.

"I'm sorry, it's out. More than likely they all are."

I forced a smile I didn't feel. "Well, thanks anyway. Maybe I'll drive over there, now that I've come this far."

Before I could reach the door, it opened and I found myself face to face with Larry.

I couldn't have said what my emotions were, besides surprise. "I thought you'd gone back to Hampton," I said, seeing the quick curiosity on Mrs. Edmonds' face.

"No." Larry, too, was aware of the proprietor of the guest house. "Where is it you want to go, Brenna? Maybe I can take you there; my car's faster than yours, I think, if you're trying to get somewhere before closing time."

134

"Jordon's Hill. My dog's in a veterinary hospital over there." I weighed the situation hastily. "I suppose they do close at five thirty. All right, why not?"

Could he read my speculations in my face? *Mrs. Edmonds saw us leave together; it's not likely he'd allow that if he planned anything sinister.* Good God, what was I thinking? This was *Larry.*

He didn't seem to notice anything amiss. As we went down the steps, with Mrs. Edmonds peering after us through the glass door, he asked what was the matter with the dog.

"He was shot." I slid into the front seat of his car, and when he came around to the driver's side, I spoke before he could pursue that line any further. "Larry, do you know where the police station is in Bascom's Point?"

"Police station! Oh, to report the shooting of the dog? Do you know who did it?"

"No." I didn't add that shooting Rudy was only part of it; I knew that I had to do something, had to contact someone in authority, someone I could trust, to find out what had happened to Tom Crane. Maybe Max would be furious when he came back, and maybe Crane was perfectly all right and would be furious as well, but what if he *wasn't* safe? I couldn't risk it, not the way things were developing.

"I think the police would probably be in the city hall, the brick building there across from the Methodist church. You want to go there first?"

"Yes," I told him, and felt both apprehensive and relieved that I'd made the decision to call for help.

Not that I found it, however, for the only legal official in Bascom's Point, it seemed, was the constable. His office was empty (it didn't boast so much as a girl to answer the telephone; he shared a secretary of sorts with the mayor and the members of the city council) and the young woman across the hall informed us that all the authorities were out on emergency business.

"They're evacuating people from along the coast, the ones that want to leave. Old people alone, you know, the ones like that. The church ladies are setting up cots and fixing food in the basement of the church." She gestured toward the white frame building we could see through the window. "Just in case, you know."

I tried to conceal my disappointment. "They expect it to be a very bad storm then? It isn't safe on the coast?"

She, too, it seemed, knew who I was. Aunt Stell had been right about small towns. "Oh, the old inn has stood for a hundred years; I don't suppose it's in any danger. There are cottages, though, you know, summer places, that aren't so sturdy. Is there any message, Miss St. John? I can tell the constable when he comes in."

Message? I thought with a moment of near-hysterical mirth. *Oh, yes, tell him somebody shot my dog and maybe shot a guest at the inn, Tom Crane, and tried to set the inn afire, and something's happened to Max, although he may be on the wrong side of the whole thing, and I'm getting colder and scareder and I'm even watching this man I'm with, the man I almost married, as if he might pull a gun on me . . . oh, yes, give him that message.*

They were both looking at me strangely, I thought, or was I imagining it. "No," I said, "no message."

[16]

THE CAR sped toward Jordon's Hill, less affected by the strength of the wind than my own small vehicle had been, yet it was impossible not to be aware of the storm.

"Why haven't you gone home?" I demanded, twisting in the seat to watch Larry's profile. He didn't take his eyes off the road.

"I was on my way out to the inn to talk to you again, to tell you I was staying over, when I spotted your car. I asked about a room out there, but your aunts said the place was full up, and I hadn't really made up my mind yet what I was going to do. But the more I thought about it, the less I liked the situation you're in. Even if I'd been able to finish my business here, I'd hesitate to go off and leave you this way . . . it seems intimidating, to say the least."

I might have responded to that with some surge of emotion, but I didn't. For the moment I was drained of emotion except for the cold, hard knot in the pit of my stomach, a knot that wouldn't go away.

"This business you're here on, Larry. What is it, exactly?"

"I told you. A client is interested in turning up those missing tapes of your uncle's."

"And what do you think you could do about finding them if you stayed in Bascom's Point?"

"I'll be damned if I know," Larry admitted. "Except that I still think the Senator left something important in the inn when he was here. Oh, I know, he was here *before* he was indicted. But he knew it was going to happen several days before that; he was running around like a madman trying to find

137

a way to stop it. He wouldn't have wasted time coming here, to a place he disliked, except for something important."

"And you think it was to leave evidence against the other people who were involved with him. Who is this mysterious client?"

"I can't tell you that." He gave me a mildly exasperated grin.

"To hell with your professional ethics, Larry. There's a killer loose, and he may not be finished with killing. You came here expecting some sort of cooperation from me, yet I have to give it blindly, without knowing who wants help. How do I know he isn't one of the guilty parties? In fact, who else would have any interest in the tapes, except the people who don't want them made public?"

"It hasn't occurred to you that a lot of innocent people might be hurt, as well as the guilty ones, has it?"

"I'm well aware of that," I said, sounding grim. "Aunt Stell, Maudie, and me . . . we were among the innocent. Only I can't see what use the evidence would be to anyone except to suppress it, and I'm not interested in being a party to that if and when the tapes do turn up."

"Look, we know there *were* other people involved in these shady deals of the Senator's, right? And it's quite possible that some of them didn't know what they were getting into, didn't know their investment, for instance, went to pay bribes. Yet they may have the very devil of a time proving that unless the Senator was honest rather than vindictive when he wrote down or dictated the story."

"Since the evidence hasn't yet come to light, they can't know if they've been accused of anything, can they? It seems unlikely to me that the Senator would have tried to drag down anyone who was innocently involved, as you say, simply with an investment."

"But not knowing is pretty rough, Brenna! How'd you like to be sitting on a time bomb, wondering when it was set to go off? I'm not trying to find the evidence and destroy it, I simply want to locate it and find out just what it is."

I found that hard to believe, although I could certainly understand how anyone who had been involved with my uncle, however legitimately, might fear being drawn into the mess. "So you have an innocent client, who invested something with the Senator, and he wants to know what the Senator said about him."

"That's about it, yes."

"But he's unwilling to have it known who he is. And when you find the evidence, if you do, you'll simply turn it over to the authorities, after you've read or listened to it. You won't try to conceal or destroy anything of a damaging nature." Skepticism must have affected my voice.

Larry had never blushed like other people; only a spot of color appeared in each cheek. "Brenna, I'm just doing a job. I have no intention of jeopardizing my future by risking disbarment, I assure you. Look, get me into that house, that inn. Let me look for what I'm convinced has to be there. You can stick right with me, see whatever I find, pass judgment on what to do with it."

"There's only one thing we could do with it," I asserted.

"OK. Whatever you say. But get me into that inn and let me look. Will you?"

"I've looked, Larry. I'm in the room the Senator had while he was there. I've looked everywhere, and I didn't find a thing."

"Let me look again. You can watch my every move. I ought to be out there keeping an eye on you anyway, just in case there's someone running around loose who thinks you know more than you do. I don't like the idea of you being out there with nobody but a bunch of elderly aunts to look after you."

I didn't answer. He turned to scrutinize me briefly before the wind made it necessary for him to concentrate more fully on driving.

"Brenna, there's no need for you to stay out there at the inn. Why don't you get away, get out of it? If you don't want to go back to Hampton, I can run you up to Washington, if you like; there's no one at my cousin's apartment right now—you remember Charlie? He's in Paris for a month, and I have his keys. You'd be quite comfortable there and no one would even have to know where you were, if that's the way you wanted it."

"I have Max."

Larry swore. "I suppose there's no convincing you that he can't be trusted. At any rate, that you can't be sure he *can* be trusted. Have you checked into his background? Made any attempt to find out why he's really here, what he's up to? You've always been such an innocent, Brenna, taking everyone at face value, and it isn't safe to assume anything about anyone in a case like this."

I might have been amused. If only he knew how little I accepted anyone at face value these days . . . quite possibly I was becoming paranoid, so that I saw dangers where there were none and villains in everyone I met. Himself included.

"Something's occurred to me," I said. I hadn't planned to say it, but once begun, I pressed on, watching him closely for any reaction that might indicate Max had been correct about this. "You've come a long way on what seems to me a fool's errand. Unless there's considerably more to it than you've said. Larry, was your father involved in one of my uncle's deals? Is he one of the people who has something to lose if the whole truth comes out?"

The heavy car swerved sharply; Larry cursed and brought it back under control, his hands hard on the wheel. "God, you'd think they'd put lights on their barricades in this weather! I didn't see it until I was right on top of it! We might have been forced off the road."

I glanced back, but the rain-blurred glass gave me too poor a view; whether or not there had actually been something in the road I couldn't tell.

His grip had relaxed now, and when he answered my question, it was with derisive amusement. "Did you think that up yourself or did your friend Von Rys drag it out to distract your attention? My God, Brenna, talk about suggestibility!"

There had been a time when his ridicule would have hurt me very much. Now it only brought a slightly firmer set to my jaw. "That sounds very much like an evasive answer, Larry. Did the Senator rope your father in on something questionable?"

His lips flattened over his teeth, and while he made a pretense of leaning forward to see through the deluge, I suspected his anger was with my question rather than with the elements that made driving so difficult. "I'm surprised you even need to ask. You've known my father for a long time; he's a man of integrity, and there's never been a hint of scandal around either him or his law firm. He had more sense than to get mixed up in anything dubious; he certainly is not involved in any of this mess."

I continued to regard him thoughtfully. When Max had made the suggestion, I had been totally unbelieving. Now I wasn't so sure. There had to be some personal reason why Larry had come here and why he was staying here. It now seemed to me quite possible that Lawrence Engle had been involved, perhaps innocently, in some deal that might reveal him in an unfavorable light, whether or not legal charges could be brought against him. My uncle had been an extremely persuasive man; I could almost hear him saying something like, "You can't lose, man, it's an easy way to pick up fifty thousand (or a quarter of a million) with little or no effort; all you have to do is give me your check for the initial investment."

If the involvement *had* been inadvertent, how far would Lawrence Engle be prepared to go to keep from being contaminated by the scandal involving the Senator? Remembering his wife, I thought he might well be pushed to fairly drastic action.

Not to the point of setting fire to the inn while there were people sleeping in it, I thought. Not to killing anyone. Shooting a dog? I didn't know about that. Mr. Engle wasn't a dog fancier, particularly; in fact, I'd never heard him express an interest in or affection for any animal, so he might have felt shooting Rudy to be expedient. Shooting a man though, that was different. And certainly Mr. Engle himself hadn't done any of these things.

I couldn't be sure a man had been shot. Tolman-Haden had disappeared; there was only the evidence of a bloody handkerchief to indicate foul play, and it could be an entirely misleading clue. As for Tom Crane . . . well, he'd walked out onto the dunes and he hadn't returned, but that didn't prove anything, did it? He might be back at the inn by now, having a predinner drink with Max. If *Max* had come back.

"Where is this place we're going? Can you give me directions?" Larry asked suddenly, and I gathered my wits to remember the way to the animal hospital.

Max had not been there, and he had not called. This news was disquieting, one more thing to worry about. Rudy, however, the doctor told me with a broad smile, had not only survived surgery, but was awake and resting comfortably. Did I want to see him?

I couldn't believe it. Rudy lifted his shaggy head when I approached his cage and licked at the hand I put between the bars.

"He lost a bit of blood and he won't be himself for a few days, but he's out of danger. Tough fellows, these Airedales."

I asked about the bullet.

The veterinarian shook his head. "Probably buried in the sand back where you found him. If he'd been hit any more solidly, he'd have been blown apart; the only reason he didn't die was that they just creased his skull. I'd guess somebody shot him with a rifle, probably from some distance off. Unless you found the shells there'd be no way to prove it, I'm afraid."

Buried in the sand . . . out where Tom Crane had gone earlier in the day . . . to discover the bullets or to retrieve them? From thinking that Crane might also have become a victim, I was now having wild pictures of the man crouched at the open third-floor window, taking potshots at my dog.

The rain hadn't come in when Rudy was shot, though; that particular puddle had been formed *today*, I was sure of it; the spatters on the sill would surely have evaporated if they'd been there since yesterday,

"Might be worthwhile to look for the bullets if you want to track down the person who shot him. On the other hand, unless you know where to look for the gun, that wouldn't help much. Bad thing, shooting dogs." The doctor shook his head. "People shouldn't be allowed to get away with shooting helpless animals."

"No," I agreed. "How long will he have to stay here?"

He opened the door of the cage and nodded approvingly when Rudy rose and staggered out onto the concrete floor. "Doing very well, he is. I shouldn't think it would hurt to take him home now actually. He won't be very frisky, and it's too soon to let him eat or drink anything . . . by morning you might give him an ice cube or two, and then by afternoon try very small amounts of food and water. Wait a bit to make sure it's going to stay down, you know, before you give him anything more. I've given him an antibiotic, and you can give him some more in tablet form for a few days, just to be on the safe side."

I stared at the shaved area where heavy black sutures had repaired the damage. "Can he walk? He didn't get very far this time."

"Oh, we can get him to your car, all right. By tomorrow he'll be getting around very well, I expect."

I didn't think Larry was overjoyed at the thought of having a large dog in the back seat of his car, but he obediently brought it around to the door; we got Rudy settled on a towel the vet provided, and I took care of the bill.

Larry paused on the threshold. "Is there a pay phone nearby? I have to make a call, and the lines are all down in Bascom's Point. They're still functioning here, aren't they?"

"Far as I know, they are. Devil of a storm, isn't it? Winds are hurricane force, according to the radio. Bad night to be out. Pay phone on the corner, up that way, service station lot."

We'd kept the man past his regular office hours; his lights went out almost as soon as we got into the car. Larry didn't volunteer any information about who he was calling. I sat in the car, one hand over the back of the seat to touch Rudy reassuringly, while Larry spoke.

If there had been any way I could have eavesdropped, I would have. The rain streamed down the windows of the cubicle, making it impossible to see Larry's face clearly, let alone try to read his lips. Not that I had any experience at such a thing.

He came back to the car, flipping water out of his hair with one hand as he slid under the wheel.

"I just talked to Jerry Lawford, Dad's partner," he said as we eased out

142

into the nearly deserted street. "He agrees that I ought to stay on and make a further effort to go over the inn with a fine-tooth comb. I can't do that without some cooperation, Brenna. Will you help me persuade the aunts it should be done?"

I forgot Rudy, staring at Larry. There was something different about him, an air of excitement perhaps.

"Is it your father then that we're trying to protect?"

"Oh, for God's sake, don't get off on that kick again. I told you Dad has nothing to do with it, and neither does Jerry; he's simply a senior member of the firm and I asked his advice," Larry said, but there was less annoyance in his tone than I might have anticipated. "How about it? What have you got to lose? You can watch me every minute—the aunts can, too. Will you ask them?"

I considered. "I'll think about it."

"Think . . . what is there to think about?"

"I don't know, but it's more than I'm willing to cope with tonight. I want to get Rudy home and settled. . . ." And find Max and Tom Crane, I thought. *Dear heaven, please let them be at the inn when I get back!*

In the end he pinned me down to allowing him to come out for breakfast in the morning. I'd ask the others what they thought about it, but I honestly couldn't see how it would hurt anything for Larry to search the inn if the rest of us were watching him. Only not tonight.

The lights of the county seat, blurred in the rain, were slipping rapidly by. It wasn't a big town. I leaned forward to peer past the swishing blades. "Do you know your way around here at all? To know where the police station is?"

His features seemed to sharpen. "To report the shooting of the dog? Or do you have something else?"

"I don't know what I have," I said, and that was the truth. "I only know I need to talk to someone. . . ." I almost added, *someone I can trust.*

"I don't know who has jurisdiction at Bascom's Point; probably not anyone here in Jordon's Hill. County sheriff, maybe, since the spit is outside the town limits. Chances are their office is closed for today, except for emergency calls; it's nearly six o'clock."

"Well, I think this is an emergency." It sure would be if I got back to the inn and found that neither Crane nor Max was there. Fine lot of bodyguards they were turning out to be, deserting me this way!

Larry was right about the police station, though. We found the sheriff's department and the Jordon's Hill police established side by side in the local courthouse, which was locked up now except for a back door. A uniformed officer informed us that everybody but himself either was having dinner or was off helping with rescue work. He was new, he didn't know much about anything; if an emergency occurred, he was supposed to make radio contact with one of the town's two patrol cars and hope they could handle it.

Frustration seethed through me as I gave it up. No doubt Max and Tom Crane would be there having dinner when I got back, anyway; if they weren't, I'd keep trying until I located the village constable.

Larry offered to take me on back out to the inn, but I protested that I'd rather have my own car there. Besides, I wasn't ready for him to push any further about searching the inn, not until I'd talked it over with someone else.

Getting Rudy transferred from one car to the other wasn't easy, for he was very wobbly and was too heavy for me to lift. Larry might have done it, but he didn't offer and I wouldn't ask him. The wind whipped car doors around so that we had to block them open with our bodies and urge the dog out of Larry's back seat and into mine.

Poor Rudy managed it with an effort; he recognized the car and seemed glad to get into it, for he made himself comfortable across the entire seat.

I slammed the door and was ready to go, but Larry put a hand on my arm. "Brenna, the wind is really howling out there on the spit; if this isn't a hurricane, it's the next thing to it. Maybe I'd better follow you out to make sure you're all right."

I stifled an exclamation of annoyance. "No, that's silly. I'll be all right. Thanks for the lift, Larry. I'll see you in the morning."

Several people came along the street, carrying odds and ends of bedding wrapped in plastic, no doubt for the emergency center set up in the church. I wondered uneasily if Larry was right, that the wind might prevent me from getting to the inn, but I didn't want him to go with me.

One of the women paused, then peered more closely at me. "Excuse me, aren't you Miss St. John?"

We turned to face her, hunching against the storm that drove the rain stingingly against any exposed flesh.

"Yes, I'm Brenna St. John."

"I thought so. I'm the postmistress. I've got a message for you."

She juggled the sleeping bags she was carrying and dug into her slicker pocket to bring out a crumpled envelope. "It's not mail proper, exactly. But that young man that's staying out there gave it to Constable Henry to pass

144

along to you when he came back from Jordon's Hill, only he's too busy so he gave it to me. I was going to take it out to the inn, but I haven't had a chance. I've been needed over at the church."

She passed it over to me and I clutched it against the onslaught of the wind. "Thank you. Do you know where the constable himself is?"

"Haven't seen him for a couple of hours." She bobbed her head to conclude the conversation and got a better grip on her sleeping bags, then headed off toward the church.

"What is it?" Larry asked.

I could scarcely be expected to read it out in this storm, even if it were light enough to do so easily. I slid into the front seat of my little car. "It's a note from Max, I expect, explaining why he hasn't come back." I put it on the seat beside me. "I'll read it when I get home. Good night, Larry."

"But aren't you going to open it?"

I didn't want to read it while he was standing there. I slammed the door and turned the key in the ignition, taking off before he could do more than take a step after me.

It was dusk now, and the trees whipped overhead as I began to creep out of town. Larry was right about one thing—the wind *was* stronger. If there had been any way to communicate with the inn I might simply have given up and stayed in town for the night.

I waited until I was out of Larry's sight before I pulled to the edge of the road and opened the note. It was written in Max's bold, sprawling hand, and the ink had run in places, for both envelope and letter were wet. It read:

DEAR BRENNA,

I put in a call to Miller at the FBI office in Washington. When I told him about the bloody handkerchief, he wanted it immediately; they haven't had a report from Bill Haden and they're concerned about him. There are no planes flying along the Eastern Seaboard, so when he insisted I bring it up to him, there didn't seem to be much choice. He's driving down to meet me halfway. I don't know how long it will take, but I'll be back as soon as I can. Maybe when I tell him everything we've talked about, he'll come back with me, I don't know. Tell Tom Crane where I've gone and he'll look after you until I get back.

Love,

MAX

145

I sat for a moment, aware of the cold and the impact of the wind on my small vehicle. There was nothing to indicate how long ago Max had left; I hoped it was hours and hours ago so that I might reasonably hope he'd return before long.

When I was heading directly into the gale, I was able to control the car fairly well. But when I turned onto the spit road, the gusts nearly put me into the bay; my hands trembled on the wheel and my mouth went dry. I made some sort of protesting sound, and Rudy's massive head lifted from his paws so that I could see him in the rear-view mirror.

"Cross your fingers, pal," I told him, "that we make it the rest of the way. Maybe I should have let Larry come, after all."

I didn't see the man until I was nearly on top of him. He was in the middle of the road, and for a moment I thought it was Tom Crane, for he was tall and wore a dark slicker.

Touching the brake was automatic. Only when he turned to face me, holding out both hands in supplication, did it occur to me to be alarmed, for he was blocking my way. There was nothing to do except stop or run over him.

I stopped, feeling the car rock dangerously, and I wondered how far I was from the water. It was impossible to tell for sure; sand and bay blended in a uniform gray murk.

Belatedly, I reached for the button that would lock the door, but I was too late. My door was wrenched open, and a strange man, rather wild-eyed and with wisps of white hair plastered to his skull, thrust his face into mine.

"Thank God—you can't imagine how glad I am to see a human being! You'll take me on out to the inn, won't you?"

"Yes, of course. Get in." The words, too, were automatic; my flare of alarm was subsiding. He was only an old man who looked drenched in spite of his rainwear. He hurried around and slid wetly in beside me, gasping and wiping at his face.

"I don't suppose you have a towel, do you?"

"I'm afraid not, but there's a box of tissues in the glove compartment."

The car rocked violently under the gusts, and I began to creep forward again, unable to resist sneaking a glance at my passenger.

"You weren't walking to the inn surely?"

"Not intentionally. The storm was so bad I decided not to try to make it tonight, and I attempted to turn around. Got stuck in the dadratted sand, and there was nothing for it but to get out and walk. I thought I was closer to the inn than to town, but I haven't been out here in twenty years, so maybe I misremember. I can't tell you how delighted I was to see your lights."

My fright had abated. He was only an old man, unfortunate enough to be stranded out here as darkness was falling.

"I'm glad for the company," I told him. "Maybe the extra weight will keep my car from blowing away."

We talked about the weather for a few minutes before we got around to introducing ourselves. He was Gavin Foster, Mr. Sherman Foster's cousin. He had once lived in Bascom's Point and had been gone for many years; he was passing through and making an unexpected visit.

When I told him my name, his interest sharpened. "St. John? You related to the St. Johns that own the inn?"

"Yes. They're my great-aunts."

"All still around? Callula and Eglantine and Grazielle? Well, well, how about that! Funny thing, you know you've lived seventy-odd years yourself, but you don't expect everybody else to have done the same thing! Get married, any of 'em?"

"No, they're all single." I didn't tell him two of them were making eyes at his cousin.

"Well, well. Too particular, those St. John girls, my wife used to say. She went to school with Callie. They had their chances, all of them, I know that . . . proposed to Zell myself when I was no more than a lad, but she wouldn't have me." He chuckled, still patting water out of his hair with my tissues. "Said I was too wild. She was right, I was. Did she get fat? Zell?"

"No. She's tiny and very trim."

That seemed to please him. "Susie got fat. My wife. She died last year. I didn't think Zell would get fat. She was a beauty, I'll tell you, when she was seventeen. Pretty enough to be particular, all right. Oh, are we there? Where's the lights, for pity's sake?"

I explained to him about the electricity being off. I parked as close to the back door as I could get, and the old man made a run for it while I got my drunken dog out of the car and into the house.

Egg came into the back hallway to meet us with a lamp held high. My apprehensions had been held in abeyance while I fought the storm, but once I was inside the inn again, they all rushed back like the shadows that lay all around us.

"Did Tom Crane ever come back?" I demanded without even considering the new visitor. Rudy had made it into the hallway but dropped onto the rag rug there as if he were exahusted.

Egg looked at him with interest. "Poor thing. Is he all right?"

"Yes . . . well, he will be. What about Tom Crane?"

Egg shook her head. "No. We cooked his chops, and yours, and Max's, but they all got cold. Nobody showed up."

I scarcely registered the reproach in her face. The lamb chops weren't the only things that were cold. Fear was an icy trickle through my veins.

Something was very wrong, and I had to do something about it, but what? What did I do now?

[17]

MR. FOSTER and I had both missed our dinner. The aunts fussed about getting us something to eat and working out a sleeping arrangement for Gavin Foster. Since there wasn't an empty room, he suggested sharing with his cousin; there was a roll-away bed that could be moved in for him.

While they were preparing our meal, I rubbed Rudy down to make sure he was quite dry and fixed him a pallet in a corner of the kitchen, where he seemed content to go to sleep at once. I asked the others (all three turned up to greet us) about Crane, and I got the same reply. No one had seen him since he'd gone out onto the beach hours before.

I felt almost as battered by emotions as I had earlier felt battered by the storm. Tom Crane had apparently walked out onto the dunes, to the spot where Rudy had been shot, and vanished. His car remained in the yard, which seemed to rule out any possibility that he'd left the spit.

I couldn't believe that he was staying away of his own volition. If only Max would come back and help me decide what to do!

I wasn't feeling hungry, yet I knew that at least part of the sickish feeling that enveloped me was due to an empty stomach, so I joined Gavin Foster at one of the round kitchen tables. Zell had a cup of tea with us while the old man ate his way through a formidable amount of food. He had gotten out of his wet clothes into some of his cousin's, apparently, for he was rather rakishly attired in a bright flannel shirt and sturdy corduroy trousers. His hair, drying now, seemed thicker and whiter, almost as luxuriant as Mr. Montgomery's.

I turned to Callie, who was bringing the teapot to the table. "Did Mr. Montgomery get home for dinner tonight?"

Callie made a snorting sound. "Didn't much of anybody get here for dinner. Oh, I know you couldn't help it, probably the rest of them couldn't either, but what do you do with eight cold lamb chops?"

"He usually has dinner here, doesn't he? Mr. Montgomery?"

"Unless he has a client to see. Most of the time he knows ahead on that so he tells me. Of course, it's hard to know all the time, with real estate men. People want to look at houses in the evening after their working hours. I can't imagine anybody wanting to house-look on a night like this, though."

I couldn't either. Was his absence significant or completely irrelevant? If the man hadn't been so persistent on behalf of his unnamed client who wanted to buy the inn, I wouldn't have given him another thought. As it was, Max felt there was something peculiar about that client, which might make Mr. Montgomery's comings and goings more important than they seemed.

Callie left the teapot and went back into the kitchen where she could be heard grumbling to her sister as they cleared away the dishes. I poked around with my fork among salad greens and kept-hot scalloped potatoes until Zell gave me a rather penetrating look.

"Brenna, is something wrong? Besides worrying about your dog, I mean?"

I looked at them, two elderly people obviously pleased to be re-establishing an old acquaintanceship, and felt an overwhelming urge to enlist someone's aid. They were old, they were frail, they were undoubtedly as helpless as I, yet they had good minds and they knew the countryside as I did not.

"There's a young man in it somewhere, I daresay," Gavin commented kindly.

I made up my mind. There was no one within hearing distance, and I couldn't conceive of either of them being in collusion with anyone else involved in criminal activities. I drew in a deep preparatory breath.

"As a matter of fact, there are several young men in it somewhere. Part of the problem is that I don't know where exactly. I'm worried and I'm scared, and maybe I'm not thinking straight anymore. Will you listen and tell me what you think?"

To do them credit, they listened to a rather incoherent story with a minimum of interruption; when one of them did speak, it was with a

150

pertinent question. Gavin Foster continued to eat and patted his mouth with a napkin when he had finished.

"That's quite a story," he said, but there was no suggestion of disbelief in his words. "No wonder you're looking rocky. I'm a bit out of touch, Zell; who's the person to get in touch with? Sheriff's department, would you say?"

Zell's head bobbed. "We're in their jurisdiction out here. Of course, from what you say they may be hard to run down, with all the rescue work going on. Lulu had the radio on, that transistor she carries around sometimes, and they said people were being evacuated from that settlement up the coast a few miles . . . lots of little summer homes and places that aren't built like this one. We could go into town and see who we could find, though. Must be somebody we could report to and get some help."

"Thank you for that 'we,' " I told her. "I've been going out of my mind trying to think what to do. If Tom Crane was shot, too . . . I'm appalled, now, that I didn't go looking for him earlier, but I thought sure he'd come back. . . ."

Gavin poured himself another cup of tea. He had fine hands, very aristocratic-looking. He ought to have had lace cuffs, I thought, not that lumberjack type of shirt. "Are there guns in the house, Zell? Rifles, that sort of thing? Something that could have been used to shoot the dog?"

Again Zell's head bobbed. "Uncle Eldon always had hunting guns; they're in a glass cabinet in what used to be his old sitting room, when all the family was home. It's closed up now because it's hard to heat and the furniture is all peeling, but the room isn't locked."

"So anybody could get to the guns." His eyes were a paler blue than Egg's and very keen. "The dog was shot from this house, and if the young man was shot, too, as you suspect, that would have been from the same place. Who that's here would know how to handle a rifle and be a good enough shot to hit what he was aiming at, at that distance?"

"I reckon every man here has hunted in his time. Mr. Rossdale used to hunt; Mr. Montgomery still does when it's the season. You and Sherman were good shots as boys, I remember."

Gavin sighed. "I'm assuming the young lady is excluding me from her list of suspects, and I'm assuming my cousin isn't on the list either. I don't know about Sherman, but I haven't fired a rifle in thirty years. I suppose I could still do it, though. No matter. It seems something must have happened to the fellow and we'd better find out what it was. Can't say I relish poking around

151

on the dunes myself in the dark and the storm, and probably we wouldn't be able to find anything anyway. No, best bet is to get the police. So what do you say we bundle up again and head for Bascom's Point and see what we can stir up?''

The relief I felt was immense. Not only had they accepted what I said as having sounded rational, they had immediately committed themselves to help. I got a flicker of the reason for this when Zell looked around cautiously and said in a conspiratorial whisper, ''I suppose it would be better if we kept it to ourselves, wouldn't it? In case anyone suspects anything. After all, it does sound as if someone here in the inn must be in on whatever's going on.'' Whatever Gavin was going to do, Zell intended to be included in, I guessed.

Gavin Foster's voice was perfectly normal. ''No problem there. We'll tell them I'm worried about my car and we're going into the village to get someone to get it unstuck. And naturally I want my luggage, which is in the car. That should give us an excuse for being gone however long it takes. I'd suggest rain gear all around.''

When we told her, Callie rolled her eyes as if she thought we'd taken leave of our senses, and Egg made only a perfunctory protest regarding the weather. We didn't talk to anyone else.

We decided on the way into town that if we couldn't rouse the constable at his house (he had a radio in his car by which means he could contact the sheriff's office), we would find out who was in charge of the emergency setup at the Methodist church.

That was where we ended up, dashing between parked cars toward the lighted side entrance. There were plenty of people, milling around with cups of coffee and sandwiches or seated on improvised beds or sleeping bags on the floor. Since Zell knew most of the people there, Gavin and I stood near the doorway and let her do the advance work. She was an earnest small figure, dwarfed by the oversized slicker she wore, moving from person to person around the big basement.

We were offered a choice of cheese or tuna sandwiches, which we declined, and coffee, which we accepted. There was a surprising air of cheerfulness, considering that most of these people had been driven out of their homes with little more than the clothes on their backs; several old men had gotten up a card game, and young children ran around playing a noisy game of tag.

Zell came back looking depressed. ''There's nobody here from any of the law enforcement agencies. Most of the able-bodied men are up near Little

Charlotte Point, putting up sandbags and nailing up windows, I guess. Somebody said Ed Reiner just got back into town, so we could probably get him to take his tow truck out after your car, Gavin, but I don't know what to do about getting a policeman.''

"I should have gone looking for Tom Crane this afternoon," I said. "I'd have had a chance of finding him while it was still light."

Gavin was matter-of-fact about this. "Yes, you could have seen something . . . and might well have been shot yourself. You know, it takes a good man to hit a target at night. Even if we had lights bobbing around, chances are he couldn't hit us."

Zell watched in a sort of horrified fascination. "Are you suggesting we go out there now, by ourselves, and look for Mr. Crane?"

"You know anything else to do? If he was shot, he's probably dead, but if he isn't . . . well, hell, he wouldn't have much of a chance of surviving through a night like this, would he?"

Remembering Rudy, I had to agree. "God knows what we'll be able to see though, even with flashlights. If there are any . . . traces of him . . . they won't be easy to see." I didn't say "blood," but they knew what I meant.

We turned when the door opened at the top of the stairs. Half a dozen teenage boys came in, laughing and jostling one another. To them this was all a lark and undoubtedly meant they wouldn't have to go to school tomorrow. One of them bumped against Gavin as they came past, then paused to say, "Excuse me, sir."

Gavin lifted one of those graceful hands. "Just a moment. Are you lads committed to some sort of action tonight, hauling sandbags, anything like that?"

The boys eyed us in a wary fashion. Then one of them laughed uncomfortably. "No. They told us to get out of the way. We could have helped, but they said they had enough men who knew what they were doing."

"How'd you like to go on a rescue mission with us?"

The reaction was one of immediate interest, written on every face. "Who needs rescuing?"

"Fellow name of Crane—he's a tourist staying at the inn out on North Spit. There's a chance he's been hurt. Do you know where we can get flashlights and a vehicle or two?"

And that's all it took to recruit them; they raided cars for flashlights, and one boy who lived next door rounded up several more for us. They seemed totally unawed by the storm, or perhaps it would be more accurate to say they accepted it as a sort of challenge.

We stopped long enough to arrange for a tow truck to go out after Gavin's car, and then the rest of us were on the way back to the spit. It was up to me to tell them where to start looking. I believed, and Gavin agreed, that the site of the demolished house where I had found Rudy was the place to start. Finding it in the dark was a neat trick. What we finally did was to drive all the way back to the inn and then return as far as I thought it should be to put us opposite the right area. There we abandoned my car; the boys had a pair of Jeeps that could take us out onto the dunes. Two of them cheerfully gave up their own places in the doubtful comfort of the vehicles so that Zell and Gavin and I could ride.

"I know the place you mean, I think," our driver said when I described it. "Cement blocks for a foundation, right? I'll drive straight out until we come to the water, and then we'll get out and work our way back until we find it."

As it happened, that wasn't necessary. We found the abandoned foundation on the first pass by driving over it with a bone-shattering wrench.

There were some advantages to raising kids by television, I thought when everyone had piled out. They knew enough to look before they stepped. The rain had slackened to little more than a heavy mist, although the wind continued to be strong enough so that it was very difficult to walk against it. Our impromptu crew of detectives plied their lights carefully, and within a very few minutes one of them gave a shout.

"Hey, it looks like somebody was here, and it couldn't have been very long ago or there wouldn't be any marks left!"

I moved with the others, eager yet apprehensive. I drew in a shallow breath when I saw the area where several lights were focused, for there was a depression in the wet sand; the rain had hardly blurred the edges of it yet, it was so recently made.

"Somebody dragged something," one of the boys said. "Cripes, are we looking for a *body?*"

"We might be," Gavin conceded. "Follow it in both directions and watch close for anything that might have been dropped or caught in the grass or on the edge of one of those cement blocks."

I hadn't the heart to go with them; quite suddenly I didn't want to know what was at either end of that track. Zell must have felt the same, for she stayed with me; we huddled inside our raincoats with our hands deep in the pockets, turning so that the stinging mist came at our backs.

"Hey, I think there's something here!" The shout brought us around; I felt shriveled inside the slicker as I waited to hear. Several lights converged upon the area, and then all but one of them started moving toward us, toward the sea.

Gavin moved more slowly than the boys; he paused to speak to us, tugging the brim of his rain hat lower to protect his face as he edged away from the wind.

"Looks like something's buried against that foundation. We didn't dig down far, but . . . well, you may have guessed right, Brenna. There's a bit of cloth showing where the boys pushed back the sand; I don't think we'd better disturb it any further, if it's what it looks like. A bit of a man's shirt, could be blood on it."

Zell's face above the yellow circle of her own flashlight reflected the dread that must be mirrored on my own. "Is . . . someone wearing it?"

"I think so. Those dratted police will have to come now; we'll go over to Jordon's Hill and call in the FBI if we have to. *They* can't all be out hauling sandbags and nailing up windows, and if this is connected with Senator McCaffey's death, either it's their jurisdiction or they can find out whose it is."

A muted yell brought us around toward the sea. For a moment it was all I could do to breathe; the wind seemed to suck away my breath until I lowered my head.

"What is it?" Gavin shouted, and, after a disconcerting moment of silence, came the reply.

"It's a guy, and I think he's dead, sir."

I remember running through the wet sand and kneeling beside the sodden lump that couldn't possibly be a human being, but it was. I remember the lights touching the white, cold face, and my own too-rapid pulses hammering, and the flash of guilty gratitude that it wasn't Max.

The boys moved aside for Gavin, only too willing to let him take charge. It wasn't a lark, an adventure, anymore.

Tom Crane lay nearly submerged in the surf; even as we stood or knelt beside him, the waves surged over our feet and would have gone into his face if the boys hadn't responded to Gavin's orders to pull him out of it.

"Can't tell much in this light," Gavin muttered. "No head wound I can see, but . . . yes, there it is. He's been shot in the chest, high, close to the shoulder. He's damnably cold, but there's just a possibility . . . can anybody feel a pulse?"

There was a silence. Nobody moved to touch the motionless figure until I

155

stretched out a hand that was shaking and so cold I doubted it was possible for me to feel anything.

"Get inside his shirt," Gavin instructed. "Lower down, below the wound."

My teeth were chattering. "He feels frozen. Even colder than I am."

"That doesn't mean anything. Can you detect any heartbeat?"

I remembered laying my ear against Rudy's chest, and without letting myself think about it, I did the same again on Crane's icy flesh.

"Anything?"

"I don't know. Maybe. I can't tell. Oh, please, let's get him to a hospital. . . ."

"I'll bring the Jeep down here," one of the boys said, and he was off into the darkness toward the headlights some distance away.

I watched while they improvised a stretcher out of a blanket and lifted the unconscious man onto it. I followed up over the dunes to the other Jeep, no longer aware of my own discomfort.

Crane was probably dead. Was it my fault? Would finding him hours earlier have made a difference, if I'd organized a search party then?

"Considering the weather," Gavin remarked from behind me, "there's a devil of a lot of traffic out here tonight."

The wind covered the sound of engines, but we could see the headlights approaching from the village, two sets of them. Max? I wondered with a surge of hope. Oh, please, let it be Max!

And then the lights merged with our own, and almost before the engines had died, the drivers were out of the vehicles, moving toward us, and Max's arms came around me in a quick hug. I smelled wet wool and listened to the babble of voices, the sharp questions and the overlapping answers, and I thanked God, for the federal agent had arrived, too.

[18]

"MILLER'S GOING on to the hospital with Tom," Max said, crawling into the car beside me. "He'll get a crew out here to dig along the foundation of that old building. I offered to go along, but he thought I'd be of more use here with you. Are you OK?"

"Yes, but it's been a bad night. How . . . do you know anything about Tom Crane?"

"He's alive. At this point I guess we're grateful for that much. He was shot, probably from quite a distance, and chances are he won't be able to tell us much when he does come around."

My lips were stiff and cold. "I think he was shot from the inn, Max. The same as Rudy." I told him about the water up on the third floor.

He swore. "Well, they'll let us know how Tom comes out. Let's get back to the inn. I'm wet and half-frozen and I haven't had time to eat since noon. I didn't get a chance to call about Rudy either, I'm sorry, but once I'd talked to Miller he was in such a hell of a hurry . . . and there was no way I could get a message to you anyway, at least I didn't think there was at the time. On the way out of Jordon's Hill I spotted the constable's car from Bascom's Point and flagged him down to send you a message. Did you get it?"

"Yes. Max, Tom was not only shot; he was dragged down to the water's edge where the tide would surely have covered him before long. He must have been shot hours ago, but we could still see the marks on the sand. . . ."

"Yeah. Well, we must be getting closer to the son of a bitch, whoever he is. Let's go—we can talk some more while I get something to eat."

Gavin's car had been pulled out of the sand, and Zell rode back with him

157

while Max and I drove our own cars. We converged on the back hall at the same time. It was Zell who stopped and spoke dramatically, aiming her flashlight at the floor.

"Look! Somebody came in just ahead of us, there's water all over the place." We all looked at one another.

"Better see if we can find out who's been out," Max said at last. "Ask the aunts, Brenna. I'm going to get out of these wet clothes. I'll be back down in a few minutes."

The watery trail ended at the rack where the rain gear was hung; the wet coat was a large one and could have fit anyone in the house. There was nothing to indicate who had worn it.

We went on along to the small sitting room without taking off our own coats. Callie and Egg were sitting there, making their granny squares and socks. The record on the Victrola was "Moonlight Bay." I remembered it from my childhood, scratches and all.

"Who just came in?" Zell demanded.

They looked at us with mild interest. "Nobody that I know of," Callie said. "What on earth are you doing running around in the rain so late?"

"They just got Gavin's car unstuck. Someone came in ahead of us; there's a wet coat."

"We didn't see anyone going in or out."

"Where is everybody?"

"Mostly gone up to their rooms, I guess. It's such a miserable night, and getting cold. We tried to light off the furnace, only something seems to be wrong with the thermostat—we couldn't get it going. So I suppose they've all curled up in bed and are reading by lamplight or going to sleep early."

My voice sounded too loud in the small room. "I'm going up and knock on all the doors and see if anybody looks wet. Or if anybody can confirm where any of the others were for the past hour."

Egg put down the sock she had begun. "Brenna, what's wrong?"

I turned and headed for the stairs; I heard Zell explaining, "Poor Mr. Crane was on the beach; he's been hurt."

That roused some interest; I could hear their voices but not the words as I made my way upstairs.

I ought to have been frightened half to death. Strangely enough, my emotion was not fear but anger.

I started on one side of the corridor and worked my way along it, knocking, waiting, insistent upon being answered.

The Avery sisters were in bed, reading. They both had their hair up in rollers. No, they hadn't been out; they'd been right here for some time, reading. Yes, certainly they'd heard other people coming and going, but they hadn't paid any attention this early in the evening. Lulu—or Clara, whichever it was—murmured a question, but I simply thanked her and moved on.

I knocked loudly on Mr. Rossdale's door. If he slept without his hearing aid, he might be very difficult to rouse, but I was determined to check on everyone presently in the house. A second hammering finally brought him to the door. For a moment the impact of his gaudy pajamas was blunted because I was looking at his hair: wet and recently combed across his pink skull.

"Yes? What's the matter, not another fire?"

"No. Have you been outside in the past hour, Mr. Rossdale?"

"How's that?" He reached up and adjusted his hearing aid.

"Have you been outside in the past hour?"

"Outside? Outdoors? In the storm?"

"Yes." I took another breath and said it. "I notice that your hair is wet."

He put up a hand and felt his hair, as if to determine the truth of the matter. "Yes, yes."

"I thought you might have been out of doors."

"No. No, I took a shower and got into bed. It's cold, something wrong with the furnace."

It was a losing battle, yet I asked one final question, "Did you see anyone else come in from outside?"

He shook his head. "No. Never paid any attention. Too cold to sit downstairs tonight, so I came up to bed."

I gave up and let him shut his door in my face.

Sherman Foster was fully dressed, complete to his tie. He carried a book, marking his place with a finger. "Oh, Miss St. John. Nothing wrong, is there?" He glanced beyond me as if expecting to see smoke billowing up the stairs.

"I'm trying to find out who was outside, who came in just ahead of us a few minutes ago."

He scratched his nose with a corner of the book. "Didn't know anybody was out except you and my cousin. I understood he went to get his car pulled out of the ditch or something. I'd have left it there myself, this kind of weather. Did he get it out?"

"Yes. He's probably come in by now. But you weren't out then?"

He shook his head. "Not me. Gavin might take a look at the furnace, if

159

you talk to him before he comes up. He used to be good at fixing such things. I took a look, but I didn't see what the problem was. Cold, tonight, the way the wind's working in all the cracks. You might mention it to Gavin if you see him.''

I promised that I would and turned away.

Nothing. Nothing whatever except that Mr. Rossdale's head was wet and Mr. Foster's was dry. Which needn't mean anything except that one of them had taken a shower and the other one had had a hat on while he was out in the rain.

I made a sound of frustration and felt the hair prickle on the back of my neck when a voice came out of the shadows behind me.

"Something wrong, Miss St. John?''

"Oh, Mr. Montgomery! You startled me!''

In the dim glow of the lamp that burned on a hall table I saw that his hair, too, glistened with a wet sheen.

He smiled. "I'm sorry. I just came up the stairs; you were talking to Mr. Foster and didn't hear me, I guess.''

"Did you just come in?''

"Yes. Worked late tonight. Had a client who wanted to look at a house. On a night like this, if you can believe it! But a sale's a sale, so what can a man do?''

I couldn't take my eyes off his hair. He'd combed most of the water out of it, but it had been thoroughly wet. Had he, indeed, just arrived from Jordon's Hill? Or had he preceded us into the house and then waited until we'd passed him in one of those unused rooms so that we'd think he'd come in behind us? I tried to remember whether or not his car had been outside and couldn't; fool, why hadn't I looked and made sure which cars were there?

"I hope you made the sale,'' I said woodenly, and he shrugged.

"Too early to say. Not many people bring out their checkbook the first time they see a property. No, they like to come back and check it out a few times. Well, good night, Miss St. John.''

He passed me and went on down the hall and into his room. I stood and wondered about him. Had he come up the stairs unheard? Or had he been elsewhere, had he listened to what I was asking the others and given me the least suspicious answers he could come up with?

So, anyway, that made one dry head (not totally without suspicion) and two wet ones.

I started once more toward the head of the stairs and was brought to a stop by a glimpse of one of the bathrooms, where the door stood open.

The bathrooms at the inn were nothing like the tiled and mirrored decorator's masterpieces of the slick magazines. They had linoleum floors and old-fashioned fixtures, with tubs up on legs so that dust balls formed beneath the tubs.

There were no showers.

I had only used the one bathroom, so I checked out the other one, just to be sure I wasn't wrong. There were only tubs, no showers.

How, then, could Mr. Rossdale have gotten his hair wet in a shower?

Irresolute, I stood there in the middle of the passageway. I had determined exactly nothing. Except for the Avery sisters and my two aunts, none of them could corroborate anyone else's alibi for the time during which Crane (or his body) had been dragged into the sea. Anyone's wetness, or lack of it, was easily explained and proved nothing.

Rage created a heat to counteract the cold of my external surroundings. Damn them, whoever they were! Someone in this house was a killer, and there must be something I could do to smoke them out!

Them—or him? I couldn't seriously consider any of the old women in the house to be on the suspect list. I doubted that any one of them was physically capable of dragging a man even a few yards through the wet sand.

A man, then, and the list was very short. At least I knew I could leave Max off it, for he'd been with the FBI man, driving down from Washington when Tom Crane was dragged into the sea.

Beside me a door opened, startling both me and Donald Rossdale. He had gotten dressed, rather hastily I judged from the way his tie was tied, and he stopped, blinking at me myopically through those thick lenses. For a moment his glasses threw me; I wondered if it was possible to see well enough through them to shoot a man and a dog over any distance.

"I . . . I thought I'd go down and see if I could maybe do something about the furnace."

I didn't reply to that; in fact, his words scarcely registered. I don't know where I found the courage or the brashness to ask my question.

"Where did you take a shower, Mr. Rossdale?"

"Eh?" He had a habit of touching his hearing aid when anyone spoke to him, as if by pressing it tighter into his ear he could make it work better.

"You said you'd taken a shower. I wondered if you'd found one that I didn't know about." My mouth was dry, yet I was aware of perspiration forming beneath the slicker I still wore.

"Oh." He transferred his fingers to his hair, patting at its dampness. "Oh, yes. Well, I meant really that I'd taken a bath. Lived for years with only a shower, just a way of speaking, you know. Shower, for bath.''

His pale blue eyes, so magnified by the thick glass, stared at me guileless-ly, and then he dodged around me and headed toward the stairs.

Well, it was possible. I had a grandmother who always referred to a refrigerator as a Frigidaire, even years after we had some other brand of appliance.

He hadn't locked his bedroom door.

Under ordinary circumstances I can't imagine anything that would have induced me to enter anyone else's room in his absence. The present circumstances were anything but ordinary, however. Only a few days before he was indicted, the Senator had come here to see someone, and it might have been Rossdale.

With the courage which came at least partially from knowing that Max was just down the hall, I hesitated for no further rationalizations, and turned the knob.

He hadn't bothered to put out his lamp, which wasn't a kerosene one such as the rest of the household were using but one of those gas lamps with mantles that were almost as bright as electric bulbs.

The room was in a state of confusion. He had been in the bed and, in getting out, had left the covers trailing onto the floor. There were newspapers scattered on the floor and in one chair. The clothes he had taken off earlier in the evening were in a heap near the bed, his discarded pajamas beside them.

Of course it was quite possible that he was simply a messy man. On the other hand, the place looked as if it had been vacated by someone in a panic, or was that only my imagination again?

I didn't know what I'd come in for, what I was hoping to find. The gun, maybe? Or something equally incriminating. There was no gun that I could find, certainly no rifle; none had been slipped into a drawer or under the bed.

Yes, I looked under the bed, and I did find something there that intrigued me enough to pull it out: a small flat case, a sort of attaché case, of dark smooth leather.

It was not covered with dust, although there was plenty of that under the bed, too; no, he'd handled it recently and wiped it clean.

It was heavy as I swung it onto the edge of the bed and reached for the zipper.

God only knows what I thought would be in it. The missing tapes or other records? Maybe, if I was thinking at all at this juncture, this was what I expected, although there was no logic to that. If this man had the tapes, he

162

wouldn't be going around invading other people's rooms in a search for them.

The case was not locked and the zipper slid noiselessly open.

It contained no tapes. I gaped at the contents, wondering if it were genuine currency.

For that's what it held, bundles of currency, all that I could see in twenty-dollar bills, although when I lifted out a few of them there were more bundles underneath, of fifties and hundreds.

I'm no good at mental arithmetic, but I didn't need to do any calculations to know that the case contained a staggering sum of money.

How had Rossdale come by it? Was it possible that the Senator had come here with this, to leave it for safekeeping when he knew his own resources were being investigated?

I had entered the room holding my breath, walking on eggshells; when I saw the case of money I forgot to be cautious, which was a mistake.

I knew that when I heard the door click softly shut and looked around into those pale, thickly veiled eyes.

[19]

SINCE THE storm was still screaming about the eaves, it was a wonder I could hear both my breathing and his, yet I could.

Although he had closed the door, he made no move in my direction. Only then did it occur to me that if this man was not connected with the Senator or what had happened to Rudy and to Tom Crane, he might legitimately be very resentful of my intrusion. I tried to believe that it was only his extraordinarily thick glasses that gave his face such a malevolent look.

"Were you looking for something, Miss St. John?"

He was a thickset man, slow-moving, ordinarily very quiet. Now I saw that the thickness was muscle, and the way he was poised on the balls of his feet suggested that he not only was ready for physical action but was quite capable of speed.

The words came out of my subconscious before I knew they were there. "He isn't dead, you know. He's going to be able to talk."

I had no way of knowing this was true; maybe he didn't know for sure that it wasn't.

The nearsighted eyes didn't flicker. I wondered if Max would hear me if I screamed, and then I wondered if I'd be able to scream, the way my throat felt.

He moved a hand, indicating the bundles of bills. "Were you going to help yourself?"

"No. Is it . . . his?"

"His?" The echo was very soft, only mildly curious.

"The Senator's. Did he bring it here just before he was indicted?"

Now Rossdale couldn't maintain the passivity of his countenance, for it twisted in anger. "His! It's nothing to do with him, it's mine! You've no claim on it, girl, none whatever."

"But it was you he came to see." How did I know that was true? Instinct, perhaps, the same instinct that told me this was a deadly dangerous man.

There was danger, now, although it was well controlled. "He shouldn't have come. He had no right to bother me, not now when I'm so close. . . ." He broke off with a strangled sound. "There was no trail to me; I'd lost them years ago until he came. The bloody bastard, he deserved what he got, dragging the Feds in on me again."

I had no idea what he was talking about. It seemed preferable to keep him talking rather than let him approach any closer.

"Did you kill him? Were you the one?" For the Senator, too, had been cut down by rifle fire.

"You won't pin that one on me, girl. I was right here in Bascom's Point the day he was shot, with plenty of witnesses."

"But he came here to see you." What was he going to do? Was it possible that if I simply walked around him he'd let me go? Or was he as dangerous as he looked?

"I told him to go to hell. You know that? Did he tell you that? Why should I stick my neck out, come out of cover when my time was almost up, for his sake? He never did anything for me, the bloody blackmailing bastard. I didn't owe him anything. 'Ace in the hole,' he said I was. Like hell! Thought he'd blackmail me into doing his dirty work! If he wanted to blackmail the rest of them into helping him out of the mess he got into, let him do it himself, and I told him so. So don't think you're going to cut in on me, any more than he did."

It was a tremendous spate of words from a usually inarticulate man. He seemed to come to that conclusion himself, for he stopped and came toward me. I was unresisting when he reclaimed the packet of bills and closed the case and picked it up.

"Since you're dressed for outdoors, there's no need to bother anybody else, is there? We'll take my car, and you can drive it."

My lips were stiff. "I'm not going anywhere with you."

He almost smiled. "Oh, yes, you are. I haven't hid out in this godforsaken backwater for almost seven years just to sit here and wait for them to come and get me at the last minute. Come on, we're going down the back stairs, and if you make any noise, I'll throttle you on the spot."

There was no doubting that he meant what he said. As if to convince me, however, he took hold of my upper arm and squeezed until I made an involuntary sound of painful protest.

"Think how that will feel on your neck," he advised, and with one hand on me in an unbreakable grip and the other on the handle of the case with the money, we moved to the doorway. "Open it. If there's anybody in sight, don't move."

I prayed that Max, or anyone, would be in the hallway, but there was no one. I inhaled deeply, thinking I'd have to chance a badly wrenched arm and yell when we came abreast of Max's door, and then I saw that the door stood ajar and there was no light. While I had been in Mr. Rossdale's room, Max had gone downstairs.

We went down a narrow secondary passageway I hadn't known existed, to the enclosed stairs that must end somewhere in the kitchen regions. I hoped to God Max was eating in the kitchen and that it wouldn't be possible to escape his notice. The fingers that gripped my arm were strong and cruel.

When he let me go, I was so unprepared that I nearly pitched ahead of him down the steep steps. But he wasn't letting me go. His voice was low and grim. "Now go slow, and don't make any noise when we get to the bottom. I'll have this aimed right in the middle of your back and it's got six shells, plenty to go around for you and anybody else we meet, so remember that."

"This" was a small handgun. I'd never seen one up close except on the screen. This was all so unreal that for a few seconds I felt as if this were all a badly written movie script, except that I was damp with nervous perspiration, and when he nudged me with the barrel of the weapon, it was cold and hard.

"Go on down," he said, "and open that door carefully. We're going out the back door, and if you don't make any alarm, nobody will get hurt."

There was nothing to do but obey. I didn't doubt that he meant what he said, that he wouldn't hesitate to shoot . . . me and anyone else who got in his way. What the devil was I going to do?

I eased open the door and peered into the back corridor, orienting myself in the half-lighted doorway. Then, slowly, his head swiveled in the other direction. There were lights there, too. Not bright ones, because everyone was using the kerosene lamps, but the other aunts must have been in their sitting room. The Victrola was playing, another record I remembered from my childhood, "The Jolly Coppersmith." The gay little tune was one of the first I'd learned to whistle. I wondered if it would be the last one I'd ever hear.

His lips formed the oath, but I didn't hear it. He jerked the little handgun

166

toward the rear of the house to indicate we were going that way, and pressed the handle of the attaché case into my hand.

"Carry that. And don't drop it or it will be the last thing you ever do."

I nearly dropped it when he let go, because it was heavy and my hand was trembling. He nudged me again, and I began the long walk toward the back door.

If Max or one of the others saw us, I had no doubt that my captor would shoot. And if they didn't see us . . . where was he taking me, what were my chances of getting away from him?

The people in the kitchen were out of our direct line of vision, a fact that was both disappointing and a relief, since I didn't want any of them shot. On the other hand, I was nearly sick with fear at the thought of leaving the inn with this man.

We had reckoned without Rudy.

He had moved from the pallet in the kitchen and lay across the rug put down in front of the door.

I saw him before Rossdale did, for I was ahead of the man. Rudy lifted his head, and in the deep shadows I saw his stubby tail twitch a greeting.

I remember a moment of panic, a flashing realization that Rudy would be killed without thought if he seemed to present any threat. When Rossdale saw him. . . .

I had forgotten that Rossdale had poor eyesight. He was close behind me and he reached around with his free hand to open the door without being aware of the dog at all. He came down with his full weight on one of Rudy's outstretched paws.

Rudy's yelp of pain coincided with several things: involuntary sounds from both Rossdale and me, a lurching effort by Rossdale to regain his balance, and my own instinctive swing with the heavy case in my hand in an attempt to deflect a shot.

The gun went off with a violence that left my ears ringing, but the case connected with Rossdale's gun hand in time to send the bullet somewhere into the shadows instead of into either Rudy or me. I'm not even sure he intended to fire it; he must have been as nervous as I was and may have simply squeezed the trigger when he lost his balance.

The attaché case slid across the floor toward the lighted doorway. Rossdale swore, and Rudy, by this time recognizing that something was going on that he didn't like, lunged to his feet and came to my aid.

The next couple of minutes are a bit confused in my mind. I do know Rudy left teethmarks in the wrist controlling the gun, and another shot was fired which we subsequently found in the ceiling. Someone was yelling (me?) and people came rushing out of the kitchen.

They didn't have guns, but by this time they didn't need them. Rossdale had given in to Rudy's persuasive methods and dropped his weapon; it skittered toward Max, who picked it up and held it as if he knew what to do with it.

Zell brought up the rear with a lamp held high, and Egg and Callie came from the other direction with their lamp as well. We stood for a few minutes, breathing heavily, looking at one another. I think Rossdale would have tried, even then, for the door, but Rudy barred the way, no longer snarling but looking quite capable of using his teeth again.

Max was the first one to regain the use of his vocal cords. "Well. Going somewhere, were you?"

Gavin nudged the attaché case with his foot. "What's this? Turned up the missing tapes, have we?"

Rossdale began a movement that ended abruptly when Max shifted position so that the gun was aimed in his direction. "It's mine. Nothing to do with Senator McCaffey, it's mine."

"It's money," I said, working to conquer the tremor in my voice. "A lot of money."

Gavin kicked the case a bit farther away from Rossdale before he stooped to open it. He whistled over the contents. "You're right. It's a lot of money. I'm afraid I'm lost. What's all this got to do with Senator McCaffey's murder? Or is that why you shot him, eh?"

Rossdale struggled with his rage; we could see how difficult it was for him to contain it, to resist the urge to take us all on at once, weapon or not. "I never killed him, I was right here in Bascom's Point the day he died, and I can prove it! She knows, she knows I was here, I wasn't in Washington!"

Zell's lamp wavered as she lowered it to a level more compatible with the strength in her arms. "That's so. He was here, with the rest of us." She stared down into the opened case. "There must be a fortune there. . . ."

Callie's words cut harshly across Zell's. "And he asked to delay paying his rent this month because he was a bit short! With all that money hidden away!"

Max let his gaze travel to Gavin's face. "Is it genuine? Can you tell?"

"Looks good to me. Not that I'm any expert, but it certainly looks good. What would you say was in there? A hundred thousand? A hundred and fifty?"

168

Max's eyes returned to Rossdale. "How much is it?"

Rossdale's mouth flattened in a sullen line.

"He doesn't want to talk. Well, maybe we'd all better go in and sit down . . . Brenna looks as if her legs might give out . . . and then we'll see if we can't convince Mr. Rossdale we need some answers."

We all moved into the kitchen and the aunts who were holding lamps found places to put them down. I didn't know about the others, but I was limp. When Rudy came to stand beside me I scratched idly behind his ears, but my attention was still on the man who had intended to kidnap me.

"What happened, Brenna?" Max asked. None of them moved or spoke while I told them.

"Well. We do need some answers, don't we? How about it, Mr. Rossdale? You aren't going anywhere, you know; whatever you planned, it's all off. We found Tom Crane on the beach, and though he's badly hurt he's still alive. An FBI man is with him, and sooner or later he'll be back here. When he does come back, you're going to be sitting here waiting for him, and you'll have to talk then. So why wait?"

Rossdale's hair had come away from his scalp in several long strands that now went in the wrong directions. The lamplight glinted off his thick glasses. I couldn't see his hands, but I'd have bet they were clenched into fists.

"Where did the money come from?" Max demanded.

I saw the muscles bunch along our prisoner's jaw, but that was all.

Gavin leaned back in his chair and spoke in a conversational tone. "I was a deputy sheriff once, back in 1922. Only six months, I wasn't really suited for it. In fact, the reason I got on the force was I got into a bit of trouble, and my daddy was a friend of the mayor, and they cooked up a little learning experience for me. I got six months on the force instead of thirty days in jail, and it was a beneficial experience, all right."

He pulled a jackknife out of his pants pocket and began to clean his fingernails with the point of one blade. Everyone watched him, except that I noticed Max didn't forget he was guarding Rossdale.

"That sheriff was one of the meanest bastards I ever met, before or since. He just plain had an aversion to prisoners that refused to talk when he asked questions."

Interest flickered in Max's eyes. "I had a sergeant like that when I was in the Marines. He knew a number of things to do to persuade a reluctant tongue."

Gavin had finished with his nails and now he took the knife and scraped at the back of his wrist. I was sitting next to him and I could see that it removed the hair as neatly as a razor.

"My daddy gave me this knife. Been a real good one, really holds an edge. Not much use having a knife unless you can keep it good and sharp. I don't imagine that FBI man will be back before morning, do you?"

"I doubt it," Max said. I was glad it wasn't me he was looking at with that speculative look on his face. Rossdale swallowed audibly, but he didn't say anything.

Gavin was inspecting his knife. "I saw a man cut a dog's leg off once, with a knive not much better than this one. Dog was all tore up on a barbed-wire fence, and it was the only way to get him loose. I'd hate to try to amputate a leg with a little bitty knife."

"On the other hand," Max said in the same perfectly ordinary tone, "it wouldn't be hard to remove something smaller than a leg. There're several parts of a man that wouldn't be too hard to cut off with a jackknife, if it's a good sharp one."

His eyes met Gavin's across the table. I didn't know whether they were bluffing or not, although I couldn't imagine them actually *cutting* anyone. . . .

Maybe Rossdale could, though. There were beads of moisture on his forehead, and he swallowed again.

"How about it, buddy?" Max almost smiled. "You going to come up with some answers, or do we have to find out how sharp Gavin's knife is?"

The words burst out amost as if beyond his control. "You wouldn't dare! The police will be here, you said so yourself, and you'd be in real trouble!"

Max's smile, if there had been one, vanished. "Maybe. I've been in trouble before and survived it. And it would be your word . . . one man's . . . against ours, as to how an 'accident' happened."

Rossdale was breathing through his mouth now. "You'd go to jail; you aren't going to risk going to jail. . . ."

"But you'd still be missing whatever it was got cut off," Gavin observed. He shaved a bit more of the hair off his arm where he'd pushed up his sleeve. "And some parts don't grow back."

The epithet Rossdale spat at them seemed to hang in the air after the actual words had died into silence. I wondered if the aunts had ever heard the phrase spoken; they had remained silent and motionless ever since we'd assembled around the table. Only Egg's slack jaw demonstrated comprehension.

"I think," Max said very quietly, "that we'd better ask the ladies to leave us alone for a little while."

When he began to push back his chair, I was unprepared for the violent movement across the table. Rossdale was on his feet, swearing, struggling to get to the doorway.

Max and Gavin were up, too; Gavin's chair fell over backward and he had to move around it. Rudy, sutured head and all, dove into the middle of the melee, adding to the confusion. I heard Max yell, "Not *me*, you damned fool dog!" and I tried to call Rudy off.

A leg got broken off one of the kitchen chairs and a lamp would have overturned except for Callie's quick action. And then Rossdale was down with Rudy nipping at his extremities while Max brought the gun into firing position.

"Call him off, Brenna! Stop it, Rudy, cut it out!"

I got Rudy by the collar and dragged him off so that Rossdale was allowed to get up. His glasses had been broken, one lens cracked under someone's foot. Gavin picked them up and handed them to him.

Rossdale seemed a different man without his glasses. Blood oozed from the wrist Rudy had bitten. His hearing aid dangled from his ear, and he seemed blind and helpless.

Max steered him back into the chair he had vacated, ignoring the rest of us, intent only on Rossdale. "OK," he said flatly. "Now are we finished fooling around—or do you want to put us to the final test?"

Rossdale's hatred was palpable in his face, but he knew he wasn't going anywhere. Even if he managed to escape, he couldn't drive his car; the only reason he'd have been able to find it was that he'd moved it up to the back door before he came back for his money and his belongings.

He swore again, but it was different this time. He was defeated and he knew it.

Gavin leaned forward with his elbows on the table. "All right. You've got that out of your system, so let's have some answers. Why did you shoot young Crane?"

And for the next quarter of an hour the rest of us listened in silence while he told us.

[20]

ROSSDALE DIDN'T tell all without prodding, of course. Several times he had to be reminded that Tom Crane was a friend of Max's, and that Max and Gavin were prepared to go to some lengths for the information they wanted. By this time they had me believing they meant it, and I was sure Rossdale believed it, too.

Rossdale's relationship with my uncle went back many years. They had never been friends, but they had been business associates. Rossdale was a banker, and some twenty years earlier he had approached the Senator for funds to cover a shortage in his accounts. Max didn't press for the details on why Harold McCaffey was vulnerable to a spot of blackmail. It had something to do with government contracts that had been granted to a construction company in which the Senator had a controlling, if silent, interest, and Rossdale had come across this information in his work at the bank.

Since the amount of money he demanded was relatively small, the Senator came up with it, and there the matter rested. Until, seven years ago, Donald Rossdale saw an opportunity to seize a fortune. A small daughter of the bank's wealthiest depositor was kidnapped. Rossdale was the man delegated to take one hundred and fifty thousand dollars in cash to the distraught father to pay the ransom.

Instead, he calmly walked out of the bank, went to a hotel room where he proceeded to dye his hair, don workingman's clothes, and leave his own suit in a garbage can. Because his glasses were extremely distinctive, he ceased to wear them; instead, he picked out a pair in the dime store that did nothing for his sight but helped round out his disguise. Thus unable to drive, he resorted to what he thought would be the least notable form of transportation: a Greyhound bus. He rode various buses, back and forth across the country, for two weeks. He got off and on at the same time as a lot of other people. He never did anything to attract attention to himself. Several times he bought different work clothes, always in secondhand stores so that they were shabby and undistinguished.

He wanted a place to go to earth, as he put it, a place where he could live unnoticed until the statute of limitations had expired, until he could safely spend the money, which consisted entirely of marked bills. He had stolen an additional amount from the bank, which he had managed to leave unmarked, but it wasn't enough to do more than subsist on. He had to be in a place that was very cheap, a place where people wouldn't ask questions or pry into his background.

He remembered that the Senator had once voiced his opinion of a place in Bascom's Point that was owned by his wife's family; McCaffey had had to spend a short time there during the early years of his marriage and had found it the epitome of dead ends. There were no interesting people, there was nothing to do, it was an impossible place.

For Donald Rossdale, it was ideal. The inn was cheap and it was isolated. Few real tourists went there, and the old people soon left him alone when they found that he didn't play cards and that his hearing made conversation difficult.

He settled in to wait out his seven years.

Afterward we wondered what he had intended to do with his hundred and fifty thousand dollars. A man who could live as he did for seven years, without friends or family, in near-poverty . . . what did he dream of, that could be paid for with his stolen money? But Max didn't ask him that, and we never knew.

Gavin did ask about the ransom. Since it was never paid, what happened to the little girl?

Rossdale looked at him myopically, blinking as if that were immaterial. In his rusty, unused-sounding voice, he said she'd been found several days later, crying in an abandoned stolen car.

"All right," Max said. "Let's get back to the present. Senator McCaffey came down here to see you just a few days before he was indicted, right? How did he know you were here?"

"He came once, when I'd been here about a year. Something about some papers his wife had to sign . . . her share of the property over to *her*, or something." He looked in my general direction. "I didn't know he was

173

here, or I would have stayed out of sight. I came downstairs and saw him
. . . and he saw me. He recognized me even if I didn't look much the same,
because of my glasses."

"And he didn't do anything? Say anything?"

A nerve twitched in Rossdale's cheek. "He said something. He grinned
and said, 'So you got away with it, did you, you son of a bitch?' That was all.
Until he came back this last time."

"And he came back to see you? What did he want?"

"He wanted me to handle some blackmail. Get several influential people
to come to his rescue. He said he'd provide the material, tell me what to say
to them. Tell them I'd go to the newspapers with proof if they didn't find a
way to keep him from going to jail."

"What people? What kind of information?"

"Different people. Senators. A couple of judges. People like that. People
who might have been able to stop the investigation, or get him off with less
of a scandal, something like that."

"And what was this information you were supposed to reveal to persuade
them?"

"Different things. He had a list all made out, but I didn't keep it. I told
him I wouldn't do it; he could do his own dirty work. Seven years I sat in this
goddamned hole; another month and I'd have been home free. They couldn't
have touched me. I wasn't going to get mixed up in McCaffey's mess."

"And how did he react to that?"

"He didn't like it. But I didn't think there was much he could do about it.
Blowing the whistle on me wouldn't have helped him any, that I could see.
So he went away."

"And you went after him and killed him, just in case?"

"I never killed him. I never saw him after he was here. I was right here,
everybody can tell you that, the day he was shot." His blind eyes roamed
around the table, although I doubted that he could see well enough to tell
which of the aunts was which.

Callie's voice was nearly as raspy as Rossdale's. "He's telling the truth
there. He was here. We all were together when we heard it on the radio, that
Harold was killed."

"You hired someone to do it then," Max suggested.

Rossdale made a snorting sound. "With what? I wasn't lying when I said I
couldn't afford to pay my rent; I'm out of money. But somehow I had to hold
out until that seven years was up; if I spent anything and they traced it to me,

174

it was all for nothing, everything I went through. I didn't give a damn about McCaffey, so long as he went away and left me alone."

We all mulled that over for a minute or so. I was still totally confused about almost everything.

Maybe Max was, too. He was tugging at one end of his mustache. "Why did you start killing people, then, if you thought you were still safe?"

I thought he'd deny it, but he didn't. He knew he was going to jail, of course; he must have been reconciling himself to that. But he intended to go in one piece, and if talking was what we insisted upon, he would talk. Since there was nothing official about our question and answer session, he wasn't really compromising himself to any extent.

"I don't know why he set the Feds on me," Rossdale said. He brought his hands up on top of the table and sat rubbing them together. I'd never noticed before what unattractive hands he had, with pudgy fingers that didn't look as strong as I knew they were. "Just plain vindictiveness, I figured when that first one showed up."

Bill Haden? I glanced quickly at Max.

"How did you know he was a federal agent?"

Rossdale rubbed at his eyes as if they hurt. "I can smell one. I knew it as soon as I saw him, and when he started poking around in people's rooms I knew I had him pegged right. There wasn't anything else I could do."

"You killed him and buried him out by that old foundation on the beach," Max summed it up. "Where Rudy started to dig him up."

Rossdale's silence was a tacit admission of the accuracy of this.

"So you shot Rudy because he wouldn't stay away from the place, and then when Crane went out to look for the shells you saw him and were afraid he'd find Haden, so you shot him, too. And then when it got dark, you went out and dragged him into the surf, figuring the storm would take care of everything else."

Rossdale continued to massage the bridge of his nose without speaking.

Zell's small voice piped up. "Did he start that fire, too?"

"Well? What was that for?" Max demanded.

For a moment it seemed that he wouldn't reply, and then Rossdale sighed heavily. "I still thought I had a chance of making it then. Only I couldn't just up and pull out without everybody wondering why. Seven years I've been here, got no mail, saw nobody, went nowhere. If I suddenly up and left without a good reason, somebody was going to wonder about it. I didn't dare take a chance on anybody getting suspicious and coming after me, not before the statute of limitations was up.''

There was a silence until Gavin asked, ''What did setting the fire have to do with it?''

''Why, if the house was damaged enough so everybody had to get out, they wouldn't think anything of it if I went somewhere else to find a place to live, would they?''

I drew in a breath, wondering if it would have bothered him if some of us had died in that fire. The aunts' faces were impossible to read.

''And you didn't do it to destroy anything the Senator might have left here?''

Rossdale blinked again. ''Left here? I didn't know he left anything here. I wouldn't have cared if he did; it was nothing to me. I just wanted to get away before it was too late, before any more investigators came around.''

It was a grim thought, that one man had been killed and another might be dying because Rossdale had mistakenly thought they were after him. If what he said was true, we were no closer than we'd ever been to determining who killed the Senator and where he'd left the evidence so many people wanted.

I remembered Larry. ''Larry Engle thinks my uncle left something hidden here. He asked if he could come out and search for it.''

A furrow formed across Max's forehead. ''Engle? Is he still here?''

''He's staying in the village. He's coming out in the morning to see if we'll let him look around.''

''What's his interest in all this?''

''He says an unnamed client wants to find some information they think the Senator left that would incriminate him, even though he was only innocently involved. Larry's convinced that Uncle Harold hid something here in the inn while he was here. Is there any reason why we shouldn't let him look?''

''Not if we keep an eye on him, I suppose. By morning I'm sure Miller will be back, and he may have something to say about it. Certainly anything that turned up wouldn't be public property; it would have to be turned over to the authorities, so I can't see what good finding it would be to Engle.''

''Maybe his client is willing to pay for finding out that he *isn't* incriminated after all,'' Gavin suggested. ''It's better than being scared to death, waiting for the ax to fall.''

''Seems like a lot of trouble to go to for that,'' Max said.

A slight smile touched Gavin's wide mouth. ''Obviously you've never spent much time sitting under an ax.''

At my knee Rudy made a sudden movement, leaning into me and pricking up his ears. Max lifted a hand for silence, although the wind was still doing its thing, and, with a shutter flapping somewhere, we couldn't hear anything else.

"Is it a car?" Max pushed back his chair and stood up. "Maybe it's Miller, with news of Tom."

It was a car, but it wasn't the federal agent. It was Larry. He looked wet and cold, rubbing his hands together as he came into the kitchen. A glance told him Egg was putting on water for tea.

"If you're fixing something hot to drink, I'd sure like some. God Almighty, what a night!" And then he saw Mr. Rossdale, with the broken glasses before him on the table, and noticed that Max carried a gun. "Hey, what's going on?"

"We're learning a few things. Sit down," Max invited, indicating the one vacant chair at the table. "Maybe you can make a contribution by telling us the name of your client, the one who's concerned about whether or not Senator McCaffey left something here in the inn."

Larry shook his head, unbuttoning his raincoat. "My client's name is confidential."

"Look, buddy." Max stood behind Zell's chair, the hand holding the gun resting on the chairback. "A man's been assassinated, a federal agent has been murdered, and a friend of mine may be dying because of this mess. My sense of humor is running a little low tonight. We aren't playing kid games anymore. The federal authorities will be swarming all over this place by daylight, looking for a body and some answers, and they're not going to be put off by a thing like that. If the guy is interested in Senator McCaffey's papers, he's got something to do with what's going on, so let's pool our resources and start clearing up some of this."

"That's what I came out here to tell you, about your friend Crane. They've got an emergency telephone hookup from Jordon's Hill, and somebody named Miller sent a message for you. The constable was the one he called, but I offered to come out and tell you; I wanted to be sure Brenna got here all right, anyway."

"What's the message?"

"Crane came through surgery in fair condition. As soon as they can they'll take him to a bigger hospital; they were waiting for an ambulance. He needs to be in an intensive care unit. The doctor says there's a chance he'll make it."

Max nodded. It wasn't great news, but it was better than nothing, as much as we could expect at this point. "OK. Now about that client's name. . . ."

177

"Pardon me, I'm not intruding on anything private, am I?"

We all turned to see the realtor, Mr. Montgomery, standing in the doorway.

A smile flickered tentatively. "I was hungry and I thought I'd make a sandwich, if it's not bothering anybody?"

"I'm glad you showed up," Max said. "We're getting some things straightened out, and you can add to the information, I'm sure. Mr. Engle is about to tell us the name of his privileged client, and then maybe you can tell us the name of *yours*. Too many people have been killed and hurt, and I think a lot of the answers are right here, in this group of people."

Montgomery's jaw went slack; only now did he take a closer look at our little group and notice the oddities.

"You first, Engle. Who are you working for?"

Those telltale spots of color appeared in Larry's cheeks. "I'm sorry. I can't tell you."

"All right. See how far you get with that when Miller shows up."

"I didn't say I *won't*, Von Rys, I said *can't*. I don't know the man's name."

"Oh, come on. . . . You expect cooperation in letting you search the inn, but it's got to work both ways."

"It's true. Jerry Lawford gave me the assignment . . . he's my father's partner. He didn't tell me the name, and there's no reason why I have to know it actually. I'm simply to find whatever the Senator left here and try to get a look at it. I'm a very junior partner in the firm, you know. It isn't even an important assignment, or Jerry would have come himself."

Montgomery was standing just inside the doorway with the lamplight full upon his face. I was caught by his expression, and Max followed my gaze to see it, too.

"What's the matter? Did he say something interesting?"

The realtor licked his lips. "You said . . . Jerry Lawford is your father's law partner?"

"That's right. Why?"

Mr. Montgomery hesitated. "I don't know if I should . . . you say you think my client has something to do with . . . with someone being *killed*. . . ?"

"Senator McCaffey was here just before he was shot," Max pointed out. "One of Engle and Lawford's clients obviously believes he left something here in the inn that's dangerous or valuable, depending on your viewpoint. So when a mysterious client wants to acquire the inn, especially when he

178

specifies he wants immediate possession, I'd certainly guess he might have something to do with all this, yes. Since you came in late, I'll give you another bit of information: One federal investigating agent has been killed, and my friend Mr. Crane was shot today on the beach and left to die in the surf. So I hope you understand why we feel it's important to get everybody to tell as much of the truth as they know, before anything more happens."

Montgomery licked his lips again. "I see. Well . . . well, I certainly wouldn't want to contribute to . . . to anything . . . although I can't be sure that my client. . . ."

"You aren't going to incriminate anyone who isn't guilty of any crime," Max assured him. "Who is this man who wants to buy the inn in such a hurry?"

Montgomery drew a deep breath. "His name is Jerry Lawford."

Larry made an abrupt movement, leaning onto the table with intense curiosity written across his face. "*Our* Jerry Lawford? From Hampton?"

"Yes. You weren't aware that he was trying to buy the inn?"

"No. He sent me here to see if I could find an opportunity to look for whatever Senator McCaffey hid here. I tried the day I came, but people kept following me around and there wasn't really a chance. He never said anything about buying the place."

"Sounds to me," Gavin put in dryly, "as if the fellow were trying to cover all bases. Anything, so long as he got hold of whatever the Senator came down here to hide."

"He didn't come here to hide anything," Rossdale grated. "He came to try to coerce me into doing his dirty work for him."

Larry tapped his fingers on the table. "Well, there seem to be two minds about that. But there's a way to find out. Because if McCaffey hid anything, I think I know where it would be, so why don't we look?"

[21]

FOR A moment no one said anything. The flames burned steadily in the lamp in the middle of the table; beyond it, Donald Rossdale looked older and as if he were beginning to collapse inward on himself. He kept rubbing the bridge of his nose.

"Where?" Max demanded at last.

"In the secret compartment." Larry looked to the aunts for confirmation of this. "There is a secret compartment, right? Jerry remembered Mrs. McCaffey talking about how they used to hide things there and play in it when she was a child. It's off one of the bedrooms on the second floor. That's all I know about it, not which bedroom it's in. Jerry was convinced that if the Senator left anything here for safekeeping that would be where he put it."

Zell's voice was childlike in excitement. "The secret compartment! Why, I hadn't thought of it in years! Remember, we pretended we were slaves in the underground railway system, being spirited to freedom!"

Callie was frowning as we all began to push back our chairs. "It isn't really a secret compartment. It's just a storage place under the stairs. There's nothing secret about it; everyone's known about it for years, all our lives."

"But there is a compartment where something might be hidden? Can we go look at it?"

"It's off the little room where Brenna's sleeping," Callie said.

"I didn't know about it," I said. "I don't remember anyone ever telling me about it."

"It's nothing but a storage place," Callie insisted. "There was nothing to

180

tell. You're welcome to look it over all you like, but I doubt Harold would have put anything valuable there."

We all went up the stairs together. Mr. Rossdale was left alone, with no guard. "Blind as a bat without his glasses," Gavin observed. "He won't go far."

The attaché case of currency Max confiscated, and he'd put the gun out of sight. He gave me a grin and a quick handclasp as we trailed along after the others. "It's about over, I think. We're coming to the end."

But we hadn't reached it yet. Callie was the one who opened the compartment, which was simply a section of the wall beside my closet which was papered like the rest of the room but slid into the wall like those doors people used to have between their front and back parlors.

"It wasn't made that way to conceal it." she told us. "It was just that there was space under the stairs, and it isn't shaped right for a regular door. There wasn't room for a door to open out into the room either, not without being very inconvenient. There, that's all there is to it."

It wasn't much, to be sure. And within a few minutes even the most optimistic among us had to admit Callie was right. There were some boxes and a trunk, all covered with dust, and odds and ends of furniture. There was no sign that anyone had disturbed the place in years, confirmed by the fact that a mass of cobwebs nearly covered the opening when the door was recessed.

It was a letdown, of course. I agreed with Rossdale; my uncle probably had come only to see him, not to leave anything here. The "secret compartment" wasn't all that good a hiding place, in my opinion, and would have been completely inaccessible to him once he'd returned either to Hampton or to Washington.

Rossdale hadn't gone anywhere in our absence. He sat in a dejected silence while the rest of us discussed our findings and deductions, or lack of them. He did accept a cup of tea and seemed oblivious of our conversation.

We were still there when Max's contact, Miller, showed up an hour later with the constable and two of the young men who had helped us search for Tom Crane.

They came into the kitchen, dripping and cold, with faces revealing their grim discovery even before anyone spoke. When offered a choice between Egg's tea and Max's scotch, they all chose the latter.

Miller might almost have been a twin to Hastings, the federal agent who had questioned Maudie and me after my uncle's death. He was tall, spare, and very neat; his light-blue eyes missed nothing.

"We found Haden, where you indicated he might be. He'd been shot. We won't have a ballistics report until tomorrow, of course." The sharp gaze traveled around our company. "What's been happening here?"

Max told him, succinctly. Miller controlled his gratification at our capture of Donald Rossdale, and fastened on the name both Larry and Mr. Montgomery had given us.

"Jerry Lawford. Have you any idea why he's involved in the case, Mr. Engle? What his interest is?"

"So far as I know he's acting on behalf of a client," Larry said. "That's what he told me. It's quite possible the same client asked him to try to buy the inn. There's no reason to think Jerry himself is involved."

Miller grunted. "Well, we'll find out. We're somewhat hampered at the moment by the fact that the telephone lines are out over half the state; we have an emergency line rigged up to the guesthouse in town, but the local authorities are still rescuing residents along the coast and won't want us to tie it up for long."

Larry had joined the other men in a drink; he replaced his glass on the table now and started buttoning up his coat. "Is there any reason why I can't go home, sir? Back to Hampton, I mean?"

Miller's eyes were flinty. "You're driving?"

"Yes. My car's outside. I've been staying at Mrs. Edmonds', but there's no reason for me to stay any longer. I'd like to get back, and I could make a few miles yet tonight."

"It's a bad night for driving. But I'm not holding you. I'll expect you to be available as a material witness if we want you, naturally." The blue eyes narrowed. "And, of course, I'll have contacted our agent in Hampton before you get there. To talk to Mr. Lawford. It wouldn't be advisable for you to try to contact him first."

"Whatever you say," Larry agreed, but I could see that he held his jaw rigidly in the way he had when he was upset.

"I suppose you don't have a more recent report on Tom Crane?" Max asked, already dismissing Larry.

"Not since the one I sent on earlier, no. He was holding his own. I think they were going to give him several units of blood after he was transferred; it may be several days before much improvement can be expected."

Larry had to squeeze between Zell and me to reach the back door. He paused to look down at me. "I'm sorry this has all been such a mess, Brenna. If there's anything further I can do, you'll let me know?"

"Yes," I said, although I couldn't think I would ever again ask Larry for anything. And then I remembered the keys. "Oh, would you take Addison's keys back to them? Mr. Addison is sort of paranoid about employees walking off with keys, and I promised him. . . ."

The key ring resisted my initial effort to remove one key; when I gave an impatient tug, it came apart and all the keys spilled onto the floor. Max and Larry both knelt to retrieve them, while Zell lifted a lamp so that they could see.

"Here. I think we've got them all." Max cupped my hand and dropped the keys into it. "Which one belongs to Addison's?"

I found the proper one and began to put the others back on the ring. "Except that Mr. Rossdale won't go around shooting anyone else, we haven't gained much, have we? We don't have the tapes, we don't know who shot my uncle . . . and for all I know somebody still thinks *I* know something about them. I don't like the idea of being a target for someone who solves his problems with a gun."

"The best thing to do would be to take a trip out of the country for a while, let things cool off," Max suggested. Larry was leaving, and several people were speaking as he worked his way through the group. Nobody was paying any attention to us. "I still have a little time off before I have to report back to work. We might even find a judge who'd give us a special dispensation to get married without waiting."

I stared at him in mild exasperation. "But it wouldn't solve anything, Max."

"It would solve some of my personal problems, and yours, too. I've got a strong hunch Jerry Lawford holds the key to this, and once Miller and the others start working him over they'll come up with the rest of the answers."

I had come to the last key to go on the ring, but now I stood scowling at it. "This one isn't mine."

"It must be. Nobody else dropped any keys."

"But I never saw it before. It isn't even a regular key, is it?"

Max put out his hand. "Let me see it."

It was small—one of those flat, inexpensive-looking ones—and there was a number on it. *Twenty-eight.*

"It looks like a locker key," Max observed. "Brenna, love, did you ever leave your key ring lying around where the Senator had access to it?"

Everyone in the room had stopped talking, watching us. Even Larry lingered in the doorway.

"Yes, certainly. I usually dropped it on the hall table when I came in and left it there until I went back out. It was easier than digging through my purse every time. Max, the number . . . do you think it's one of those bus station lockers or something. . . ?''

"No, those are only good for twenty-four hours. If the Senator tucked his tapes away he'd pick a better place than that. Not a bad idea, you know, putting the key on your ring. Granted, he knew you weren't in sympathy with his activities and so he didn't ask for your cooperation. But he could have figured you'd come through in a pinch, get the stuff for him when he wanted it, and, with as many keys as you were carrying, you weren't too likely to notice one more. If this is the only key to a locker somewhere, it would explain why they didn't find anything on him except the decoy tapes, if that's what they were.''

I felt excited and yet half-sick. "But we don't know what it fits or where the locker is. . . .'' I stared around at the newly revived faces, aware that Miller was moving toward us, holding out a hand for the key. "He belonged to a club in Washington . . . I forget the name, but Maudie will remember it. I think . . . I think they have lockers there for the use of the members. Those wouldn't be twenty-four-hour ones, would they?''

"We'll find out,'' Miller said with crisp certainty as Max relinquished the key.

And so it proved. There were some things we never learned, for most of the people involved could not be induced to say anything that would further incriminate themselves.

Donald Rossdale, in bitter frustration, did confess to the authorities as he had under pressure to us. If I hadn't known how callous he'd been about other people's lives, I might have found him an object of pity as he was led away.

It was not until two days later, when the storm had blown itself out to sea, and communications were reestablished with the outside world, that we learned that the final pieces of the puzzle had fallen into place.

Although the wind had fallen, it was still cold and wet, a day unsuitable for outdoor exercise. So it was that Gavin found us with Rudy in front of the fireplace in the main lobby, sitting on the floor mapping out our itinerary on Max's map of the United States. We had decided to go somewhere not likely to be subject to hurricanes and were debating between mountains and beaches.

Max looked up at the tall old man grinning at us. "Well, you're looking awfully pleased with yourself.''

Gavin nodded. "Matter of fact, I am. Callie and Egg and I just got back from signing the papers making me a half interest in this place.''

"What? Why on earth do you want a share in a ramshackle old unprofitable hotel that will probably go down in the next high wind?"

"Didn't go down in the last one; chances are it will last a few years more. As long as we'll need it anyway. I have a little money to invest, and I've been living in a different kind of hotel, one of those where everybody sits around doing nothing but feeling sorry for himself. Put a new roof on this place, fix up the third floor so the rooms can be rented, there ought to be a mite of profit in it. Zell convinced me I'd enjoy myself here; did you know she's a champion chess player—or used to be? Gave me a run for my money this morning, she did." He nudged our map with his toe. "What you planning? Your getaway to Mexico?"

"Something like that. Maybe by the time we come back all the danger will be over, although I expect I can take care of my wife by myself anyway."

Gavin's toe tapped on the floor. "If that's the only reason you're planning to marry the girl, I can save you the trouble and the expense."

Max sprang up, offering a hand to me. "What's that mean? You've got news?"

Gavin was nodding. "Sure have. Met the constable in the village, and he's been talking to your friend Miller. Been a busy feller since we saw him."

"Well, don't keep us in suspense. Did they find the guy that shot McCaffey?"

"Did indeed. Jerry Lawford, who wasn't fronting for a client, at all. I didn't get all the details, but the gist of the story seems to be that McCaffey offered Engle and Lawford in on a deal a few months back. Engle didn't like the smell of it and said so, but Lawford couldn't resist the chance to make a killing . . . figuratively, of course. He put up a sizable sum of money on the Senator's promise he'd double it in six months. Might have worked, too, except that McCaffey got caught. The whole deal was crooked as a broken leg. Lawford tried to get out and couldn't. I guess he finally had to go to his partner and admit he was involved, and they tried to recover the incriminating evidence in whatever way they could. They didn't tell the boy"—he shot a look at me as if to assess how I felt about Larry—"he thought he was working for a client.

"Everybody figured it was a hired assassin, but it wasn't. Lawford panicked—he knew he was going to lose everything he had when they discovered he was involved in the Senator's scandal. McCaffey told him to his face he was going to get dragged right down with *him*.

"Lawford didn't dare try to hire a killer; he was afraid of leaving himself open to blackmail that way. He's a hunter, a good shot, so he did it himself. He knew where McCaffey was going, and when, and he set it up and shot from the office building across the street. He knew the Senator wasn't carrying all the evidence on him because McCaffey had told him outright it was hidden where nobody'd ever find it until he wanted them to. Scared hell out of Lawford when he found out there were tapes in the attaché case—until he learned they were blanks.''

Max's arm came around me, pulling me against him. "So it's all over."

"All over," Gavin confirmed. "They found the tapes in the locker at the club in Washington. Sounds like there was a string of names a mile long, people that were connected in some way with the construction frauds. Just as well you're changing your name, Brenna. 'St. John' is going to have bad connotations for a while, I'm afraid.''

My voice wavered. "I'm glad Aunt Stell isn't here to know about it.''

Max squeezed me. "*Our* lives aren't over—they're just about to get interesting. We're leaving in the morning, Gavin. The honeymoon will be short, but we'll continue it when we get back to Pennsylvania." He rubbed thoughtfully at the back of one thigh, where Rudy had nipped him during the fracas with Mr. Rossdale. "We're leaving Rudy here with Callie and Egg. I couldn't face that dog on a honeymoon. Or turn my back on him either.''

He released me and stepped back so he could look me in the face. "There's just one stipulation I'm going to make about this marriage, and I'm going to say it in front of a witness.''

"Oh? What's that?''

"No dog in the bedroom. Ever.''

As if he recognized that he was being talked about, Rudy lifted his head and looked at us, wagging his stumpy tail.

"Agreed," I said. And then Max kissed me, with Gavin looking on, grinning, and I was glad I'd come back to Bascom's Point, in spite of all that had happened.

For once, running had been the right thing to do.